The Premier
The Train

Two Novels by Georges Simenon

The Premier

The Train

A Helen and Kurt Wolff Book
Harcourt, Brace & World, Inc. / New York

The Premier

Translated from the French by Daphne Woodward

CHAPTER *1*

For more than an hour he had been sitting motionless in the old Louis-Philippe armchair, with its almost upright back and shabby black leather upholstery, that he had lugged around with him from one Ministry to another for forty years, till it had become a legend.

They always thought he was asleep when he sat like that with eyelids lowered, raising just one of them from time to time, to reveal a slit of gleaming eyeball. Not only was he not asleep, but he knew exactly what he looked like, his body rather stiff in a black coat that hung loosely on him, something like a frock coat, and his chin resting on the tall, stiff collar that was seen in all his photographs and which he wore like a uniform from the moment he emerged from his bedroom in the morning.

As the years went by his skin had grown thinner and smoother, with white blotches that gave it the appearance of marble, and by now it clung to the prominent cheekbones and sheathed his skeleton so closely that his features, as they became more strongly marked, seemed to be gradually fining down. In the village once he had heard one little boy call out to another:

"Look at that old death's-head!"

He sat without stirring, scarcely a yard away from the log fire, whose flames crackled now and then in a sudden downdraft, his hands folded on his stomach in the position in which they would be placed when his dead body was laid out. Would anybody have the nerve, then, to slip a rosary between his fingers, as someone had done to one of his colleagues, who'd also been several times Premier and a leading Freemason?

He had got more and more into the habit of withdrawing like this into immobility and silence, at all times of day, but most often at dusk, when Mademoiselle Milleran, his secretary, had come in noiselessly, without stirring the air, to switch on his parchment-shaded desk lamp, and gone away again into the next room; and it was as though he'd erected a wall around himself, or rather as though he had huddled up tightly into a blanket, retiring from everything except the sense of his individual existence.

Did he sometimes fall into a doze? If so he wouldn't admit it, convinced that his mind was ceaselessly alert; and to prove this to himself and to those around him, he would sometimes amuse himself by describing their comings and goings.

This afternoon, for instance, Mademoiselle Milleran—her name was the same, but for one letter, as that of a former colleague who had been President of the Republic, though not, it was true, for long—this afternoon, Mademoiselle Milleran had come in twice on tiptoe and the second time, after making sure that he wasn't dead, that his chest was still rising and falling as he breathed, she had pushed back a log that threatened to roll out onto the carpet.

He had chosen for himself, as his own corner, the room nearest to his bedroom, and the massive, unstained, unpolished wooden table was as plain as a butcher's chopping block.

This was his famous study, so often photographed that it, too, now belonged to the legend, like every nook and corner of Les Ebergues. The whole world knew that his bedroom was like a monk's cell, that the walls were whitewashed, and that the Premier slept on an iron bedstead.

The public was familiar with every angle of the four low-ceilinged rooms, converted stables or cowsheds, whose interior doors had been removed and whose walls were entirely lined with pitch-pine shelves packed with books.

What was Milleran doing, while he kept his eyes shut? He hadn't dictated anything to her. She had no letters to answer. She didn't knit, didn't sew. And the morning was her time for looking through the newspapers and marking with red pencil any articles that might interest him.

He was convinced that she made notes, rather in the way certain animals heap up in their lair anything and everything they come across, and that once he was dead she'd write her memoirs. He had often tried to catch her at it, but never succeeded. He'd been no more successful when he tried to tease an admission out of her.

One would have sworn that in the next room she was keeping as still as he and that they were spying on each other.

Would she remember the five o'clock news?

Ever since morning a gale had been blowing, threatening to carry away the slates on the roof and the west wall, rattling the windows so that you would have thought someone was continually knocking on them. The Newhaven-Dieppe steamer, after a difficult crossing that had been mentioned on the radio, had had to make three shots at getting into Dieppe harbor, after being almost forced to turn back.

The Premier had insisted on going out, all the same, about eleven o'clock, muffled in his ancient astrakhan coat that had been through so many international conferences, from London to Warsaw, from the Kremlin to Ottawa.

"You surely don't mean to go out?" Madame Blanche, his nurse, had protested on finding him dressed up like that.

She knew that if he wanted to she wouldn't be able to stop him, but she put up a fight in the forlorn hope.

"Dr. Gaffé told you again only yesterday evening . . ."

"Is it the doctor's life or mine that's involved here?"

"Listen, sir . . . At least let me call up the doctor and ask him . . ."

He had merely looked at her with his light-gray eyes, his steely eyes as the newspapers called them. She always began by trying to stare him out, and at such moments anybody would have felt certain they hated each other.

Perhaps, after putting up with her for twelve years, he really had come to hate her? He'd sometimes asked himself. He wasn't sure of the answer. Wasn't she, perhaps, the only person who wasn't awed by his fame? Or who pretended not to be?

In the old days he'd have settled the question without hesitation, confident of his judgment, but as he grew older he was becoming more cautious.

In any case, this woman, who was neither young nor attractive, had ended by absorbing more of his attention than he gave to so-called serious problems. Twice, in a moment of anger, he had thrown her out of Les Ebergues and forbidden her to come back. As it was he wouldn't let her sleep there, although there was a spare room; he made her take lodgings in a house in the village.

Both times she had turned up next morning, in time for his injection, her hard, commonplace, fifty-year-old face entirely devoid of expression.

He hadn't even chosen her. The last time he had been Premier, ten years ago, he'd found her at his side one night when, after speaking for three hours in the Chamber of Deputies in the teeth of relentless opposition, he'd fainted away.

He could still remember his astonishment at finding himself lying on a dusty floor and seeing the white-overalled woman with a hypodermic syringe in her hand, the only serene, comforting face amid the general anxiety.

For some time after that she had come every day to give him treatment at the Hôtel Matignon; and later, when the government fell, to his bachelor flat on the Quai Malaquais.

Les Ebergues had then been still just a country hide-out, bought at haphazard as a place for brief holidays. When he had decided to retire and live there permanently, she had announced, without consulting him:

"I shall come with you."

"And suppose I don't need a nurse?"

"They won't let you go away there without someone to look after you."

"Who are *they?*"

"Professor Fumet, to begin with . . ."

He had been his doctor and friend for more than thirty years.

"Those gentlemen . . ."

He had understood, and the expression had amused him. He still used it to refer to the few dozen people—were there as many as that?—who really ran the country.

"Those gentlemen" didn't mean only the Premier and the Cabinet, the Council of State, the Bench, the Bank of France, and a few senior permanent civil servants, but also applied to the Sûreté Générale, in the Rue des Saussaies, which was concerned that no ill should befall the famous statesman.

Had not two detectives been sent to Bénouville, the village nearest to Les Ebergues, where they had taken up residence at the inn so as to mount guard over him, while a third, who lived at Le Havre with his wife and family, came on his motorcycle at intervals to take his turn of duty?

At this very moment, despite the squalls and rainbursts that seemed to come from sea and sky at the same time, one of the three would be standing leaning against the wet trunk of the tree by the side gate, with eyes fixed on the lighted window.

Madame Blanche had come to Bénouville. For a long time he had supposed she was a widow, or that, although a spinster, she, like many old maids in jobs, had herself addressed as "Madame" to enhance her dignity.

It was three years before he discovered that she had a husband in Paris, a certain Louis Blain, who kept a bookshop near Saint-Sulpice, specializing in religious works. She had never mentioned it to him, she simply went up to Paris once a month.

One day when he was in a bad temper he had growled, while she was attending to him with her usual calm face:

"You must admit you're a stiff-necked woman! I might almost say a depraved woman, in one sense of the word. There you are, fresh as if you'd just got up, not a hair out of place, mind and body alert, and you come into the bedroom of an old man who's gradually rotting away. Incidentally, does my room stink in the morning?"

"It smells like any other bedroom."

"Before I grew old myself I used to be sickened by the smell of old men. But you, you pretend not to notice. You have the satisfaction of saying to yourself:

" 'The man I see every morning, ugly and naked, half dead already, is the same one whose name is in all the history books, and who any day now will have his statue, or at least his avenue, in most of the towns of France. . . .' Like Gambetta! . . . Like poor Jaurès, whom I knew so well. . . ."

She had merely inquired:

"Are you keen on your name being given to avenues?"

Perhaps it was precisely because she saw him naked, a weak old man, that he resented her?

And yet he didn't resent Emile, his chauffeur and valet, who was equally familiar with his sordid, unadorned privacy.

Was that because Emile was a man?

Anyhow, Madame Blanche and Emile had gone out with him, into the north wind that forced them to bend double, Madame Blanche with her cape, which flapped like a loose sail. Emile in his strict, black uniform with the tight-fitting leather gaiters.

There were no excursionists to photograph them that morning, and no journalists, nobody except Soulas, the swarthiest of the three detectives, smoking a damp cigarette beneath his tree and beating his arms across his chest now and then to warm himself.

The house, which had no upper story except for three little attic rooms above the kitchen, consisted of two buildings that had been connected together, and stood all alone, or rather crouched on the cliff-top, about a quarter of a mile from the village of Bénouville, between Etretat and Fécamp.

As usual, Emile walked on the Premier's left, ready to prop him up if his leg gave way, and Madame Blanche, obeying the orders he had given her once and for all, followed a few paces behind.

This daily walk had also been publicized by the press, and in summer a tourist agency at Fécamp would bring busloads of excursionists to watch from a distance.

A narrow lane, starting from behind the house, wound through the fields till it joined the coast-guard path, at the very edge of the cliff. The land belonged to a local farmer who turned his cows out to graze there, and from time to time the ground would crumble beneath the hoofs of one of the beasts, which would be found three hundred feet below, on the rocks of the shore.

He knew he was wrong to go out in bad weather. All his life he had known when he was wrong, but all his life he had persisted, as though challenging fate. Had he done so badly, after all?

The drifting sky was low. One saw it moving in from the open sea, bringing dark clouds that broke into tatters, and the air tasted of salt and seaweed; the same wind that was whipping up evil-looking white horses on the surface of the water was storming the cliffs to fling itself savagely on the countryside.

Through the roar he heard Madame Blanche's voice coming faintly from behind:

"Sir . . ."

No! He had made up his mind to go to the edge, to watch the wild sea, before going back to be an invalid in the Louis-Philippe armchair.

He was being careful about his leg. He knew it well, better than Gaffé, the young doctor from Le Havre who came every day to see him, better than Lalinde, the former staff doctor, who paid a "friendly visit" from Rouen once a week, better even than Professor Fumet, who was only sent for on serious occasions.

It might happen any moment. Since the attack three years ago, that had kept him in bed for nine weeks, and then on a chaise-longue, his way of walking had never been quite natural. His left leg seemed to float, as it were. It seemed to take its time about obeying, and whenever it moved forward there was a slight sideways motion, at each step, that he couldn't prevent.

"I waddle like a duck!" he had said jokingly at the time.

Nobody had laughed. He'd been the only one who'd made light of the business. And yet he followed, with almost impassioned interest, everything that went on inside him.

It had begun one morning when he was out for his walk, just like today except that in those days he used to go farther, as far as the dip in the cliffs which was known as the Valleuse du Curé.

He'd never had a moment's anxiety except about his heart, which had played him a few tricks, and he'd been advised to take care of it. It had never occurred to him that his legs, let alone his hands, might let him down as well.

That day—it was in March; the weather was bright and cold; the white cliffs of England had been visible in the distance—he had felt in his left leg, beginning at the thigh and creeping slowly downwards, a skin-deep warmth accompanied by the prickly sensation that one feels, for instance, after sitting for a long time beside a stove or in front of a log fire.

With no uneasiness, curious as to what was happening to him, he had gone on walking, his faithful stick in his hand (his pilgrim's staff, as the papers called it), until, without thinking, he had rubbed his thigh with his hand. To his stupefaction, it had been rather like touching another person's body. There was no contact. He was touching his own flesh, pinching it, and he felt it no more than if his flesh had been cardboard.

Had that scared him? He had turned around to tell Madame Blanche about it when, all of a sudden, his leg had given way, slipped from under him, and he had found himself huddled up at the side of the path.

He felt no pain, had no sense of any danger, was simply conscious of his ridiculous posture and the rotten trick his leg had so unexpectedly played him.

"Help me up, Emile!" he had said, stretching out his hand.

In the Chamber of Deputies, where everyone, or almost everyone, uses "*tu*" and affects Christian-name terms with everyone else, he had never addressed anyone in that way; nor did he even use "*tu*" to his cook-housekeeper, Gabrielle, who had been with him for more than forty years. He called his secretary by her surname, Milleran, as if she were a man, without ever using "*tu*," and Madame Blanche was always Madame Blanche as far as he was concerned.

"You didn't hurt yourself?"

He had noticed that the nurse, bending over him, had turned

pale, for the first time in his acquaintance with her, but he hadn't attributed any importance to it.

"Don't get up for a moment," she had advised. "Tell me first of all whether . . ."

He was struggling to stand up, with Emile's help, and then his eyes had, despite himself, become a little set, his voice had been slightly less assured than usual, as he observed:

"Funny thing . . . It won't take my weight any more. . . ."

He had lost his left leg. It wasn't his, any longer. It refused to obey him!

"Help him to sit down, Emile. You'll have to go and fetch . . ."

She must have known, just as the others knew later on. Fumet, who understood his character, had offered to tell him frankly what had happened. He'd said no. He refused to be ill. He didn't want to know his illness, and not for a moment had he been tempted to open one of his medical books.

"Can you carry me, Emile?"

"Certainly, sir."

Madame Blanche protested. He didn't give in. It was impossible to bring the car along that narrow path. They'd have to fetch a stretcher, probably from the priest, who doubtless kept one in reserve for burials.

He preferred to cling with his arms around the neck of Emile, who was strongly built and had firm muscles.

"If you get tired, put me down in the grass for a bit. . . ."

"It'll be all right."

Gabrielle watched them coming, standing in the door of her kitchen. This was before he'd taken on young Marie to help her.

Less than half an hour later, Dr. Gaffé, who must have driven like a lunatic, was by his bedside, and almost at once he rang up Dr. Lalinde at Rouen.

It wasn't till about four o'clock that, glancing at his hand, the Premier noticed it looked funny. He moved his fingers playfully, like a child, and these fingers didn't take their usual positions.

"Look at this, Doctor!"

It hadn't surprised Gaffé, who had not gone home to Le Havre for lunch, nor Lalinde, who had arrived about two o'clock and had afterwards made a long telephone call to Paris.

Later on, he learned that for several days one of his eyes had been fixed, his mouth twisted.

"A stroke, I suppose?"

He could hardly speak. They hadn't answered him, one way or the other, but the professor had arrived that same evening, followed by an ambulance which, a little later, took the lot of them off to Rouen.

"I give you my word, my dear Premier," Fumet said, "that you won't be kept in the clinic against your will. It's not a matter of getting you into hospital, only of taking X rays and making tests that aren't possible here. . . ."

Contrary to his expectation, it wasn't an unpleasant memory. He remained very detached. He watched them all: Gaffé, who hadn't begun to breathe more freely until Lalinde had arrived to share his responsibility; Lalinde himself, sandy-haired, rosy-cheeked, blue-eyed, with bushy eyebrows, trying to give an impression of self-confidence; then Fumet, the big man, used to distinguished patients and to the little court of admiring disciples that followed him from bed to bed as he made his rounds.

When they felt obliged to withdraw into corners to talk in low tones, he amused himself by studying the characters of the three men, and the idea of death didn't even occur to him.

He'd been seventy-eight years old at that time. The first question he had asked at Rouen, while he was being undressed and the X-ray apparatus was got ready, was:

"Did the inspectors come along behind?"

Nobody had paid attention, but they were surely there, or one of them at least, and the alarm had certainly been given to the Ministry of the Interior.

There had been some unpleasant moments, particularly when he'd been given a lumbar puncture and again when they'd taken an encephalogram. But he had never stopped joking, and at about four in the morning, when they were busy in the laboratory, he asked whether someone could get him a quarter bottle of champagne.

The funny thing was that they'd found him one, in a rather

shady Rouen night club that was still open, and probably it was one of the policemen, one of his watchdogs, as he sometimes called them, who had been sent on the errand.

That was a long time ago, now. It was no more than a story to tell. For two months the village of Bénouville had been invaded by French and foreign journalists determined to be in at his death. In the newspaper offices the obituary notices had been written, blocks made of photographs with some claim to be historic, and the printers stood by ready to set it all up.

Wouldn't the same articles be used sooner or later, with a change of date and a few details, for he had taken no part in politics since then?

He'd never fallen again, like a tripped hare, but now and then, though less acutely, he'd had the feeling that his leg was taking its time to obey him. It sometimes came over him at night, too, in bed, a sort of cramp, or rather, a numbness that didn't hurt at all. When it happened out walking, Emile would notice almost at the same time as himself. A kind of signal passed between them. Emile would come closer and the Premier would clutch his shoulder, stand still, though without taking his eyes off the landscape. Madame Blanche would come up then, and hand him a pink tablet, which he would swallow without a word.

The three of them would wait in silence. It had happened once in the middle of the village, when people were just coming out of mass, and the peasants had wondered why they stood riveted to the ground like that, for the Premier didn't appear to be in pain, or out of breath, and he made it a point of vanity to keep smiling vaguely all the time.

He hated it to happen on days when Madame Blanche had urged him not to go out, and so this morning he'd paid more attention than usual to the behavior of his leg. For fear of putting the nurse in the right, he had not stayed out long; all the same, he had sneezed twice.

When they got back he had flung at her triumphantly:
"You see!"
"Wait till tomorrow to find out if you've not caught a cold."

That was her way. One had to take her as she was. Whereas Milleran, the secretary, never resisted him, was so unobtrusive that he hardly noticed her presence in the house. She was pale, with soft, blurred features, and anybody who had only seen her two or three times would probably not have recognized her again. All the same she was efficient, and at this moment, for example, he felt sure she had her eye on the little clock in her office, waiting to come in on the dot and turn on his radio.

The ministerial crisis had lasted a week, and as usual the Republic was said to be in danger. Cournot, the French President, had sent for about a dozen political leaders in succession, and didn't know where to turn next.

He'd known Cournot as a very young man, fresh from Montauban, where his father sold bicycles. He was a militant Socialist, one of those who sit in gloomy offices, dealing with tiresome secretarial work, and are seldom heard of except at annual conferences. He hardly ever spoke in the Chamber, and when he did it was usually at night sittings, to almost empty benches.

Had Cournot realized, when he chose that self-effacing line, that it would lead him one day to the Elysée, where his two daughters, with their husbands and children, had moved in at the same time as he did?

One eyelid slightly raised, his hands still folded on his stomach, sitting stiff-backed in the Louis-Philippe armchair, he was watching the clock, like his secretary next door; but his clock, presented to him by the President of the United States during a state visit to Washington, was a historic piece, which would end up in some museum.

Unless Les Ebergues were itself to become a museum, as some people were already suggesting, and everything should stay in its place, with Emile as custodian.

He felt sure Emile had been thinking about it for several years, the way another man might think of his pension. Wasn't time beginning to drag for him, as he looked forward to the little speech he would make to visitors, to the tips they would slip into his hand on leaving, and the souvenir postcards he might perhaps sell?

At two minutes to five, fearing Milleran might be the first to move, he put out his hand noiselessly, furtively, and turned the knob on the radio set. The dial lit up, but for a few seconds no sound came. In the next room, for there was no door between it and the Premier's study, the secretary got to her feet and at the very moment when she came tiptoing in, music blared out, a jazz tune in which the trumpets seemed to be challenging the noise of the storm.

"I'm sorry . . ." she murmured.

"You see, I wasn't asleep!"

"I know."

Madame Blanche, in such circumstances, would have smiled, sarcastically or disbelievingly. Milleran simply vanished as though she had melted into thin air.

"At the third pip it will be precisely . . ."

It was too early yet for the proper news bulletin, which would be broadcast at a quarter past seven, but there was a short summary of the latest headlines, between two musical programs:

"This is Paris-Inter calling . . . After devoting last night and this morning to consultations, Monsieur François Bourdieu, Leader of the Socialist Group, was received by the President of the Republic at three o'clock this afternoon and informed him that he was giving up his attempt to form a Cabinet. . . ."

The Premier's face betrayed no sign of his feelings, as he still sat motionless in his armchair, but his fingers were clenched now and the tips had gone whiter.

The announcer had a cold and coughed twice over the microphone. There came a rustle of papers, then:

"According to unconfirmed rumors circulating in the corridors of the Chamber, Monsieur Cournot is said to have requested Monsieur Philippe Chalamont, Leader of the Left Independent Group, to visit him late this afternoon, and to be intending to ask him to form a coalition government. . . . Argentina . . . The general strike which was called yesterday at Buenos Aires, and which had brought out about seventy per cent of workers . . ."

The voice broke off without warning in the middle of a sentence; at the same time the lights in the study and the neighboring rooms went out, and now there was nothing except the sound of the wind, the dancing firelight.

He didn't move. Milleran, next door, struck a match, opened the drawer where she kept a supply of candles, for it was not the first time this had happened.

There was a brief flash as the lights seemed to be coming on again, the bulbs gave out a cloudy glow, like those of certain night trains, then they faded slowly and it was complete darkness.

"I'll bring you a candle at once. . . ."

Before she had had time to stick it upright on a china ashtray, a light appeared, moving along a passage that connected the former cowsheds with the kitchen and the rest of the house. This passage, which had not existed in the old days and which the Premier had had built, was known as the tunnel.

It was Gabrielle, the old cook, who was coming through the tunnel now, brandishing a big oil lamp with pink flowers painted on its globe.

"The young doctor has just arrived, sir," announced Gabrielle; she always referred thus to Dr. Gaffé, who was just thirty-two, to distinguish him from Dr. Lalinde.

"Where is he?"

"In the kitchen, with Madame Blanche."

This made him suddenly angry, perhaps because of the name that had been mentioned on the radio and the news that had been broadcast.

"Why did he come in by the kitchen?"

"Well now, I never asked him!"

"What are they doing?"

"They're having a chat, while the doctor warms his hands at my stove. After all, he can't touch you with icy-cold hands."

He loathed not being informed of comings and goings in the house.

"I've told you a hundred times . . ."

"I know, I know! It's not me you ought to tell. It's the people that come; I can't shut the door of my kitchen in their faces."

There was a front door by which Milleran was supposed to let in visitors. It was perfectly visible, being lit by a lantern. But more often than not people would persist in coming in through the kitchen, whence a murmur of unknown voices would suddenly become audible.

"Tell the doctor I'm waiting. . . ."

Then he called:

"Milleran!"

"Yes, sir."

"Is the telephone working?"

She tried it.

"Yes, I can hear the click."

"Ask the electric company how long it will take them to repair . . ."

"Very good, sir . . ."

He received Dr. Gaffé in a cold, unsmiling silence which made the doctor, who was shy by nature, feel more awkward than ever.

"Madame Blanche tells me you went for a walk this morning?"

The young doctor made this remark in a casual tone while opening his bag, and he received no answer.

"In weather like this," the doctor went on, embarrassed, "it was perhaps a little unwise . . ."

Madame Blanche came forward to help the Premier out of his coat. He stopped her with a glance, took it off himself, rolled up his shirt sleeve. Milleran's voice could be heard on the telephone, then she came in to announce:

"They don't know yet. There's been a general breakdown. They think it's the cable that . . ."

"Leave us."

Dr. Gaffé came to see him every day at the same time, and nearly every day he solemnly took his blood pressure.

The Premier had asked him once:

"You think it's necessary?"

"It's an excellent precaution."

"You make a point of it?"

Gaffé had got flustered. At his age he still blushed. He was so much in awe of his patient that once when he had to give him an injection he had fumbled so badly that Madame Blanche had been obliged to take the hypodermic away from him.

"You make a point of it?" the Premier had insisted.

"Well, the thing is . . ."

"Is what?"

"I think Professor Fumet makes a point of it. . . ."

"It's he who gives you instructions?"

"Of course."

"And he alone?"

What was the use of forcing the doctor to tell a lie? Fumet himself must have had orders from higher quarters. Because the Premier, while still alive, had become a historical personage, he wasn't allowed to take care of his health just as he thought fit. They pretended to obey him, the whole pack of them, but who gave them their real orders? And to whom, God knows when, God knows how, did they report?

Was it also by order that visitors went to the kitchen instead of ringing at the front door?

Gabrielle had told the truth: Gaffé's hands were still cold and the Premier thought he looked ridiculous, squeezing the little rubber bulb and staring very solemnly at the needle on the round dial.

Because he was cross, he deliberately refrained from asking, as he usually did, out of politeness as it were:

"How much?"

Nonetheless, Gaffé murmured, his satisfaction no less absurd than his solemnity:

"Seventeen. . . ."

The same as the day before, the day before that, every day for months and months past!

"Any pain, any discomfort during the night?"

"Nothing."

"And your leg?"

He was feeling his pulse and the Premier couldn't restrain himself from glaring resentfully at him.

"No respiratory difficulty?"

"No respiratory difficulty," he replied curtly, "and I may as well tell you at once that I made water in the usual way."

For he knew that would be the next question.

"I wonder if this electric failure . . ." muttered Gaffé.

Without listening to him, the Premier was putting on his coat, with the same sour expression, taking care to avoid Madame Blanche's eye, for he did not want to lose his temper.

Probably because of the electric failure, the consequent silence of the radio which was his only contact with the outside world, he felt like a prisoner in this cottage flattened on the cliff-top, between the black hole of the sea and the black countryside which was not even dotted any longer with the little twinkling lights that indicated the presence of life.

The oil lamp in his study, the candle in Milleran's office, its flame wavering with each draft, reminded him of the stickiest evenings in his childhood, when the houses didn't yet have electric light and gas had not been brought to Evreux.

Hadn't Gaffé said something just now about respiratory difficulties? He might have answered that he suddenly felt as though he were being physically and morally smothered.

He had been shut up at Les Ebergues and the few human beings who surrounded him had become his jailers, whether they wanted to or not.

He was forgetting that it was he who had left Paris, swearing dramatically that he would never set foot there again, in a sulky mood, because . . . But that was another story. His reasons were his own business, and everybody, papers and politicians alike, had misinterpreted his retirement.

Was it he who insisted that this young doctor, a nice young fellow, but a silly greenhorn, should come every day from Le Havre to take his blood pressure and ask him some footling questions, always the same ones? Was it he who was forcing two poor devils of police inspectors to live at the inn at Bénouville, and a third to settle at Le Havre with his wife and children, so as to mount guard under the elm beside the gate?

All right, so he was in a bad temper. These fits of anger had come over him all his life, just as some people feel the blood running to their heads, or some women grow suddenly depressed. For forty years his rages had been the terror not only of his own staff but of many people in high places, including generals, leading magistrates, statesmen.

The effect on him was the same as that produced on other people by alcohol, which doesn't always cloud the intelligence but sometimes stimulates it, and his bouts of ill-temper didn't throw him off his course. Far from it!

The electric failure was going to last, he knew it was. He didn't go so far as to suggest that they had engineered it on purpose, though that would have been perfectly possible.

"I'll be here tomorrow at the same time, Premier . . ." faltered the doctor, whom Madame Blanche was about to escort through the tunnel again.

"Not that way!" he protested. "By the proper door, please."

"I beg your pardon. . . ."

"Not at all."

It was he who went to the tunnel, and called out:

"Emile!"

"Yes, sir."

"Bring the car under the window and fix it like last time. You can manage it?"

"Certainly."

"Get it going by seven o'clock, if the lights haven't come on again."

"I'll see to it at once."

At that moment the telephone rang. Milleran's flat voice could be heard saying:

"Les Ebergues, yes . . . Who is speaking? . . . A call from the Elysée? . . . Just a moment, please. . . . Hold on. . . ."

He suspected nothing, let himself be caught, as on previous occasions.

"Hello?"

As soon as he heard the voice he understood, but all the same he listened to the end.

"That you, Augustin?"

A pause, as usual.

"Xavier here. . . . You'd better hurry, old chap. . . . Don't forget I've promised to be at your funeral, and here I am in hospital again. . . ."

A whinnying laugh. Silence. At last, a click.

Milleran had understood.

"I beg your pardon," she stuttered, taking the blame on herself and fading into the semidarkness of her office.

He had a book on his knees, the *Mémoires de Sully*, but he was not turning the pages, and Milleran, her ear cocked in the next room, was about to come in and make sure the oil lamp was giving him enough light, when he spoke to her. He would sometimes keep silent for two hours and then give her an order or ask her a question as though she'd been sitting in front of him, and he felt so sure of her that he would not have forgiven any lapse in her attention.

"Ask the post office where that call came from."

"I'll do it at once, sir."

Still staring at the page of his book, he heard her at the telephone, and she soon informed him, without leaving her chair:

"Evreux."

"Thank you."

He had suspected as much. Yet Xavier Malate's last call, two months earlier, had come from Strasbourg; the previous one, much further back, from the Hôpital Cochin in Paris.

In the whole course of his life the Premier had avoided forming an attachment to anybody, not so much from principle, or from hardheartedness, as to safeguard his independence, which he prized above all else. The only woman he ever married came into his life for a brief three years, long enough to bear him one daughter, and that daughter, now a woman of forty-five, married, with a son in his first year of Law School, had always been a stranger to him.

He was eighty-two years old. All he wanted now was peace, and that he thought he had attained. Strangely enough, the only human being who still clung to him and had the power, at a distance, to disturb him so much that he couldn't read, was a man for whom he cared nothing, now or at any other time.

Was this Malate's importance due to the fact that of all the members of his own generation with whom he had had any degree of intimacy, he was the sole survivor?

Malate used to declare confidently, as though announcing a certainty:

"I'll be at your funeral."

He himself had been in hospital a dozen times, in Paris and elsewhere. A dozen times the doctors had given him only a few weeks to live. Each time he'd bounced up again, returned to the surface, and he was still there, with his obsession about outliving his old schoolfellow.

A long time ago somebody had said:

"He's a harmless imbecile."

The speaker, whoever he was, had been astonished by the reaction of the Premier, whose cordiality had suddenly vanished as he answered curtly, as though touched on the raw:

"There is no such thing as a harmless imbecile."

After a pause he had added, as though he had been wondering whether to speak his mind to the full:

"There is no such thing as an imbecile."

He had proffered no further explanation. It was difficult to put into words. Underlying a certain kind of stupidity, he suspected something Machiavellian that frightened him. He refused to believe it could be unconscious.

By what right had Xavier Malate irrupted into his life and stubbornly kept his place there? What feelings or thought processes prompted him to the tricks, never twice the same, that brought his boyhood friend to the telephone to listen to the mean message he delivered in his harsh voice?

The Premier knew the hospital, in the Rue Saint-Louis at Evreux, from which this latest call had been made. It was only a few yards from the house where Malate's father had had his printing works, at the corner of the next street, to be precise.

He and Xavier had been at the town *lycée*, in the same form; and it must have been in the third form, when they were both a little over thirteen years old, that the thing had happened.

Later on, Malate had claimed that it was the future Cabinet Minister and Premier who had had the original idea. That was possible, but by no means certain, for the Premier himself could not remember making the suggestion, which didn't seem like him.

All the same, he had joined in the conspiracy. At that time they had an English master whose name he had now forgotten, like those of at least half his schoolmates, in spite of the important part the man had played in his life for four years.

He could still see him pretty clearly, however, short, badly dressed, always wearing a black jacket too big for him and shiny with age, his hair hanging in gray elf-locks under his bowler hat. He reminded one of a priest, especially as he was a bachelor and was perpetually reading a black-bound volume of Shakespeare that looked like a breviary.

He seemed very old to the boys, but he could not have been more than fifty-five to sixty, and his mother was still alive; he used to visit her at Rouen from Saturday evening to Monday morning.

People called him an imbecile too, because he conducted classes without appearing to see his pupils, for whom he seemed to feel a lofty contempt, if not a measure of disgust, and his only reaction, if one of them grew restless, was to give him two hundred lines.

It was too late to find out what he had really been like, what he used to think.

The practical joke had taken some time to prepare, for success depended on the most careful planning. With the help of an old workman employed by his father, Xavier Malate had undertaken the hardest part, the setting up and printing of about fifty invitations to the teacher's funeral, on paper with a deep black border.

These had been posted one Saturday evening, for delivery on the Sunday morning, for in those days letters were still delivered on Sundays. They had made quite sure that the English master had set out by train for Rouen, whence he would return at seven minutes past eight on the Monday morning, in time to drop his bag at home before his first lesson at nine o'clock.

He lived in a humble street, on the first floor, above one of those local grocer's shops whose windows display jars of sweets, tinned foods, a few vegetables, and whose door rings a bell as it opens.

The funeral invitations had said that the coffin would be fetched at half past eight, and they had managed, heaven knows how, to get the hearse used for paupers' burials in front of the house on the minute.

Some ingenuity had been displayed in selecting the people to whom the invitations were sent: several town councilors, other local authorities, some shopkeepers who supplied the *lycée*, and even the parents of a few younger boys, who were not in the secret.

The conspirators had not been there, since they had a class at eight o'clock. What exactly had happened? The Premier, though he remembered the preparations in some detail, had entirely forgotten what occurred afterwards and could only depend on what Malate had told him, years later.

In any case there had been no English lesson that morning. The master had stayed away for over a week, ill, so they said. The headmaster had opened an inquiry. Malate's guilt had been easily proved, and for several days there had been speculation as to whether he would give away his accomplices.

He had held his tongue, thus becoming a kind of hero. A hero never seen at the *lycée* again, by the way, for in spite of wire-pulling by his father, who was the printer of the little local paper, he had been expelled and sent to boarding school at Chartres.

Was it true that he had run away from there, been found by the police at Le Havre, where he was trying to stow away on board a ship, sent as an apprentice to an uncle who had an import business at Marseilles?

It was perfectly possible, and of no real importance. For the next thirty years, as far as the Premier was concerned, Malate had ceased to exist, like the English master and so many of his other schoolfellows.

He had met him again when he was forty-two years old, a Cabinet Minister for the first time, at the Ministry of Public Works in the Boulevard Saint-Germain.

Every day for a week, at about ten in the morning, the office messenger had brought him a slip bearing the name X. Malate, with the space left for the purpose of visit filled in by the words "Strictly personal," underlined twice.

In his memory the name was vaguely associated with a face, hair that needed cutting, and thin legs, but that was all.

Seven times running he had told the messenger:

"Say I'm at a meeting."

The eighth time he had given way. As a Deputy, he had learned by experience that the only hope of getting rid of a certain type of pest is by seeing them. He remembered an old lady, always dressed in black, with a wheezy dog tucked under her arm, who had haunted various government offices day after day for two years, trying to get her brother into the Académie Française.

Malate had come into the rather austere-looking office, and the thin, knobby-kneed lad had grown to be a tall, fat man with the unhealthy red face of a heavy drinker and bulging eyes. Very much at ease, he held out his hand as though they had seen each other only the day before.

"How are you, Augustin, old boy?"

"Sit down."

"Don't you recognize me?"

"I do."

"Well then?"

His eye had a slightly aggressive glint, which meant, of course: "So now you're a Minister you cut your old pals?"

At ten o'clock in the morning he already smelled of drink, and though his suit was well tailored it showed traces of the kind of bohemian negligence that the Premier detested.

"Don't be frightened, Augustin. I'm not going to waste your time. I know it's valuable, and I've not got much to ask you. . . ."

"It's true, I'm extremely busy."

"Heavens! I realize that all right. Since we left Evreux, I first, you'll remember, a lot of time has gone by and we've grown from kids into men. You've done well, and I congratulate you. I've not done so badly either, I'm married, I have two kids, and if I can get just the slightest bit of help, everything will be grand. . . ."

In cases like this the Premier turned to ice, not so much from hardness of heart as from clear-sightedness. He had realized that, whatever one did for him, Xavier Malate would all his life be in need of just a bit more help.

"A contract for enlarging the harbor at Algiers is to be given out next month, and it just so happens that I work in a big engineering concern in which my brother-in-law is a partner. . . ."

A surreptitious touch on the bell warned the messenger, who promptly opened the door.

"Take Monsieur Malate to see Monsieur Beurant."

Malate must have got the wrong idea, for he broke into effusive gratitude:

"Thank you, old man. I knew I could count on you. You realize, don't you, that if it hadn't been for me you'd have been expelled from school too, and then you'd probably not be here now? Ah, well! Honesty is the best policy, whatever they may say. I suppose it's practically in the bag?"

"No."

"What d'you mean?"

"That you must put your case before the head of the contracts department."

"But you'll explain to him that . . ."

"I'm going to ring through and ask him to give you ten minutes. That's all."

He had eventually used "*tu*" to him, after all, and he regretted it as a weakness, almost a piece of cowardice.

Later on he had received nauseating letters in which Malate talked about his wife, who had twice attempted suicide, and so he daren't leave her alone any more, his children who hadn't enough to eat and couldn't go to school because they had no decent clothes.

He had stopped asking for a government contract, but was pleading for help of any kind, for a job, however humble, even as a lock-keeper or as watchman on road works.

Malate had no suspicion that his former Evreux schoolfellow had asked for his police record from the Rue des Saussaies, and he persisted, his letters growing steadily longer and more tedious, or more harrowing.

He had been inditing such letters, which were nearly all on café notepaper, for over twenty years, sometimes changing his victim, occasionally achieving his aim, and though he had married and was a father, he had deserted his wife and children ten years ago.

"He's here again, sir," the messenger would announce from time to time.

Malate altered his tactics, taking to hanging around the ministerial building, looking seedy and unshaven, in the hope that his one-time schoolmate would take pity on him.

One morning his former friend had walked straight up to him and declared curtly:

"The next time I see you anywhere near here, I'll have you arrested."

In the course of his career he had disappointed other hopes, had shown himself unrelenting to quite a number of people.

Malate was the only one who had taken a kind of revenge, and the years had not softened his hatred.

He had succeeded up to a point, for on several occasions the Premier had approached the Rue des Saussaies to find out where he was.

"*I'm in hospital at Dakar with a stiff bout of malaria. But you needn't gloat. I shan't peg out this time, because I've sworn I'll be at your funeral.*"

He really was at Dakar. Then in prison at Bordeaux, where he'd been given twelve months for writing rubber checks. From there he had written, on a sheet of prison paper:

"*Life's a funny thing! One man becomes a Cabinet Minister, another becomes a convict.*"

The word "convict" was exaggerated, but dramatic.

"*All the same, I'll be at your funeral.*"

The office of Premier didn't intimidate him, and in fact it was to the Hôtel Matignon that he first began to telephone, giving the name of some politician or celebrity.

"Xavier here . . . Well? How does it feel to be Premier? . . . All the same, you know, I'll still be at your . . ."

The electric lights had not come on again, and Milleran, too, had an oil lamp now. The treacly-looking circles of light in the dusky rooms recalled his old home at Evreux. The Premier even remembered, all of a sudden, the peculiar smell his father's clothes used to have when he got home, for, being the local doctor, an odor of camphor and phenol used to trail around with him. Of red wine, too.

"Call up and find out what's happening about the electricity."

She tried, announced before long:

"The telephone's cut off as well, now."

Gabrielle appeared, to announce:

"Dinner is ready, sir."

"I'm coming at once. . . ."

He didn't feel he was to blame about Malate, and he was only annoyed with himself for allowing his former friend's threat to get on his nerves. He, who believed in nothing except a certain human dignity he could hardly have put into words, in freedom too, at any rate in a measure of freedom of thought, was beginning to suspect Xavier Malate of having baleful powers.

Logically, considering the unhealthy life he had been leading for forty years and more now, the printer's son should have been dead. Not a year went by without his paying a visit, long or short, to some hospital or other. He had even been found to have tuberculosis and sent to a mountain sanatorium where patients died every week, and from which he had emerged cured.

He had had three or four operations, the last two for cancer of the throat, and now, going round and round in imperceptibly diminishing circles, he was back at his starting point, Evreux, as though he had decided to die in his native town.

"Milleran!"

"Yes, sir?"

"Call up the hospital at Evreux tomorrow and ask them to read you the record of a man called Xavier Malate."

It was not the first time she had dealt with the matter, and she asked no questions. Through the window Emile could be heard, bringing the Rolls alongside the house. The black limousine, with its old-fashioned wheels, was more than twenty years old, but like so many other things in this place it belonged, as it were, to the Premier's personality. It had been presented to him by the Lord Mayor of London, on behalf of the citizens of the English capital, when he had been given the Freedom of the City.

Walking slowly, with his hands behind his back, he went along the tunnel to the dining room, with its blackened beams, where a solitary place was laid on a long, narrow table that came from some former convent or monastery.

Here too the walls were whitewashed, as they are in the poorest villager's cottage, and there was not a single picture or ornament; the floor was paved with the same gray, worn flagstones as the kitchen.

An oil lamp stood in the middle of the table, and it was not Gabrielle who served, but young Marie, taken on two years ago when she was only sixteen.

The first day he had heard her asking Gabrielle:

"What time's the old boy have his dinner?"

He would never be anything more to her than "the old boy." She had heavy breasts, her dress was too tight, and on her weekly day off she made herself up like a tart. Looking out of his window one evening, the Premier had seen her under the elm, her skirts hitched up to her waist, her hands behind her clutching the trunk of the tree, placidly satisfying the needs of one of the policemen. He was doubtless not the only one, and in the overheated rooms she gave off a strong feminine odor.

"Do you think it's proper, sir, for you to have a girl like that here?"

His only answer to Gabrielle's question had been a rather melancholy:

"Why not?"

After all, in earlier days hadn't he occasionally come across Gabrielle in intimate converse with a delivery man, and once with a policeman in uniform?

"I can't understand you. You let her do whatever she likes. She's the only person in the house who's never scolded."

Perhaps that was because he didn't expect her to be faithful or devoted, only to do the heavy work for which he had engaged her. Perhaps, too, because she was eighteen years old, healthy, sturdy, and common, and the last person of that type that he was likely to have about him?

She represented a generation about which he knew nothing, to which he was and would remain just the old boy.

His dinner was always the same, having been prescribed once and for all by Professor Fumet, and Marie had found that astounding, too: a poached egg on dry toast, a glass of milk, a bit of cottage cheese, and some fresh fruit.

He had ceased long ago to feel this as a privation. He even felt surprised, almost disgusted, at the thought that intelligent men, with serious problems to solve every day of their lives, could bother about food and, in the company of pretty women, so much enjoy talking about it.

One day when he had been walking with Emile down a street at Rouen, he had stopped short outside a food shop and gazed for a long time at the trussed fowls, a pheasant *en gelée* still decked with its many-colored tail, a ewe-lamb lying on a bed of fresh, costly greenstuff.

"What do you think of that?"

"They say it's the best shop in Rouen."

He had spoken for his own benefit, not for Emile's:

"Man is the only animal who finds it necessary to decorate the corpses of his victims in order to whet his appetite. Look at those neat rounds of truffle slipped under the skin of the capons to make a symmetrical pattern, that cooked pheasant with his beak and tail so artistically put back in place. . . ."

It was twenty-five years since he had last smoked a cigarette, and only rarely was he allowed a glass of champagne.

He didn't rebel, felt no bitterness. He obeyed his doctors, though not for fear of dying, for death had long since ceased to frighten him. He lived with it in an intimate relationship which, if not cheerful, was at least resigned.

He had been mistaken just now in thinking that he and Xavier Malate were the only survivors of their generation. Unless Eveline had died since his last birthday. She was a sort of counterbalance to the printer's son. His recollection of her was rather vague, although he'd been in love with her when he was about twelve years old.

Her father had kept the ironmonger's shop in the Rue Saint-Louis, nearly opposite the *lycée*, and she'd been two or three years older than himself, so she would be about eighty-five now.

Had he ever spoken to her? Two or three times, perhaps. He wasn't even sure, at that, that he wasn't mixing her up with her sister or some other little girl in the district. On the other hand, he was positive that she'd had red hair, fiery red, was thin and lanky, with two pigtails hanging down her back, and wore a pinafore with small red checks.

She had waited before writing to him, not only till he became a Minister but until he was Prime Minister, on the eve of an international conference where the destiny of France was at stake, or so people believed, as they always do. Didn't he believe so himself at the time?

Eveline didn't ask him for anything, but sent him an envelope containing a little medal from Lourdes, with a note saying:

"*I shall pray that you may succeed in your task. This will help you to save the country.*

"*The little girl from the Rue Saint-Louis—*
                    "*Eveline ARCHAMBAULT.*"

She had never married, presumably, for Archambault was the name he could see in his mind's eye, in big black letters above the ironmongery. When she sent him this little token she was well over fifty, and the address on the back of the envelope showed that she still lived in the same street, the same house.

She was there to this day. He sometimes imagined her, a little old woman dressed in black, trotting along, close to the house walls, on her way to early mass on some gray morning.

Since that first medal she had formed the habit of sending him birthday wishes every year, and the envelope always contained some pious object, a rosary, a religious picture, an *Agnus Dei.*

He had made inquiries through the Prefecture, learned that she was quite well provided for, and had sent her a signed photograph.

The glass panel in the door between the dining room and the kitchen was covered with a red-checked curtain, in the style of a village inn. He could see Gabrielle's shadow moving to and fro on the other side. Madame Blanche had already left, for it was Emile who helped the Premier to get to bed. The telephone had been installed in the house where she lodged, at the near end of the village, and she took her meals at Bignon's inn, known nowadays as the Hôtel Bignon, where the policemen put up.

He heard Emile's footsteps, then caught sight of his shadow against the curtain, as he came into the kitchen from out of doors, announcing:

"All right now! It's working."

"What's working?" Gabrielle mumbled.

"The radio."

The old cook wasn't interested in the radio; she went on grilling herrings for the servants' supper, while Emile slumped down on the bench and poured himself a glass of cider.

Since five o'clock the Premier had been deliberately avoiding the thought of Chalamont, who had been mentioned in the Paris-Inter broadcast, and the telephone call had come like a dispensation of Providence to take his mind off the subject. In any case he had trained himself to accomplish that feat easily: to turn his thoughts in a given direction and prevent them from straying in any other.

It was too soon to think about Philippe Chalamont, for there were only rumors so far, and even if the President of the Republic asked him to form a Cabinet, Chalamont would not necessarily agree.

Young Marie stood behind him, vacant-eyed, watching him eat; she could hardly have looked sloppier, and it was obvious she would never learn, but would end up sooner or later in her right place, as a barmaid in some harborside café at Fécamp or Le Havre.

"Will Monsieur take a *tisane?*"

"I *always* take a *tisane*."

He went off, with hunched shoulders, not knowing what to do with his arms, which, now that his body had shrunk, had become too long. He used to say to himself:

"If man is descended from the apes I must be returning to my origin, for I look more and more like a gorilla."

Emile had put the loud-speaker on the table, with the extension cord going out through the window frame and connected up with the car radio. When the time came for the news, he would only have to switch on. Emile had thought of this himself, during their first year at Les Ebergues. With a storm just like tonight's blowing, the electricity had failed in the middle of an unusually violent debate in the U.N.

The Premier, furious, was prowling around his office, lit, as now, by an oil lamp, except that they hadn't yet found a globe for it, when Emile had knocked on the door.

"If you will allow me, sir, I would like to make a suggestion. Have you thought of the radio in the car, sir?"

On that occasion he had gone out in the dark, swathed in a rug made of wildcat skins—it was a present from the Canadians—and sat in the back of the Rolls, with the dial of the radio as his only light, until the midnight news.

Since then Emile, who enjoyed playing the handyman, had improved the system, bought a second loud-speaker which only needed connecting with the radio set.

There was no electric failure in Paris, and they probably didn't realize that in Normandy the storm was bringing down trees, telegraph poles, and chimneys. Journalists and photographers were mounting guard in the courtyard of the Elysée, where it was raining, and in the corridors and bar of the Chamber little knots of overexcited Deputies were forming in the window nooks.

An anxious calm would be reigning in the Ministries, where every crisis improved or endangered the prospects of promotion of hundreds of civil servants, and the Prefects, each in his own fief, would be waiting with equal anxiety for the seven-fifteen news.

For forty years, on such occasions, it had invariably been his name that had been put forward in the last resort. He had usually remained secluded in his flat on the Quai Malaquais, the one he had moved into when first called to the Bar.

Milleran had not been his secretary in those days. She was still a little girl, and in her place, waiting silently in the room with him, ready to jump on the telephone, there had been an ungainly young man with a pointed nose, whose name was Chalamont.

There was a difference of twenty years in their ages, and it had been curious to see how the secretary took on the gait, voice, posture, and even the mannerisms of his chief. Over the telephone it was so marked that most people were taken in and addressed him as "Minister." Wasn't it even stranger, perhaps, to note that the face of this lad of twenty-five was as impassive as that of a middle-aged man who had had many years to harden him?

Was it because of this mimicry, because one could feel that his admiration was intensely sincere, that the Premier had kept him on, carrying him along from one Ministry to the next, first as attaché, then as secretary, finally as Principal Private Secretary?

Chalamont was now Deputy for the sixteenth arrondissement, and lived with his wife, who had brought him a large fortune, in a flat overlooking the Bois de Boulogne. He didn't need to make a living out of politics, but he stuck to the political world from choice, some people said as a vice, for he was a savage fighter.

And yet, though he was the leader of quite a large group, he had only once been in the Cabinet, and then only for three days.

Wasn't it characteristic of him that on that occasion he had chosen to be Minister of the Interior, and have the police records at his disposal?

What the public, and a good many political men, did not know was that during those three days there had been an almost uninterrupted series of telephone calls between Les Ebergues and Paris, and that Bénouville had noticed an unusual number of cars whose number plates indicated that they came from the Seine Department, all making for the house on the cliff.

On the morning when the new government had presented itself in the Chamber there had been no electric failure, and the old man of Les Ebergues had been listening, with a gleam of ever-increasing satisfaction in his eyes, to the course of the debate.

The proceedings had lasted just three hours, and the newborn government had been defeated before Chalamont had even had time to move into his office in the Place Beauvau.

Was the Premier still as powerful as that today? Hadn't people rather forgotten the statesman who had retired haughtily to the Normandy coast and whom children, learning about him at school, imagined to have died long ago?

"May I go to dinner, sir?"

"By all means, Milleran. Tell Emile to turn on the radio at ten past seven."

"Will you need me?"

"Not this evening. Good night."

She had a room between Gabrielle's and Emile's, above the kitchen, and young Marie slept in a small ground-floor room, once a storeroom, which had had a window put in its outside wall.

Alone in the book-lined rooms, only two of which had any light this evening, the Premier moved slowly from one to another, scrutinizing certain shelves, certain bindings, now and then running his finger along the top of a volume. One day young Marie had caught him at this kind of suspicious inspection, and she had asked:

"Have I left some dust?"

He had turned slowly toward her, had given her a long stare before replying briefly:

"No."

It might be she, it might be Milleran, or even Emile, and he wouldn't allow himself to suspect one of them rather than another. He had known about it for months, and felt sure there must be at least two of them hunting, one inside the house and one outside, possibly one of the detectives.

He had been neither surprised nor annoyed, and at first it had rather amused him.

For a man who had nothing left to do except die in a manner worthy of the legend that had grown up around him, this was an unhoped-for diversion.

Who? Not only, *who* was ferreting among his books and papers, looking for something, but *who* had set them to it?

He, too, had been Minister in the Place Beauvau, not for three days but, on several occasions, for months, once for two whole years. So he knew the methods of the Rue des Saussaies as well as he knew the records that were such a temptation to fellows like Chalamont.

Nearly every evening since making his discovery, he had distributed through the four rooms a number of reference marks, "witnesses," as he privately termed them, which were sometimes no more than a thread of cotton, a hair, a scarcely visible scrap of paper, sometimes a volume just slightly out of alignment.

In the mornings he made his round, like a fisherman going to pick up his lobster pots, for he had always forbidden anybody to go into those rooms before he did. The housework was left until he was up, and then done not with a vacuum cleaner, which he hated the noise of, but with broom and feather duster.

Why had they thought first of all of the memoirs of Saint-Simon? One morning he had found that one of the volumes, which he had pushed in by a quarter of an inch the previous evening, was back in line with the rest. The detectives living at the Bénouville inn could not have guessed that Saint-Simon had been among his favorite bedside books all his life.

A calf-bound folio of Ovid, whose size would have made it an ideal hiding place, had been handled next, then, a few weeks later, an entire row of illustrated books on art, most of which were bound in boards.

It had all begun about the time when he had told a foreign journalist that he was writing his memoirs.

"But you have already published them, Premier, and they were even printed in the biggest magazine in my country."

He was in a good humor that day. He liked the journalist. It amused him to give the fellow a scoop, if only to annoy certain other journalists whom he couldn't stand.

"My official memoirs have been published," he retorted.

"So you didn't tell the whole truth in them?"

"Perhaps not the *whole* truth."

"And you're going to tell it this time? Really the whole of it?"

His mind was not made up then. It had all been in the nature of a joke. He had indeed begun, for his own amusement, to write a commentary on the events he had been mixed up with, giving little sidelights that no one else knew about.

It had become a kind of secret game, and now he was still wondering, with amusement, who would find those notes in the end, and how.

They were already looking. So far, nobody had looked in the right place.

Naturally the entire press had printed the information about his "secret notebooks," as they were called, and the reporters had come to Les Ebergues in greater numbers than ever before, all asking the same questions:

"Are you going to publish during your lifetime? . . . Will you have them held back until some years after your death, as the Goncourts did? . . . Are you revealing the shady side of twentieth-century politics, foreign as well as domestic? . . . Are you bringing in other world statesmen you've known? . . ."

He had given evasive replies. The journalists had not been alone in the interest they took in those memoirs, and several important personages, including two generals, whom he hadn't seen for a number of years, had visited the Normandy coast that summer, as though by chance, and felt impelled to pay their respects to him.

They were no sooner seated in his study than he began to

wonder when the question would come. They'd all taken the same tone, casual, joking.

"Is it true you've written something about me in your private papers?"

All he would say was:

"The press reports were very exaggerated. I've only just begun to jot down notes, and I don't know yet whether anything will come of it. . . ."

"I know some people who are trembling at the idea. . . ."

He would reply innocently:

"Ah!"

He knew what was being said on the quiet, what two newspapers had had the temerity to say in print: that, piqued at being left in silence, forgotten, he was revenging himself by suspending this undefined threat over the heads of hundreds of the Establishment.

For a few days he had even wondered whether there might not be a grain of truth in this, and his conscience had been uneasy.

But if it had been like that he wouldn't have gone on, and he would in fairness have destroyed the pages he had already written.

He had reached an age at which a man can no longer fool himself.

It was actually because of Chalamont, his former secretary, whose name would be mentioned over the radio in a few minutes, that he had decided against drawing back; not that Chalamont was important, but his case was typical.

As had been more or less announced just now, would not the President of the Republic probably be going to give him the job of forming a government?

Chalamont would undoubtedly remember that once when his old chief was asked about his prospects of receiving a portfolio, he had replied curtly:

"He'll never be Premier as long as I'm alive."

After pausing as he always did when he wanted to stress the importance of his pronouncements, he had added:

"Nor when I'm dead, either."

At this very moment, when the storm outside was wrenching

at the roof tiles and a shutter was banging, Chalamont would be at the Elysée and the journalists would be in the rain-swept court-yard, waiting for his answer.

The door of the Rolls opened and closed again. Almost at once, the loud-speaker, standing on the oak table, began to crackle faintly, and the Premier sat down in his Louis-Philippe armchair, folded his hands, closed his eyes, and waited too.

CHAPTER 3

First of all came the news agencies' reports, terse and impersonal:

"*Paris . . . Latest developments in the political situation . . . At five o'clock this afternoon the President of the Republic received Monsieur Philippe Chalamont, leader of the Left Independent Group, at the Elysée and asked him to form a coalition Cabinet. The Deputy for the sixteenth arrondissement postponed his reply until tomorrow morning. At the end of this news bulletin we shall broadcast a short interview with Monsieur Chalamont by our representative, Bertrand Picon. . . .*

"*Saint-Etienne . . . The fire that broke out last night in an electrical equipment factory . . .*"

The Premier sat motionless, no longer listening, keeping an eye on a log which was threatening to roll onto the floor. Two or three gusts of wind made it shake and crackle, and finally he got up, squatted down by the hearth, cautiously, for he was not forgetting his leg, took the tongs, and tidied up the fire.

He would have half an hour to wait. The French radio correspondents were speaking, one after another, from London, New York, Budapest, Moscow, Beirut, Calcutta. Before settling into his armchair again he took several slow turns around the table and regulated the wick of the oil lamp.

"*And now we come to today's sport. . . .*"

Another five minutes and it would be Chalamont's turn.

When the moment arrived there was a brief interruption while they switched from the live broadcast to the tape, for the interview was a recorded one. That was perceptible from the sound, which had changed, and from the voices, which had a different timbre, so that one could tell that the two speakers had been out of doors.

"*Ladies and gentlemen, it is a quarter to six and we are in the courtyard of the Elysée, I and a number of newspaper reporters. . . . This wet, windy day is the eighth that has gone by since the government fell, and as usual Paris has been full of gossip.*

"*At the present moment the question is: Are we to have a Chalamont government?*

"*Just over half an hour ago, Monsieur Philippe Chalamont, summoned by Monsieur Cournot, arrived in his car and strode rapidly past us and up the steps, with no more than a wave of his hand to indicate that he had nothing to say to us yet.*

"*The leader of the Left Independent Group and Deputy for the sixteenth arrondissement, whose photograph has often appeared in the papers, is a vigorous man who looks younger than his sixty years. He is very tall, with a bald forehead, and rather stout. . . .*

"*As I said before, it is raining. There is not room for all of us under the porch of the main entrance, where the doorkeepers are indulgently turning a blind eye to our presence, and a charming lady among our number has valiantly opened a red umbrella. . . .*

"*Outside the gate, in the Faubourg Saint-Honoré, the Munici-*

pal Guards are keeping a discreet watch over the small crowd that gathers in little knots and disperses again. . . . Hello! . . . I believe . . . Yes . . . Is that he, Danet? . . . Thanks, old man. . . .

"*Excuse me . . . I'm told that at this very moment Monsieur Chalamont is crossing the immense hall of the Elysée, which is dazzling with light. . . . Yes, as I bend down I can see him my-self. . . . He's just put on his overcoat. . . . He's taking his gloves and hat from the attendant. . . . Close to us, his chauffeur has opened the door of the car. . . . So in an instant we shall know whether he has taken on the the job of forming a Cabi-net. . . .*"

There was the sound of a bus going past, then some confused noises and a kind of scuffle, with voices in the background:

"*Don't push . . .*"

"*Let me through, old man . . .*"

"*Monsieur Chalamont . . .*"

Then again the well-pitched, faintly conceited tones of Ber-trand Picon.

"*Minister, I would like you, sir, to tell our listeners . . .*"

Although Chalamont had only been a Cabinet Minister for three days and, indeed, had spent only a few hours in the office in the Place Beauvau, ushers, journalists, and all habitués of the Palais-Bourbon would address him for the rest of his life as "Min-ister," just as others, simply because they had once presided over some vague Parliamentary Committee, were known as "Presi-dent."

"*. . . first of all, for what reason Monsieur Cournot sent for you this afternoon. . . . I am correct, am I not, in thinking that it was in order to ask you to form a coalition Cabinet? . . .*"

The old man's fingers whitened as he sat still in his armchair. He heard an embarrassed cough, and then, at last, the voice:

"*—As a matter of fact the President of the Republic has done me the honor . . .*"

A car hooted, emerging from the confused background noises. What gave the old man at Les Ebergues the impression that Chalamont was peering around, in the wet, gloomy courtyard of the Elysée, as though looking for a ghost? There was a strange note of anxiety in his voice. For the first time, after a lifetime of effort, he had been asked to lead his country's government, and he knew that someone, somewhere, was listening, he couldn't possibly fail to think of it, someone who was silently bidding him to refuse.

Another voice, not Picon's, probably that of a journalist, broke in:

"May we tell our readers that you have agreed and that you will begin your interviews this evening?"

Even over the radio, especially over the radio, which is merciless, one could sense a blank, a hesitation; then came laughter, inexplicable at such a moment, and whispers of mirth.

"Ladies and gentlemen, you can hear the press representatives laughing, but I assure you their amusement has no connection with what has been said on either side. A moment ago Monsieur Chalamont suddenly flapped his hand, as though something had touched it unexpectedly, and we noticed that the umbrella of the lady journalist I told you about was dripping on it. . . . Excuse that aside, Minister, but our listeners wouldn't have understood. . . . Would you please speak into the microphone. . . . You were asked whether . . ."

"I thanked the President for the honor he had done me, which I very much appreciate . . . and . . . er . . . I asked him" (a car hooted very close by, in the Faubourg Saint-Honoré) *". . . to allow me . . . to allow me to think things over and give him my reply in the morning. . . ."*

"But your group met at three o'clock this afternoon, and it is rumored that you were given a free hand. . . ."

"That is the case. . . ."

It seemed as though he were trying to get away, to dive into his car, whose door the chaffeur was still holding open.

The speaker had felt impelled to mention that he was rather stout because that was what struck one at the first glance; he had the portly appearance characteristic of men who were thin for a good deal of their lives and don't know how to carry off the fat that has accrued to them. His double chin and low-slung belly looked like padding, whereas his nose, for instance, was still sharp and his lips were so thin as to be almost nonexistent.

"Minister, sir . . ."

"With your permission, gentlemen . . ."

"One last question. Can you tell us who are the chief people you intend to consult?"

Another blank. They might have cut out these pauses when they edited the tape. Had they refrained because they, too, realized that there was something unusual and pathetic about such hesitancy? The photographers on the steps must be sending up a barrage of flashlights during the interview, lighting up the driving rain and bringing Chalamont's face out of the darkness for a second to emphasize its pallor and anxiety.

"I can't answer that question yet."

"Will you be seeing anyone this evening?"

"Gentlemen . . ."

He was almost suppliant, as he struggled to escape from the cluster of people who were cutting him off from his car.

Suddenly there came a sharp, piercing voice which might have been that of a little boy, but the Premier recognized it as belonging to a highly esteemed reporter, as it snapped:

"Aren't you intending to spend the night on the road?"

An unintelligible stutter.

"Gentlemen, I have nothing more to say. . . . Excuse me. . . ."

Another pause. The slam of a car door, the sound of an engine, the crunch of gravel, and finally, silence; then Bertrand Picon again, speaking in more measured tones from a different setting, the studio:

"You have been listening to the interview with Monsieur Philippe Chalamont which was recorded as he left the Elysée. Refusing to make any further comment, the Deputy for the sixteenth arrondissement drove back to his home on the Boulevard Suchet where a group of journalists, undismayed by the bad weather, is mounting guard outside the door. We shall know tomorrow whether France has any immediate prospect of emerging from the deadlock which has now existed for over a week, and whether we are soon to have a government.

"Paris-Inter calling . . . That is the end of the news. . . ."

Music. The door of the Rolls opened and there came a tap at

the window, outside which Emile's face could be seen as a pale blur. A sign told him that he could turn off the radio, and the noise of the storm grew stronger.

In the soft light of the oil lamp the old man's face looked haggard, and his immobility was so striking that when, shortly afterwards, Emile came into the study, bringing with him a little of the cold and damp from outside, he stopped with a frown.

The Premier kept his eyes closed, and Emile, standing at the entrance of the tunnel, gave a cough.

"What is it?"

"I came to ask you whether I'm to leave the Rolls outside until the final news?"

"You can put it in the garage."

"You're sure you don't want . . . ?"

"Quite sure. Is Milleran at table?"

"She's having dinner."

"And so are Gabrielle and young Marie?"

"Yes, sir."

"Had your supper?"

"Not yet. . . ."

"Then go and get it."

"Thank you, sir."

Just as the man was going away, he called him back:

"Who's on duty tonight?"

"Justin, sir."

Inspector Justin Aillevard was a fat, melancholy little man. It was no use sending him word to go to bed, or even suggesting that he might come in out of the rain, for he took his orders from the Rue des Saussaies and it was to the Rue des Saussaies that he was responsible. The most that Gabrielle could manage now and again was to invite the policeman on duty to come into the kitchen for a moment and give him a glass of cider or calvados, according to the weather, and perhaps a slice of cake still warm from the oven.

As the Premier did not say he could go, Emile still waited, and he had to wait a long time before hearing the hesitant words:

"We may perhaps have a visitor tonight. . . ."

"Do you want me to stay up?"

The chauffeur realized that for some mysterious reason his reactions were being closely watched, and that those eyes, open now, were studying his face more keenly than usual.

"I don't know yet . . ."

"I'm quite ready to stay up. . . . You know it doesn't bother me. . . ."

In the end he was dismissed, with a touch of impatience:

"Get along and eat."

"Very good, sir."

This time he really did go, and a moment later he was straddling the bench to sit down at the kitchen table.

Could Loubat—the name had just come back to him—the sharp-voiced journalist who'd questioned Chalamont, have information that the Premier didn't possess? Or had he merely spoken on the off-chance, on the strength of thirty years spent behind the scenes in the Chamber of Deputies and the various Ministries?

It was twelve years since the two politicians had last come face to face. During the Premier's last period in Paris they had occasionally been at the same sitting at the Palais-Bourbon, but one was on the government bench and the other with his Parliamentary group, and they had taken care not to meet.

Their quarrel, as some people called it, or, as others put it, the hatred between them, was well known, but a variety of theories existed as to its origin.

An explanation favored by young parliamentarians, those of the new generation, was that the Premier accused his former colleague of having been the mainspring of the plot that had kept him out of the Elysée.

In the first place, that credited Chalamont with an influence he was far from possessing; in the second place it revealed ignorance of the fact that for certain definite reasons it would have been political suicide for Chalamont to have taken such an attitude.

The Premier preferred not to dwell on that episode of his life, even though his motives had been very different from the ones attributed to him.

He had been at the apex of his glory in those days. His energy, his uncompromising spirit, and the measures he had relentlessly adopted had saved the country from the very brink of the abyss. His photograph, surmounted by a tricolor cockade or ribbon, was enshrined in the shop windows of every town in France, and allied nations were inviting him to triumphant receptions.

When the Head of the State died, he had been on the point of retiring from political life, in which he had spent long enough, and it was neither vanity nor ambition that had made him change his plans.

He had talked about it to Fumet one day later on, when he was dining with the Professor in his flat in the Avenue Friedland. He'd been in a good temper that evening, though still with the slightly crabby undertone that characterized his personality.

"You see, my dear Doctor, there is a fact which is overlooked not only by the public, but by those who shape public opinion, and it always bothers me when I read the life of a famous statesman. People talk about the leader's interests, his pride or his ambition. What they forget, or refuse to see, is that beyond a certain stage, a certain level of success, a statesman is no longer himself, he becomes the prisoner of public events. Those aren't quite the right words . . ."

Fumet, who had a nimble mind and who was the doctor, and in most cases the personal friend, of everybody who was anybody in the country, was watching him through a cloud of cigar smoke.

"Let's put it this way, that there comes a moment, a rung of the ladder, at which a man's personal interests and ambitions become merged with those of his country."

"Which is tantamount to saying that at a certain level treason, for example, becomes unthinkable?"

He had sat for a moment in silence. He would have liked to give a definite, clear-cut reply, and he followed up his thought as far as he could:

"Sheer treason, yes."

"On condition, I take it, that the man is worthy of his office?"

At that moment he had thought of Chalamont, and answered: "Yes."

"And that isn't always the case?"

"It always would be, if it were not for certain forms of cowardice which are to some extent collective, and above all, for certain kinds of indulgence."

It was in this spirit that he had felt it his duty to stand for the Presidency of the Republic. Contrary to the rumors that had been spread, he had had no intention of changing the Constitution, or of reducing the prerogatives of the executive.

He was perhaps said to have brought a rather sterner spirit into politics, and those who knew him best had spoken of his secular Jansenism.

He hadn't gone to Versailles himself. He had stayed in his flat on the Quai Malaquais, alone with Milleran, Chalamont's successor.

At the luncheon that followed the opening meeting his chances were already being discounted, and with a few words over the telephone he had withdrawn from the contest.

Three weeks afterwards he left Paris, a voluntary exile, and though he kept his bachelor flat he hadn't set foot in it since.

Had his departure made Chalamont think he could get forgiveness more easily, and that the road was at last open? The Deputy for the sixteenth arrondissement had put out feelers, and his way of doing it had been typical of the man. He hadn't written, or come to Les Ebergues. The frontal attack was never in his line, and his schemes were usually very long-term affairs.

One morning the Premier had been surprised to see his son-in-law, François Maurelle, arrive at Les Ebergues, by himself. He was a nonentity, colorless but conceited, who had been working as a surveyor somewhere outside Paris when Constance first met him.

Why had she chosen him? She wasn't pretty, a bit on the masculine side, and her father had always regarded her with a curiosity in which there was more surprise than affection.

Maurelle's own intentions had been clear; less than a year after the marriage he had informed his father-in-law that he intended to stand for Parliament.

He had been defeated twice: the first time in the Bouches-du-Rhône, where he had been ill-advised to stand at all; next time at Aurillac, where at a second attempt he had finally worn down the voters' resistance.

The couple lived in the Boulevard Pasteur, in Paris, and spent their summer holidays in the Cantal.

He was a big, flabby chap, always dressed up to the nines, always with his hand held out and his lips ready to smile, the kind of fellow who won't express his views even on the most harmless subject without first peering at you to try to guess what yours may be.

The Premier had done nothing to help him, merely staring at him as malevolently as if he'd been a slug in the salad.

"I was at Le Havre, after driving a friend to the boat, and I thought I'd just like to drop in on you . . ."

"No."

That was an unpopular trick of his. His "no" was celebrated, for he brought it out frequently, without anger or any other inflection. It wasn't even a contradiction: it simply took note of an almost mathematical fact.

"I assure you, my dear Premier . . ."

The old man waited with a faraway gaze.

"As a matter of fact . . . Though in any case I'd have come specially . . . It just so happens that the day before yesterday I was talking about my trip to a bunch in the Chamber . . ."

"To whom?"

"Give me a little time . . . And please don't think I'm trying to influence you. . . ."

"That would be impossible."

"I know. . . ."

He smiled, and if one had slapped his face one's fingers would perhaps have got stuck in those plump, flaccid cheeks.

"I suppose I ought not to have done it—I hope you don't mind. . . . I only promised to give you the message. . . . It's from somebody who used to work with you and who's very much upset about a situation . . ."

The Premier had picked up a book from the table and seemed to be absorbed in it, paying no further attention to his visitor.

"As you'll have guessed, it's Chalamont. . . . He doesn't bear you any grudge, he realizes that you acted for the best, but to quote his own words he thinks he has perhaps been sufficiently punished. . . . He's not a young man now. . . . He could aim very high if you . . ."

The book snapped shut.

"Did he tell you about the luncheon at Melun?" asked the Premier as he rose to his feet.

"No. I know nothing about the business. I suppose he did something he shouldn't, but it's twenty years ago now. . . ."

"Sixteen."

"Excuse me. It was before I was in the Chamber. Do you think I may tell him . . ."

"That the answer is no. Good evening."

With that, leaving his son-in-law stranded, he had gone into his bedroom and shut the door.

This time Chalamont wouldn't rest content with sending him a fellow like Maurelle. This was not a question of some secondary post in a Cabinet. The stake now was the ambition he'd been pursuing all his life, the part he'd been rehearsing since he was twenty years old, and which he'd at last been invited to play.

The years he had spent as the Premier's secretary, or rather as his fervent disciple, his marriage to a rich woman, the humdrum work he had done for various committees, the elocution lessons he had taken, at the age of forty, with a teacher from the Conservatoire, and the three languages he had mastered, his tremendous erudition, his foreign travels, his entire life, private and social, all of this had been undertaken solely with a view to the high office to which he would one day accede.

And now, as he stood in the courtyard of the Elysée, under the rain that was making its cobbles glisten, someone had asked him an innocent yet terrible question:

"Aren't you intending to spend the night on the road?"

The man who put that question had known that it would fling Chalamont into confusion.

At this moment the arbiter of his fate was an old man, cut off from the outside world even more completely than usual owing to an electric failure and a telephone breakdown, who sat in a Louis-Philippe armchair, with the sea beating against the cliff

hard by and squalls of wind threatening, at ever-diminishing intervals, to carry away the roof of his house.

Twice, three times, the Premier muttered to himself:

"He won't send anybody. . . ."

Then, hesitantly:

"He'll come. . . ."

At once he would have liked to take back his words, for he
was not so sure. At forty years old, or at fifty, he had still believed
himself to be a good judge of men, and would pronounce his ver-
dicts without hesitation or remorse. At the age of sixty he had
already been less sure of himself, and now he did no more than
grope in the dark for momentary truths.

The definite fact was that Chalamont had not refused the Head
of State's invitation. He had got himself a breathing space. But
that couldn't mean that he intended to defy the taboo laid on him
by his former chief.

So he hadn't lost hope. . . .

A cracking sound from outside the house—a branch being mal-
treated by the wind—roused a doubt, a suspicion, in his mind,
and although he had already made his daily inspection he got up
and walked through Milleran's office, where the lamp threw a
dim light into the two rooms beyond. He went to the fourth
room, the farthest from his bedroom; here were the books he
never opened, but kept because they were presentation copies
with inscriptions, or because they were rare editions.

He was no bibliophile and had never bought a book for the
sake of its binding or its rarity. He had never indulged in any
passion, craze, or hobby, as the English call it, holding aloof from
fishing, shooting, and all other sports, sailing and climbing, novels, paintings, and the theatre, and he had wanted to reserve his
whole energy for his duties as a statesman, a little as Chalamont,
his pupil, had tried to do.

He had not even wanted to be a father, his married life having lasted hardly three years, and though he had had mistresses
he had only looked to them for relaxation, an interval of charm
and elegance usually, with just a touch of affection, and had never
repaid them with anything more than brief, condescending attention.

In this respect, too, legend was far from the truth, especially on the subject of Marthe de Créveaux, the Countess as she was called at the time, and as her faithful admirers continued to call her after her death.

Would he go on to the end of his notes, his genuine memoirs, which in a way were corrections, or would he leave behind him, uncaring, the image that had grown up by slow degrees and had so completely ousted the real person?

Before bending down to the lowest shelf he crossed the room and drew the curtain, for he never allowed the shutters to be closed until he was getting into bed. Once they were closed he felt as though he were shut up in a box, already removed from the world, and the irregular throbbing of his heart would sometimes seem to his ears like an alien sound. Once, in fact, he had listened more attentively, convinced that it had stopped beating.

The *Roi Pausole* was in its place, a very handsome edition illustrated by distinctly licentious drawings; the artist had sent him this inscribed copy when he was Premier. It was printed on handmade Japanese paper, in unbound sections, each followed by its set of loose-leaf illustrations, and protected by a gray cardboard case.

Would it occur to anyone, when he died, to leaf through his books, one by one, before sending them to the Salle Drouot to be scattered by auction?

His daughter, from what he knew of her, wouldn't open them. Nor would her husband. They might perhaps keep a few as souvenirs, but certainly not this one, for the illustrations would shock them.

It was amusing to imagine the fate of documents of the greatest importance, carried by the chances of an auction into the hands of people who hadn't even known they existed.

Not long ago he had moved Chalamont's confession, written in a feverish hand on paper with the heading of the Prime Minister's office, and had put it into this book by Pierre Louÿs. He had chosen that particular book because he had suddenly noted a resemblance between his one-time secretary, now that he'd put on flesh, and the King of Boeotia as depicted by the illustrator.

Several of his hiding places had been selected owing to equally unexpected comparisons, many of them humorous. As for the celebrated memoirs, they were not in the form of a connected manuscript, as everyone imagined; they were simply notes, explanations, and corrections, in tiny writing, in the margins of the three volumes of his official autobiography. Only instead of the French edition he had used the American one, which stood on the shelf side by side with the Japanese edition and some twenty other translations.

The paper he was looking for was in its place, in the second section, between pages 40 and 41, and the ink had had time to fade a bit.

"I, the undersigned, Philippe Chalamont . . ."

Hearing a sound, he started and put the book back in place, as furtively as a child surprised in a prank. It was only Emile, turning down his bed for the night, and Emile could not see him from the bedroom.

Had the man been surprised at not finding him in his study, and had he glanced into Milleran's office? If so, was he wondering what the Premier could possibly be up to in the semidarkness of the fourth room?

Had Chalamont tried to telephone from Paris? Had he set out, with his chauffeur? In that case, even with the bad weather, it would hardly take him more than three hours.

"Young Marie wants to know if she can go to the village."

He replied indifferently:

"Let her go."

"She says her mother's going to have a baby during the night."

Young Marie already had six or seven brothers and sisters, he wasn't quite sure how many, and it didn't matter anyhow. But an idea did occur to him.

"How will they let the doctor know?"

The nearest doctor was at Etretat, and it would not be possible to telephone to him.

"It's not the doctor who's delivering her, it's old Babette. . . ."

He didn't ask who Babette was. He'd only meant to offer the car. But if they didn't need it . . .

"Will you be going to bed as usual?"

"Yes, at ten o'clock." He had no reason for making any change in the pattern of his life. He invariably went to bed at ten o'clock, whether tired or not, and invariably got up, winter and summer alike, at half past five in the morning.

The only member of the household who'd protested against this timetable had been young Marie, although before coming to work for him she'd been a farm-hand and used to get up at four to milk the cows.

"Shall I make up the fire?"

The Premier was edgy, impatient, and this made him angry with himself, for he considered it humiliating to be affected, however slightly, by other people's actions or opinions.

If at the age of eighty-two he still was not secure from outside influences, what hope was there that he ever would be?

This reminded him, for a second, of the death of one of his friends, also an ex-Premier, the most ferocious anticlerical of the Third Republic, who to everyone's astonishment had sent for a priest at the last moment. . . .

He sat down in his usual place and opened Sully's memoirs, while Emile went back to the kitchen, whence he would return in due course to put him to bed.

He didn't read, however. He felt obliged to run over the Chalamont business again, as though searching his own conscience. He always thought of that chapter as entitled "the luncheon at Melun," and there were at least three people, apart from himself, for whom those words had the same sinister ring.

It had happened in June. The weather was bright and hot. Cars were rushing out of Paris, three abreast, toward the Forest of Fontainebleau. The Parisians were off for a day in the country, all unaware of the drama in progress, or else telling themselves, out of habit or from laziness, that those whom they had elected for the purpose would bring it safely to an end.

The financial crisis was probably the blackest the country had been through since the *assignats* of the Revolution. Every expedient had been attempted and they had gone almost hat in hand to beg the help of foreign governments. Every day the country was being drained of its substance, like a body bleeding to death, as the newspapers put it, and the outlook could hardly have been gloomier.

Three weeks earlier the Chamber had granted full powers to the government, after a stormy and inglorious night sitting. Every morning since then the papers had been asking:

"How are they going to use them?"

The Governor of the Bank of France was sending hourly messages, each more alarming than the last. Ascain, the Finance Minister, who had known, when he accepted that office, that it would bring him nothing but unpopularity and might mean the end of his political career, was conferring every morning with the Premier.

After the disastrous experiments made by previous governments, which had lived from day to day, robbing Peter to pay Paul, the only solution was a large-scale devaluation. And even that, if it were to be effective, must happen at the right moment, abruptly and unexpectedly enough to prevent speculation.

There were journalists on guard day and night outside the Hôtel Matignon in the Rue de Varennes, others in front of the Ministry of Finance in the Rue de Rivoli, and others, again, in the Rue de Valois, where the Governor of the Bank of France lived.

The three men with whom the decision rested were spied upon continually, their words, their mood, their slightest frown interpreted in one way or another.

But little by little the details of the operation had been settled, and all that remained was to fix the new exchange rate and the date of the devaluation.

Nerves were so strained in the Bourse and the foreign Stock Exchanges that the three men responsible ended by being afraid to be seen together for fear it might be taken for a signal.

So they decided to meet for luncheon, one Sunday, at a country house belonging to Ascain, just outside Melun. The appointment had been kept so secret that even their wives did not know about it, and Madame Ascain had not been there to receive her guests.

When he had arrived with Chalamont, who was then his Principal Private Secretary, the Premier had caught a frown on the face of Lauzet-Duché, the Governor of the Bank, but he had not felt called upon to give any reason for bringing the younger man.

Had not Chalamont become almost his shadow? Besides, even before his time, hadn't the Premier felt the need of a silent presence by his side?

The house was built of golden yellow stone; it looked onto a sloping street and was surrounded on three sides by a lovely garden, enclosed by iron railings and walls. It had belonged to Ascain's father, who was a solicitor, and the mark left by the brass plate could still be seen, to the left of the gate.

They had talked of nothing in particular during luncheon, in front of the servants; then they had taken coffee under a lime tree at the far end of the garden. As they were more secure from inquisitive ears in that spot than anywhere else, they had sat on in their wicker armchairs, around a small table loaded with liqueurs that nobody touched, to decide the rate of devaluation and fix the zero hour, which, for technical reasons, had to be Monday, just before the Bourse closed.

Reaching their decision after weeks of nervous strain, they had felt so relieved at the idea that matters were now out of their hands, that Ascain, who was short and plump, had suddenly pointed to a corner of the garden which was screened by a row of plane trees and suggested:

"We ought to have a game of skittles."

It was so unexpected, immediately after their serious conversation, that they had all burst out laughing, including Ascain, who had thrown out his proposal as a joke.

"There's a proper skittle alley over there, behind the plane trees," he explained. "My father had a passion for the game and I still keep the place in order. Like to have a look?"

Lauzet-Duché, a former Inspector of Finance, seldom relaxed his grave manner, which was enhanced by a square-cut pepper-and-salt beard.

Still not knowing what they were going to do, the four men walked across the lawn to the plane trees and there, indeed, was the skittle alley, with its cindered track and a big flat stone on which the Finance Minister, bending down, began to arrange the skittles that were lying about.

"Shall we have a go?"

The newspapers had never got hold of that story. For more than an hour the four men who had just determined the fate of the franc and the fortunes of millions of people, had played skittles, at first condescendingly and then with growing enthusiasm.

The next day, fifteen minutes after the opening of the Bourse, the telephone in the Prime Minister's office rang, and Chalamont picked it up, listened in silence, and then said:

"Just a moment, please."

And, turning to his chief:

"Lauzet-Duché wants to speak to you personally. . . ."

"Hello?"

"Is that you, Premier?"

Right away he had sensed trouble.

"Forgive me for asking, but I suppose you have told nobody about the decision we took yesterday? And you haven't mentioned it in talking by telephone to Ascain, by any chance?"

"No. Why?"

"I don't know anything definite yet. It's only an impression so far. I'm told that when the Bourse opened there were some rather disturbing dealings. . . ."

"By which bank?"

"It's too soon to say. I'm to have a report every fifteen minutes. . . . May I ring you back?"

"I shan't budge from my office. . . ."

By half past two over thirty thousand million francs' worth of government stock had been thrown onto the market. By three o'clock the Bank of France was beginning to buy back on the quiet, to prevent a collapse.

Lauzet-Duché, the Rue de Rivoli, and the Premier were in constant touch by telephone, and things reached a point where they wondered if the devaluation would not have to be postponed. This unexpected, unforeseeable speculation had already robbed it of much of its effect.

On the other hand, to draw back now might start a panic.

The Premier was livid when he finally gave the signal, in much the same spirit as a general launching a battle half lost in advance.

This would no longer be a bloodletting operation, affecting

the whole of France to a more or less equal extent. Those in the know had already escaped, and what was more they had made huge profits at the expense of the medium and small investors.

During all these discussions Chalamont, as white-faced as his chief, had remained in the office, lighting one cigarette after another and throwing each one away after a few tense puffs.

He was not fat in those days. The caricaturists usually depicted him as a raven.

In a few minutes the news-vendors would be out on the boulevards with special editions. The telephone switchboards at the Premier's house, the Ministry of Finance, and the Bank of France were overwhelmed with calls.

In the spacious office with its carved paneling the Premier sat tapping his blotter with the end of his pencil, his eyes fixed on some detail of a tapestry that hung on the opposite wall.

When at last he stood up, he moved like an automaton.

"Sit down, Chalamont."

His voice was clear, firm, with no more warmth than a machine.

"No. Not there. At my desk, please."

He began to walk up and down, hands behind his back.

"Take a pen and a sheet of paper. . . ."

And then he dictated, still walking up and down, with head lowered and hands clasped behind his back, pausing now and then for the right word:

"*I, the undersigned, Philippe Chalamont . . .*"

There was the sound of the pen moving over the paper, the sound of heavy breathing, and, about halfway through the dictation, a sound that resembled a sob.

"I can't . . ."

But the voice cut him short:

"Go on!"

The dictation went on till the bitter end.

CHAPTER *4*

"Do you really think anybody will come in this weather?" muttered Emile skeptically.

It was five minutes to ten. At about half past nine the electric bulbs had lit up feebly, as though trying to come back to life, but after blinking two or three times they had gone out again. A little later, Emile had come in and asked:

"How are you going to manage for the night, sir?"

Seeing that the old man had not immediately realized what he meant, he explained:

"About the light. . . . I went to the ironmonger's and bought the smallest oil lamp I could find, but I'm afraid even that will be too strong. . . ."

For several months the old man had given up sleeping in the dark; he had a tiny electric light, a special type that had been ordered from Paris. This decision had been taken on his doctor's insistence, after a distressing incident that had deeply humiliated him.

For a long time the doctors, Gaffé and Lalinde, had been urging him not merely to let the nurse stay at Les Ebergues instead of going off to sleep in the village, but to have her all night within call, on a camp bed in his study, for instance, or in the tunnel.

He had flatly, obstinately refused, and Fumet, to whom they had finally appealed to persuade him, had advised that, on the contrary, he should not be harassed about it.

He understood that for a man who in the whole of his life had never relied on anybody, prizing his independence above everything, the nurse's presence would be tantamount to surrender.

The fact that his chauffeur now turned into a valet, morning and evening, to help him to dress or to get to bed, was quite distressing enough for a man who had always jealously guarded his privacy.

"If I need help I can always ring for it," he had said, indicating the pear-shaped bellpull that hung above the bed.

"Or if not," he had added, "I shall be too far gone for anyone's help."

As a precaution, a very loud bell, shrill as would have befitted a school or a factory, had been placed, not in Emile's room because he might happen to be away, but on the first-floor landing, above the kitchen, so that there were three people to hear it.

But one night that had proved inadequate. In the middle of a nightmare he couldn't entirely shake off, though he was unable to recall it later, he had sat up in bed, in pitch darkness, oppressed, his body bathed in cold sweat, with a sensation of horror that he had never experienced before. He knew there was something he ought to do, that it was agreed on, that *they* had insisted he must do it, but he couldn't quite remember what it was, he was groping in the dark.

It was like a night he had been through at about eight years old, when he had mumps and had seen the ceiling coming slowly down on top of him, while his eiderdown floated up to meet it.

He struggled with his torpor, wanting to do as they had advised, for he was not hostile to them, whatever they might think, and feeling around in the emptiness, his hand touched a smooth, cold surface. Without realizing it, he had been trying to find the switch of the lamp on his bedside table, and all at once there was a crash on the floor; the tray, the bottle of mineral water, and the glass had been knocked over.

He still couldn't find the cord of the lamp, or the switch. They must have pulled the bedside table farther away; that was a little mystery he would try to clear up later. Meanwhile he felt an urgent, imperative need of action.

Then, leaning forward, he had tipped over and fallen heavily to the floor, all of a piece, landing in a position as ridiculous as on the cliff path the day his left leg had played him that dirty trick.

He could feel splinters of glass all around him, and felt sure that blood was running over his hand, though he didn't know where it came from. He tried to get up, but in vain, there was no strength in his legs, and in the last resort the instinct of the baby in its cot returned to him and he began to shout.

There had been no storm that night. And yet, incredible as it might seem, of the three whose bedrooms were above the kitchen, not so far off, not one had heard him; it was young Marie, so difficult to wake in the morning, who had arrived in her nightdress, smelling of bed. She had turned on the light and stood there for quite a while, as though on her guard, hesitant, suspicious.

Had she believed him to be dead or dying? In the end she, too, had uttered a cry and, instead of giving him a hand, had rushed off upstairs to call the others. When they had come hurrying she had lagged behind, still half frightened.

His wrist had been bleeding, but it wasn't a deep cut. Gaffé had been unable to decide exactly what had been wrong with the Premier.

"It happens to everybody, at any age. Probably a nightmare, brought on by cramp or by a momentary disturbance of the circulation. That would explain why you couldn't get up. . . ."

He had talked again about having Madame Blanche there on

a camp bed. The Premier's only concession had been to sleep from then on with a faint light in his room. They'd found him this lamp, hardly bigger than the bulb in a pocket flashlight, and he had grown accustomed to the night light, which had gradually come to form part of his world.

Emile had remembered it this evening, and, without saying anything, had gone down to the village and bought the little oil lamp. As luck would have it, at the very moment when he mentioned it, the electric current made a spasmodic return, died away again, then revived, and at last one could feel, from the brightness of the light, that this time it had come back for good.

"I'll fix you up the oil lamp all the same, just in case . . ."

Morning and evening, for his valeting duties, Emile wore a white linen jacket, and it was probably the way in which the white of the jacket emphasized his black hair and rugged, irregular features that had prompted someone to remark:

"Your man looks more like a thug than a servant. . . ."

He'd been born at Ingrannes, in the depths of the Forest of Orléans, in a family whose men had been gamekeepers, from father to son, for longer than anyone could remember, and he and his brothers had been brought up with the dogs. But he made one think of a poacher rather than a gamekeeper. In spite of his sturdy frame and bulging muscles, he moved about the house more softly than the ethereal Milleran, and a disturbing glint sometimes came into his mocking yet guileless eyes.

The Premier had taken him over the year he had become Foreign Minister. He had found Emile, just released from military service, among the chauffeurs at the Quai d'Orsay, where he had been accepted through the influence of his local "Squire," and he contrasted so strongly with the well-schooled chauffeurs of the Quai that he had found him amusing to watch.

It hadn't been easy to tame him, for at the least approach Emile's face would close up and one would be confronted with an expressionless, irritating wooden mask.

That particular Cabinet had survived for three years, and when it had been finally defeated Emile had muttered hesitantly, hanging his head and fidgeting awkwardly with his cap:

"I suppose there's no chance I could go along with you?"

He had gone along with him for twenty-two years, hanging around him like a dog at his master's heels, and had never spoken of getting married. Presumably he felt no need to do so, but the moment a passable unmarried woman, thin or fat, young or middle-aged, came into his field of vision he would cover her as a cock or a rabbit might, without hesitation but nonchalantly, as though it were part of his natural functions.

The Premier had more than once amused himself by watching his goings on, for he felt that in his dealings with women his chauffeur revealed the same instinct as a poacher dealing with game. When a new victim came along, Emile scarcely appeared to notice her, except that his small black eyes became more set and his movements slower and more silent than usual. He melted into his surroundings at such times, just as a poacher in a forest becomes a tree or a rock, and waited patiently for an hour, a day, or a week, till the propitious moment arrived. Whereupon, with an unerring instinct, he pounced.

Young Marie had certainly had her turn in the first week, if not on the first night, and the Premier would not have been surprised to learn that from time to time Milleran submitted, passively but not unwillingly, to the attentions of the only active male in the household.

Once in Paris he had been almost an eye-witness of one of these forthright conquests, which were an aspect of natural history and had a touch of its rough poetry. It was at the Ministry of Justice, when he was Keeper of the Seals. There had just been some changes in the staff, and on the morning of a big luncheon party a housemaid had arrived from the country, young and dewy, with the bloom still on her.

The great house had been the scene of feverish activity and things had been a bit confused. About nine o'clock in the morning, the Keeper of the Seals had happened to be in a room that was being turned out, just in time to witness the meeting between Emile and the new maid.

He had sensed what was happening. Some people maintain that cock and hen birds communicate with each other by a kind of telepathy, and if so, Emile must have possessed the same faculty of emitting and receiving waves, for on merely catching sight of the girl from behind he made a dead set and his brown pupils contracted.

Later on, as the Premier came out of his own suite, where he had gone to put on his morning coat, he had seen Emile come into the corridor, emerging from the linen room and closing the door noiselessly behind him; his face was flushed and wore a satisfied expression, and he paused to tidy himself up.

The two men's eyes met, and Emile simply gave an imperceptible wink, as much as to say:

"That's that!"

As though he had just snared a rabbit at the expected spot.

Girls would pester him, claiming that they were pregnant by him. Their fathers would join in now and then, and some of them wrote to the Premier, who still remembered one typical phrase:

". . . *and I rely on you, Minister, to see that the skunk puts matters to rights by marrying my daughter. . . .*"

To which Emile would reply, unabashed:

"If a fellow had to marry every girl he put in the family way! . . ."

What kind of stories would Emile relate, in future years, to sightseers who came to Les Ebergues? And what did he really think about the old man he served?

"If you've no objection I'll stay in the kitchen and make myself some coffee. Like that, if the gentlemen were to come . . ."

Was it he who had hunted through the volumes of Saint-Simon and various other books?

Milleran was equally devoted, and would be much more afflicted by his death. She would find it difficult, at forty-seven, to submit to a new kind of discipline and get used to another employer. Would she yield to the insistence of the publishers who would try to persuade her to write about his private life, so far as she knew it?

Those idiots were unaware that he'd never had any private life, and that at the age of eighty-two his entire store of human relationships—he would not venture upon the word "friendship" or "affection"—consisted of the few people who lived at Les Ebergues.

Gabrielle, whose surname was Mitaine, and who came from

the Nièvre, had been married. Widowed at forty, left with one little boy, she had come into his service, and even now she went once a month to Villeneuve-Saint-Georges, to see her son, who was now a man of forty-nine, married, with three children, and worked as head steward in a dining car on the Paris-Ventimiglia line.

Gabrielle was just turned seventy-two. Didn't the thought of death probably haunt her far more than it did her master?

As for young Marie, she would hardly remember the years she had spent working for the "old boy."

Perhaps it would be Madame Blanche who'd remember him longest, although he was more often gruff with her than with any of the others.

In point of fact there were just two people with whom he was on close terms, to whom he really mattered, two who were poles apart and offset each other, so to speak: Xavier Malate, who pursued him with a hatred as tenacious as unrequited love, and was clinging to life so as not to leave it before he did; Eveline, the sandy-haired girl in the Rue Saint-Louis, who, after losing sight of him for sixty years and more, was now sending him consecrated medals every year.

His daughter, his son-in-law, and his grandson didn't count, they had never been part of his existence. They were outsiders, almost strangers.

As for Chalamont . . .

Was he really driving toward Le Havre at this moment? Was the Premier right to be going to bed, when he might perhaps have to get up again at any moment?

"If they come, what room shall I show them into?"

He hesitated for a second. He didn't want to leave Chalamont alone in the studies. This house was not a Ministry, there were no ushers and no waiting room. When a visitor arrived, Milleran left him to wait in one of the book-lined rooms.

At least one visitor came almost every day. Usually only one was allowed, on Professor Fumet's advice, for despite his apparent coldness he exerted himself too much for his guests.

Milleran would say warningly to the newcomer, the moment she let him in:

"Don't keep the Premier for more than half an hour. The doctors say he mustn't tire himself."

Those who arrived like this, or at least those who gained admission, were statesmen from almost every country in the world, historians, university professors, students.

They all had questions to ask. Some of them, those who were writing a book about him, or a thesis, brought along imposing lists of specific questions.

Almost invariably he began the conversation grudgingly, finding it irksome, and seemed to withdraw into his shell.

Then, after a few minutes, he grew lively, and not every visitor noticed that he was now asking the questions instead of submitting to them.

Some people, when the half-hour was up, would conscientiously prepare to take their leave. Or Milleran would appear, silently, in the doorless opening between the two studies.

"We shan't be a minute. . . ."

The minute would stretch out, the half-hour would become an hour, two hours, and sometimes one of these passing visitors, much to his surprise, would be asked to stay to lunch.

This exhausted the Premier, but it cheered him up, and when he was alone again with Milleran he would rub his hands gleefully.

"He came here to pick my brains, and I've been picking his!"

At other times he would inquire jokingly, before an appointment:

"Whom am I to put on my act for today?"

There was some truth in the jest.

"I have to take care of my statue!" he had declared once, in a gay mood.

Without admitting it even to himself, he did take an interest in the impression he was to leave behind him, and there were occasions when the surly retorts for which he was celebrated were not entirely sincere, but formed part of his act. At such times he wouldn't have Milleran around, for he felt rather ashamed of himself in front of her, just as in front of Madame Blanche he felt ashamed of his weakened body.

"Do you need anything else, sir?"

The old man glanced around him. The bottle of water and the glass were in the usual place; so was the sleeping tablet he took every night. The tiny, flat light was switched on. The oil lamp was ready to replace it if need be.

"Good night, sir. I hope I shan't have to disturb you before morning. . . ."

The central light went out, Emile's footsteps drew further away, the kitchen door opened and closed again, and the room was left to silence and solitude, rendered almost intangible by contrast with the storm outside.

Since he had grown old, he scarcely felt the need of sleep, and for years he had lain in bed like this, for two or three hours every evening, quite still, his eyes shut, in a state of suspended animation.

It was not exactly insomnia. He felt neither annoyance nor impatience and it was by no means disagreeable. Far from it! During the day he sometimes thought with pleasure of the moment when he would thus be left to his own company.

Now he had taken to the little glowing disk it was still more pleasant, for its pinkish light helped, even through his closed eyelids, to create an atmosphere of secret, inner life.

At such times everything softened and mingled, the walls, the furniture, every gleam on which was known to him, the familiar objects he saw without looking at them, whose weight and substance even seemed palpable, the wind, the rain, the cry of a night bird or the sound of the waves at the foot of the cliff, the creak of a shutter, the movements of somebody undressing in one of the bedrooms, everything, even to the stars twinkling in the silent sky, played its part in a symphony of which he, as he lay apparently inert, was the center and to which his heart beat time.

Was this how death would come, taking him unawares on some not far-distant night? He knew that everybody in the household was expecting to find him, one morning, cold and stiff in his bed. He knew, too, that old people often did die in their sleep, unawares.

He sensed that Milleran's fear was rather that it would happen at nightfall, while he sat, dozing as it seemed, in his armchair, hands folded on his stomach.

In bed, too, he took that position, the attitude of a dead man prepared for his last journey, and he didn't do it on purpose, but because his body had gradually come to find it comfortable and natural.

Was that a portent?

He didn't believe in portents. He refused to believe in anything, even in the value of his lifework. At least ten times in the course of his life he had felt bound to make a superhuman effort, believing it to be indispensable, and for weeks, months, years he had led a hectic existence, pursuing his objective in the teeth of universal opposition.

On those occasions his energy, his vigorous metabolism, which used to amaze Professor Fumet, would spread not only to his immediate collaborators and to the Chamber, but to the whole country, to the invisible nation, which, after a period of mistrust and uncertainty, would be surprised to find itself following him blindly.

Because of this almost biological faculty, it was always at difficult, desperate moments that he was called in.

How often he had heard the same words uttered by a Head of State driven to the last ditch: "Save France . . ." or: "Save the Republic . . ." or perhaps: "Save freedom . . ."

Every crisis had found him with faith unimpaired, for without that he could have done nothing, a faith so firm that he could sacrifice everything for it, not only himself but others, which had often been harder.

Cold sweat broke out on him even now, he still felt physically unwell, when he recalled his first action as Minister of the Interior; he saw himself, in a black, relentless setting of coal mines and blast furnaces, holding a final parley, all alone between men on strike, whose leaders had turned them into rioters with hate-filled hearts, and the soldiers he had called in.

All the time he was trying to make himself heard, his voice had been drowned by jeering. Then, when he had stopped, a somber and probably grotesque figure, his arms falling helplessly to his sides, there had been a long, vibrant silence, betraying irresolution, hesitation.

The two camps were watching each other closely, defying

each other, and suddenly, as though at a signal—it was proved afterwards that there actually was a signal—bricks, cobblestones, and scraps of cast iron came flying through the air, while the soldiers' horses began to whinny and paw the ground.

He knew he would be blamed for his decision to the end of his life, that tomorrow, and for many a long day, most of his countrymen would curse him.

He knew, too, that it was necessary.

"Colonel, give the order to charge."

A week later there were posters on the walls showing him with a hideous grin and with blood dripping from his hands, and the government was overthrown.

But order had been preserved.

Ten times, twenty times, he had withdrawn from the lime-light in this way, having completed his task, and had sat, grumpy and silent, on the opposition benches, until he was needed again.

On one occasion some man or other, a nonentity, a kind of Xavier Malate, had come to ask him for a job to which he had no right and, on being refused, had put a bullet through his head in the waiting room, as he left his office.

For some time now, on the advice of his doctors—his Three Musketeers—he had been taking a light sedative at bedtime, which didn't send him off to sleep at once, but brought on a gradual, delicious drowsiness to which he had grown accustomed.

Sometimes he didn't swallow it immediately, but gave himself the pleasure of prolonging, for half an hour or more, his clear-headed wakefulness, his conversation with himself. He had begun to hoard his life. He felt he had a whole lot of problems left to solve, not only with calm and composure, but in the completely dispassionate mood that he could achieve only at night, in bed.

This was the most secret of all his tasks, concerning no one except himself; he would have liked to finish it before taking his departure, leaving nothing obscure, looking everything straight in the face. Was it not to help himself in this that he had begun to read so many volumes of memoirs, confessions, private diaries?

Coming to the end of one of these books, he was invariably disappointed, irritated, feeling the author had cheated. He wanted pure truth, truth in the raw, as he was trying to find it in his own case, even if it turned out to be sickening or repugnant.

But all the writers he had come across had *arranged* their material, he was far enough on in life to know that. All of them held, believed they held or pretended to hold, a truth, and he, despite his grim search for truth, had not found it.

Just now, hearing Chalamont's voice over the radio, he had been compelled to brace himself. Had he felt any doubt about being in the right when, in his office in the Hôtel Matignon, he had dictated that letter of infamy which his assistant, bathed in sweat so that the whole room stank of it, had taken down, to the last word, and signed?

If he had needed further proof than that submissiveness, he received more than enough in the next few days, when discreet investigation by the Ministry of Finance revealed the fact that Vollard's Bank had been behind the last-minute speculation which had cost the country thousands of million of francs.

Vollard's Bank, in the Rue Vivienne, little known to the general public, was a private firm, working in close co-operation with one of the biggest financial concerns in Wall Street, and Etienne Vollard, its Chairman, was Chalamont's father-in-law.

Didn't the Premier, aware of this family connection, bear a heavy responsibility for taking his assistant to the luncheon party at Melun and insisting that he should be present?

Not for an instant had it occurred to him that Chalamont might betray him. In Ascain's garden, whether before the skittle game or afterwards, he had felt as sure of his assistant as of himself.

Looking at it more closely, his confidence had been in the mission rather than the individual. It all tied up with what he had said to Fumet, in the Avenue Friedland. He had felt certain that Chalamont had once and for all crossed the invisible frontier beyond which the individual man ceases to count, all that matters being the task he has set himself.

That day, the day of the dictation, the Premier's world had tottered and almost collapsed.

He remembered how, the letter written, his Secretary had made for the door and clutched the handle. The idea that he might commit suicide, as the unsuccessful petitioner had done, had not occurred to him and would anyhow not have influenced him.

"Stay here!"

Chalamont still had his back turned, would not wheel around and face him, but he did stop where he was.

"It is impossible for me at present, and will be for some time, to accept your resignation or to kick you out."

He spoke rapidly, in an undertone, jerking out the syllables.

"Imperative reasons make it impossible, unfortunately, for me to bring you into the courts, with your father-in-law and his accomplices."

It was true that legal proceedings, with the resultant scandal, at such a moment, would have destroyed public confidence and led to even greater tragedy.

That, much more than the personal disappointment he had suffered, was the reason for his resentment against Chalamont. The latter knew that whatever might happen, they would have to shelter him, keep quiet, cover up the matter. Vollard's Bank had been gambling on a certainty, and Etienne Vollard, with his pearl-gray top hat, would be seen tomorrow in the owners' stand at Longchamp or Auteuil, where he had horses running. If he won the President of the Republic's Stakes the week after next, the Head of the State could hardly avoid shaking hands with him and congratulating him!

"Until further notice you will carry out your duties as usual, and in public there will be no change in our relationship."

This strain had gone on for a fortnight, though the Premier had been so busy that he could give little thought to his assistant.

When they were alone he avoided speaking to him and, if forced to do so, gave him his instructions in an impersonal tone.

On several occasions Chalamont had opened his mouth as though tormented by the need to say something, and at such times he would gaze pathetically at his chief.

He was no longer a boy, a young man, or even what is known as a budding politician. He was a mature man, his face already lined, and this made his humility disgusting rather than tragic.

How was he behaving in the evening, at dinner with his wife?

What had he said to his father-in-law and his partners? What thoughts were revolving in his head when he got into his car and told the chauffeur, seated in front of him, to drive to the Hôtel Matignon?

One morning the Premier found on his desk a letter addressed in his Principal Secretary's writing, and as Chalamont was not there, he left it untouched until the man came in; then he picked up the unopened envelope, holding it between finger and thumb, and tore it into small pieces which he dropped into the wastepaper basket.

Now they were to have their last conversation. It was brief. Without deigning to glance at the other man, as he stood at the far side of the desk, he said:

"From now on you are relieved of your duties with me."

Chalamont did not move, and his chief, picking up a file, added:

"I was forgetting. . . . You can consider our acquaintance at an end. . . . You may go now."

He had opened the file and picked up the red pencil he used for making notes on documents.

"I said, you may go now!"

"You absolutely refuse to listen to me?"

"*Absolutely*. Leave the room, please."

Lying in bed, he started, for he heard a noise outside. Straining his ears, he recognized the footsteps of one of the policemen, who was stamping his feet to warm them.

During the last week poor Cournot had appealed to all the political leaders in succession. Some had refused outright. Others had opened negotiations which had dragged on for a day or two. On those occasions arrangements had taken shape, names had been mentioned, lists of probable Ministers had even been put forward, but then each time the structure collapsed at the last moment and the party leaders again began to file through the Elysée.

But where others had failed, Chalamont had a chance of success. His group was a small one, but influential because of its position, halfway between the center and the left, and it had the further advantage of not being committed to any hard-and-fast policy. Moreover, at a time when the different parties held divergent views about economic questions and about wages, the public found something reassuring about the Left Independents.

Among Chalamont's other trump cards were his adaptability, his skill in trimming his sails, and the fact that at the age of sixty he was beginning to count as one of the old guard at the Palais-Bourbon, where he could rely on long-standing friendships and on a network of connections built up by services rendered and minor compromises.

What would the Premier say now, then and there, if they came and asked him:

"Do you think Chalamont can find a way out of the crisis?"

Would he venture to keep silent, or would he frankly say what he thought:

"Yes."

"Do you think that his coming to power would prevent the general strike that is threatening the country?"

There again, the answer was undoubtedly:

"Yes."

When Chalamont had been his right hand he had twenty times helped him to settle disputes with the unions, and although he was the son-in-law of a banker, lived on the edge of the Bois, and sat in the Chamber for the wealthiest arrondissement in Paris, he could handle the workers' representatives as no one else could do.

The Premier tried to halt his argument, which was making him feel uncomfortable, but he wanted to play fair.

"Is Chalamont cut out to be a statesman?"

He hesitated and refused to answer that question, but then it led to another:

"Which of today's politicians would make a better Premier?"

Oh, very well! He could think of nobody! Perhaps he was the victim of old age, which ends by distorting even the soundest judgment? If so the newspapers seemed to have grown old with him, which was true to some extent, for many of them still had as their editors, or on their board of directors, men whom the Premier had known in those positions thirty or forty years ago.

However that might be, every time a government fell they, too, would allude to "the great team," lamenting the dearth of

men of the former mold, not merely in France but among the
leaders of her allies.

Had the world really experienced an age of genuinely great
men, of whom the Premier was the sole survivor except for
Count Cornelio, the Italian, who was ending his days in a mental
home outside Rome?

Again he listened, and this time it was Emile, in the kitchen,
who had joggled the bench as he got up. He nearly rang for him,
to tell him to go to bed. His thoughts had taken a disagreeable
turn, and he was tempted to swallow the pill that lay beside the
glass of water.

Outside, the Antifer light, off Etretat, and the lighthouse of
Notre-Dame-du-Salut, above Fécamp, must be sweeping the
lowering sky with their beams, which would meet almost directly over Les Ebergues.

There would be boats out at sea, with men, stiff in their oilskins, wearing sou'westers and rubber boots, standing on slip-
pery decks and hauling at wet, cold tackle. In the village there
would be at least one lighted window, that of the room where
young Marie's mother was having her baby.

He hadn't had the curiosity, before getting into bed, to find
out whether the telephone was working again. Most likely not.
Telephone breakdowns always lasted longer than electricity fail-
ures.

It was eleven o'clock. Suppose Chalamont's car had broken
down, too, somewhere by the side of the deserted road?

Had he really, during the last few years, been attempting to
get back the confession he had signed in such dramatic circumstances?

Save for that paper, already yellowing, there was no evidence
against him except the bare word of an old man whom many
people now thought of as disappointed, embittered, with a lasting
grudge against the world for not allowing him to end his career
as President of the Republic.

Ascain had died in his fine house at Melun, to which he had
retired after being heavily defeated at the polls, and where he
had presumably spent his last years in playing skittles. He had
left no memoirs. He had left no money either, and his two sons,

one a vet and the other a traveler in patent medicines, had sold the property that had come down to them from their grandfather, the solicitor.

Ascain would bring no charge now. As for Lauzet-Duché, he had been the first to go, carried away by a stroke while making a speech at the end of a banquet in Brussels.

The others didn't know. In any case, how many still survived, even of the civil servants who had been merely on the outskirts of the affair, each knowing only one small part of it?

All that remained was a scrap of paper.

Was that what someone had been seeking at Les Ebergues for several months past? Up and down the house, in other books besides *Le Roi Pausole*, there were a hundred documents as dangerous to various people as that one was to Chalamont. Anyone who spends a great part of his life, particularly a life as long as his own, not only in the political arena but in the wings as well, is bound to witness any number of cowardly and disreputable actions.

And if someone were to ask him now:

"Do you know one single politician who in the entire course of his career has never . . ."

He cut his thought off short, as he used to cut off other people's words.

"No!"

He wasn't going to play that game. He'd been about to fall into his own trap, and with a brusque movement he propped himself on one elbow, seized the pill, and swallowed it with a mouthful of water.

He needed sleep and wanted to get to sleep quickly, without thinking any longer.

The last picture to drift more or less coherently through his mind was that of a man, whose features he could not distinguish, lying in a hospital bed. This was supposed to be Xavier Malate, and while a nun was changing him, handling him like a baby, he was tittering and explaining that they wouldn't get him to die out of turn.

"Augustin first!" he said with a wink.

CHAPTER *5*

Without needing to open his eyes he knew it was still night, and that the little flat lamp was shedding a faint light in one corner of the room, like a tiny moon. He also knew that something unusual was happening, though he couldn't have said what, something missing, a *lack,* rather than something too much, and when he had roused up sufficiently he realized that what had disturbed him was the silence surrounding the house after the storm that had been raging for days, as though all at once the universe had ceased to vibrate.

There was a ray of light under the door into the study, he could see it through the tiny slit between his eyelids. To see the time by his alarm clock he would have to turn his head, and he didn't feel like moving.

He listened. There was someone moving in the next room, without excessive caution, not furtively, and he recognized the sound of logs being dumped on the hearth and the familiar crackle of the kindling. When the smell of the burning wood began to reach his nostrils, not before, he called out:

"Emile!"

The chauffeur opened the door; he had not yet shaved or put on his white jacket, and the sleepless night had clouded his eyes.

"Did you call, sir?"

"What time is it?"

"A few minutes past five. It suddenly turned cold, late in the night, and now it feels like frost. So I'm starting the fire. Did I wake you?"

"No."

After a short silence, Emile remarked:

"So you see, nobody came, after all."

The old man repeated:

"Nobody came, you're right."

"Would you like your tea right away?"

From his bed he could watch the flames leaping in the study fireplace.

"Yes, please."

Then, as Emile reached the door, he called him back:

"Open the shutters first, if you don't mind."

Just as, in the evening, he liked to cloak himself in solitude, in the morning he was eager to resume contact with life, eager in an anxious, almost frightened way.

Day was still far off, there was no sign of dawn, and yet the night was not black but white, and a light, pale-colored vapor, which was actually fog, had time to float into the room while Emile leaned out to push back the shutters.

"The cold's as sharp as midwinter, and later on, with this damp rising as though the ground were a sponge, we shan't be able to see as far as the garden gate."

During this brief contact with the outer world they had heard the foghorn wailing, muted, in the distance. At some point during the night the wind had fallen to a flat calm, but ordinary life, in abeyance during the tempest of the last few days, had not yet got under way again and the countryside still lay, as it were, in limbo.

"I'll bring your tea in five minutes."

Coffee had been forbidden, and now he was only allowed weak tea. Of all the privations he had to endure, this was the only one he found painful, and he sometimes went into the kitchen, while Gabrielle was getting breakfast for the staff, just for a whiff of the coffee they were to drink.

Chalamont hadn't come, but it was too soon to think about that, nothing definite being known as yet. But not to have received the visit he had regarded as almost certain was a disappointment, though still vague and unacknowledged. He felt ill at ease, anxious, as though he, too, suddenly lacked something, as though there were something missing in life.

Sitting up in bed, he drank his tea, while Emile prepared his linen and his suit, for he was always fully dressed first thing in the morning, and very few people could boast of having seen him with his toilet incomplete. Even a dressing gown, he considered, belonged to the privacy of the bedroom, and he never wore one in his study.

On his way to take a shower—he had had to give up baths—he glanced out of the window and saw the glowing tip of a cigarette close to the house.

"Is that still Aillevard?"

"No. Rougé took over from him just before two o'clock, about the time when the weather changed, and I gave him a cup of coffee a while ago."

The house was starting to stir again. There was a light in Gabrielle's room—she'd be coming down to start her fire—and in Milleran's as well. Water was running through a pipe. A cow mooed in the nearest barn and another answered it from farther off, more faintly. While the storm lasted not a cow had been heard.

He took his shower, tepid and very short, as he had been advised, after which Emile helped him to dry himself and get into his clothes. Emile smelled strongly of cold cigarette, especially in the early morning. It made the Premier feel queasy, but he didn't like to ask the man to stop smoking.

"If you don't need me I'll go up quickly to change and shave."
Usually this, too, was an hour he enjoyed. In summer it was already light and he could see children taking cattle to pasture in the fields along the cliff-top. Closer to him the house would be gradually waking up and he would stroll about idly, without impatience, in the four low-ceilinged rooms, going from one shelf to another, pausing, moving on, halting on the threshold to sniff the smell of damp soil and grass which, only quite recently, had gone back to being the same as in his childhood.

In autumn and winter he watched the slow dawn breaking, and there was nearly always a thin mist rising from the ground, in a sheet of unequal density, pierced with holes through which one sometimes glimpsed the church belfry.

Today the dawn was colorless, sketched with white gouache and charcoal, and only the whiter glow of the thickening fog showed that the light was strengthening.

The others were in the kitchen, eating. The tree near the front door was growing visible in misty outline, with its trunk that leaned eastward because of the sea wind and its leafless branches which all stretched eastward too; then the dim, ghostly figure of the policeman on guard came into view beside it. He seemed very far away, in another world, and even his footsteps were inaudible, as though the fog was muffling sounds as well as blurring forms.

Now and again the Premier looked at the time, then at the little white radio set on his desk. Before the moment had come to switch it on, he saw young Marie advancing through the fog, growing gradually taller and clearer, her red jersey striking the only note of color in the landscape.

Tiny drops of moisture must be clinging to her untidy hair, as they did to every blade of grass she walked over. When she noisily opened the kitchen door, exclamations could be heard, laughter from Emile. Her mother must have had the baby, but he didn't call her to make sure.

He was counting the minutes now, and he turned on the radio too soon, had to put up with a stupid popular song followed by the whole of the weather report, to which he paid no attention. Thursday, November 4th. Feast of St. Charles. Paris market prices. Fruit and vegetables . . .

"And here is our first news bulletin. Home news. Paris. As we anticipated yesterday evening, there was considerable activity all night in the Boulevard Suchet, where Monsieur Philippe Chalamont, entrusted by the President of the Republic with the task of forming a Cabinet on a multi-party basis, was visited by a number of prominent politicians belonging to various parties. Leaving the Deputy for the sixteenth arrondissement's flat at about four o'clock this morning, Monsieur Ernest Grouchard, leader of the Radical Party, whose visit had immediately succeeded that of the leader of the Socialist group, declared his satisfaction at the way the negotiations were proceeding. It is thought that Monsieur Chalamont will go to the Elysée fairly early in the morning, to give the Head of the State his definite reply, as promised. Marseilles. The Mélina, a liner belonging to the Messageries Maritimes, on board which . . ."

He switched off, without noticing that Milleran had come into the study. His reaction was a gloomy amazement, a sensation of emptiness not unlike what he had felt earlier when the noise of the storm had suddenly given out.

He had been waiting for Chalamont, almost certain he would come. Had he been secretly hoping for the visit? He didn't know. He didn't want to know, especially not just now.

While he had been imagining his former subordinate driving through the rain and wind, and had even gone so far as to think he might have had a breakdown on the way, Chalamont had been in his flat in the Boulevard Suchet, coldly playing the game, receiving the political leaders, one by one.

It was so unexpected, so monstrous, that he could not shake off his stupefaction, and at one moment he put the tip of his first finger to the corner of his eye, which was slightly moist.

Realizing that his secretary was standing in front of him, he asked her, as though collecting his thoughts from a great distance and resentful of her intrusion:

"What is it?"

"I wanted to ask whether I should ring up Evreux right away."

He took a little time to remember, while Milleran went on:

"A hospital is open night and day, so perhaps there's no need to wait till nine o'clock?"

He still sat sluggishly in his armchair, and his set, vacant stare began to worry Milleran, though she knew from experience that she must pretend not to notice it. Simply to break the silence, she announced:

"Young Marie has a little sister. That's the fifth girl in the family."

"Leave me alone for a while, if you don't mind."

"May I go into my office?"

"No. Somewhere else. Wherever you like."

There remained one explanation, on which he pinned his hopes: that Chalamont's confession had vanished. To check this theory, he was sending Milleran away, and as soon as she was in the kitchen he went to the farthest bookcase and, with a feverish hand, pulled out *Le Roi Pausole* in its heavy cardboard case.

At that moment he was hoping . . .

But the second folder opened of its own accord at page 40, and there lay the sheet of paper with the heading of the Premier's office, ironical, looking no more important than an old love letter or a four-leaf clover forgotten between the pages of a book. And indeed it was of very slight importance, despite its dramatic statement and the care he had taken of it, for it had not prevented anything.

"*I, the undersigned, Philippe Chalamont . . .*"

With a gesture of impatience such as he had rarely indulged in during his life, and of which he was at once ashamed, he hurled the book to the ground, so that he suffered the humiliation of being obliged to get down and pick up the scattered parts, the loose engravings, the original drawings.

Because of his ex-secretary, he was reduced to watching the door, for fear someone might suddenly come in and find him on all fours on the floor. And he'd look even more ridiculous if his leg suddenly played him one of its tricks while he was in this position!

Milleran waited in the kitchen, unaware of what was going on, listening hard, and it was at least ten minutes before the bell recalled her to the study.

The Premier had gone back to the Louis-Philippe armchair. His strained manner had disappeared, replaced by a calm that she found uncomfortable because it was obviously artificial, like his voice, which had an unaccustomed, unnaturally suave note when he said:

"You may telephone now."

He cared nothing for Malate just then, but it was important for life to go on as usual, for the little everyday events to follow one another in the expected order. That was a kind of moral hygiene and the only way of keeping a cool head.

If the paper had disappeared from the Pierre Louÿs book he would have understood Chalamont's behavior, accepted it, perhaps even approved it, and it would not have affected him personally.

With the document still in his hands, things were different. That meant that his former secretary had reached the cynical conclusion that the way lay open, that the obstacle that had delayed him on his way up the political ladder had in his opinion ceased to exist.

The old man was still living, of course, on the top of some cliff in Normandy, but the scrap of paper he had brandished for so long had lost its value as a scarecrow, just as the ink of the writing on it was fading.

Chalamont was behaving as though the Premier were dead.

He had made his decision during the night, with his eyes open, knowing what he was about, weighing the risks, foreseeing every eventuality.

It had not occurred to him to call up. The breakdown had nothing to do with his silence. He had not set out for Les Ebergues, had sent nobody, this time, to plead his cause or negotiate on his behalf.

"Hello? Is that Evreux hospital?"

Was the Premier really going to bother about that maniac who had been haunting him for so many years? Had he come down to that? He was tempted to rush into the next room, take the telephone away from his secretary and ring off. Everything was annoying him, including the fog, too motionless and stupid, which was pressing against the window and making the outside world look unearthly.

"Yes . . . You say he's . . . I can't quite hear you, mademoiselle . . . Yes . . . Yes . . . That's better . . . You didn't know how long he's been there? . . . I understand . . . I shall probably ring you again later . . . Thank you. . . ."

"Well, so what?" he snarled, when Milleran came in, looking embarrassed.

"Dr. Jaquemont, or Jeaumont, I couldn't get the name clearly, is operating on him now. . . . He went into the theater at a quarter past seven. . . . They expect it to take a long time. . . . It seems that . . ."

"Why did you say you'd call back?"

"I don't know . . . I thought you'd want to know. . . ."

He grunted:

"You aren't here to think!"

It was all too idiotic. Here he was, worrying about the fate of a man who meant nothing to him, who ought to be shut up in a lunatic asylum, for no earthly reason except that the fellow had been assuring him for forty years:

"I'll be at your funeral."

Now it was Malate who was on the operating table, at the age of eighty-three—for he was a year older than his former schoolfellow—with a cancer of the throat that two previous operations had done nothing to cure. Whether he died or whether he didn't, what difference would it make? What did it matter?

"Tell Emile to take the car and go to Etretat for the papers."

"I think the barber's arriving," she announced, looking out of the window and seeing a man on a bicycle, distorted by the fog to an apocalyptic monster.

"Let him come in, then."

The barber, Fernand Bavet, who was also a saddler, came every morning to shave him, for the Premier was among the survivors of a period when men did not shave themselves, and he had always refused to do it, just as he had refused to learn to drive a car.

Bavet was a florid, full-blooded man with a throaty voice.

"Well, sir, what do you think of this pea souper? One can't see three yards in front of one's nose, and I nearly ran into one of your guardian angels . . ."

Most barbers' hands smell of cigarette smoke, which is unpleasant enough. Bavet's smelled of fresh leather as well, of newly slaughtered animals, and his breath stank of calvados.

As the Premier grew older he became more sensitive to smells, and was disgusted by things he never noticed in the old days, as though his body, as it dried up, was being purified by a kind of disincarnation.

"Now tell me, you who're in the know, are we going to have a government, after all?"

Bavet's good humor met with no response and he lapsed into resigned silence, a little vexed, all the same, for he was fond of telling his café cronies:

"The old man? I shave him every day and with me he's just like anybody else, I speak as straight to him as I would to one of you. . . ."

Still, everybody has good days and bad ones, haven't they? His job finished, the barber put away his instruments, bowed to his customer, and went off to the kitchen, where Gabrielle always gave him a drink. The engine of the car was running; Emile was warming it up before starting out to fetch the papers from Etretat, since the grocer's at Bénouville only took one local daily, printed at Le Havre, and two or three Paris papers which arrived very late.

A three-minute news bulletin was being broadcast every hour, and at nine o'clock the Premier listened again, but only to hear a repetition of what he knew already.

Thereupon, turning to Milleran, who was opening the letters, he inquired, so impatiently that she jumped:

"Well? Aren't you going to call up Evreux?"

"I'm very sorry. . . ."

She hadn't dared, not quite knowing, as things were, what she should do and what she shouldn't.

"Get me Evreux, mademoiselle. . . . Yes, the same number as before. . . . A priority call, yes. . . ."

For each successive government had had the courtesy to leave him the right to priority over the telephone, as though he were still in office. Would that favor continue under a Chalamont government?

Why did the day still seem so empty? It was no different from any other, and yet he felt as though he were going round and round in space, like a fish in a bowl, opening and shutting his mouth soundlessly, just like one.

On other days the hours were never too long. In a few minutes, when she had finished opening the envelopes and setting aside bills, prospectuses, and the invitations some people persisted in sending him, Milleran would bring him the letters to read, and usually he enjoyed this; there was an element of surprise that he appreciated, and it didn't bore him to say what answers should be sent, or to dictate a few letters when he thought it worth while.

In the last few days he hadn't cursed the storm, which ought to have annoyed him, but now he was glowering at the foggy scene outside as though suspecting that nature was perfidiously scheming to smother him.

He felt some difficulty in breathing. In a quarter of an hour Madame Blanche would arrive to give him his injection, and because of yesterday's outing, which she had tried to prevent, and his two sneezes, which she hadn't failed to notice, she would watch him distrustfully, suspecting that he was concealing something from her.

He couldn't stand women who looked at one as though one were a child caught telling a fib. Madame Blanche had threatened him with a cold, and she'd be watching for the symptoms of a cold. Wasn't it often from a cold that old people died when they had no other illness?

"Hello? Yes . . . What did you say? . . . No, don't disturb him. . . . Thank you, mademoiselle. . . ."

"Disturb whom?"

"The surgeon."

"Why?"

"I was talking to the matron and she thought you might want to hear details. . . ."

"Details of what?"

Before she had time to reply, he went on sharply:

"He's dead, isn't that it?"

"Yes . . . During the operation . . ."

With a rudeness in which he seldom indulged, he exclaimed:

"What the hell do you suppose I care about that? Wait! Send a line to the director of the hospital to say they're not to chuck him into a pauper's grave. He's to have a decent funeral, but no more. Ask what it will cost and make out a check for me to sign."

Did he feel relieved that Xavier Malate should have been the first to go, in spite of his bragging? His old schoolfellow had been mistaken. He'd clung to life for no purpose. His last chance now was for their two funerals to take place on the same day, and the Premier was determined that shouldn't happen.

There was only one person left now who had known the Rue Saint-Louis in his time, the little redheaded girl of those days. Was she going to die too, and leave him to be the last?

For quite a long time, on his way to the *lycée*, he used to gaze with an agreeable agitation at the chalky-white sign with its black letters, including an N written backwards, which composed the words: "Ernest Archambault, Ironmonger." There was no actual shop. From the front the house looked just like others in the district, with lace-curtained windows and ferns in copper pots. At the end of a dank alleyway one could see the yard and a glass-roofed workshop from which the clang of hammers emerged, audible as far as the *lycée*.

In the classroom Xavier Malate had sat two rows away from him, near the stove, which it was his privilege to stoke up. Between them sat a boy who was taller than the others, better dressed, with a rather affected manner, who lived in a château outside the town and sometimes came to school on horseback, wearing riding boots, carrying a crop, and followed by a servant mounted on a heavier animal. He was a Count, whose name he had forgotten like so many others.

Who was the present occupant of the house where he had been born and lived until he was seventeen? Had it been pulled down? In his time the bricks had been almost black, there had been a green-painted door and a brass plate announcing his father's surgery hours.

He still had, put away somewhere, a box full of old photos he'd always meant to sort out. There was one of his father, who'd had a sandy mustache and a little pointed beard like Henri III, and he could still remember how he had smelled of sour wine.

He had scarcely known his mother, for she had died when he was five and was still, apparently, a chubby little boy as fat as butter. An aunt had arrived from the country to look after him and his elder sister, and later on his sister, still almost a child, with short skirts and pigtails, had run the house with the help of one maid, who for some mysterious reason was always changing.

In actual fact nobody had brought him up. He had brought himself up. He could still recall the names of certain streets which had perhaps influenced his career.

The Rue Dupont-de-l'Eure, for instance. He even remembered the dates, for he had always had a memory for figures, including, later on, telephone numbers. *1767-1855. Patriot. Politician renowned for his integrity.*

Rue Bayet (1760-1794).

A patriot, too, and a Girondist Deputy during the Revolution. But it was not on the scaffold that he had died at the age of thirty-four. He had committed suicide at Bordeaux, which he had chosen as his exile after being deserted by his party.

Rue Jules-Janin. Writer and critic, Member of the Académie Française . . .

At the age of fifteen, because of Janin, he had dreamed of the Académie Française, and had almost chosen literature as his career.

Rue Gambetta (1838-1882) . . .

Come to think of it, he might have met Gambetta if he'd lived in Paris instead of at Evreux.

Rue Jean-Jaurès (1859-1914) . . .

As a schoolboy he hadn't known that one day he would sit in the Chamber as Jaurès' colleague and would witness his assassination.

He didn't admit it in his memoirs, not even in the secret ones: but right from boyhood he had known he, too, would one day have his street, even his statue in public places.

In those days he had felt nothing more than pitying condescension for his father, who spent his time, day and night, in all weathers, hastening from one patient to another, carrying his heavy, shapeless bag of instruments, or in his office, with its frosted glass windows, seeing an endless stream of poor patients who filled the waiting room to overflowing and were often to be found sitting on the stairs.

He resented, as a piece of humbug, the way his father carried on in practice although he didn't believe in medicine, and it was not until much later, after his father's death, that he began to reflect on something he'd been fond of saying:

"I do my patients as much good as other doctors, who believe in their vocation, and I run less risk of doing them harm."

So his father had not been the uncouth, slightly bohemian, rather drunken fellow that he had imagined, in whom, as a child, he had refused to take any interest.

At the age of twenty he had returned to Evreux for his sister's marriage to one of the clerks at the Town Hall. Had he seen her three times after that, before she died of peritonitis when she was getting on toward seventy? He hadn't gone to her funeral, and he seemed to remember that he'd been on an official visit to South America at the time. He had nephews and nieces with children of their own, but he'd never felt any desire to get to know them.

Why had Milleran rushed off to the kitchen as soon as she had seen Madame Blanche approaching the house? To tell her he didn't seem quite himself, or that Xavier Malate's death had upset him?

In the first place, it wasn't true. And in the second place, as he always said, he loathed the sidelong glances they gave him, as though they were constantly expecting . . .

Expecting what?

When the nurse came in, carrying the little bowl with the syringe, he looked her straight in the eye and forestalled her inquiries by declaring:

"I feel perfectly fit and I haven't a cold. Give me my injection quickly and leave me in peace."

It cost him an effort every morning, in his bedroom, the door of which she always closed behind her, to let down his trousers in front of her eyes and expose his livid thigh.

"The left side today . . ."

Left and right, on alternate days.

"Have you taken your temperature?"

"I have not, and I don't intend to."

The telephone rang. Milleran knocked on the door; nothing in the world would have induced her to open it, for she knew the reception she would get.

"What is it?"

"A journalist who insists on speaking to you. . . ."

"Tell him I'm busy."

"He says you'll remember his name. . . ."

"What is his name?"

"Loubat."

It was the squeaky-voiced reporter who had thrown Chalamont off his stride the previous evening, in the courtyard of the Elysée, by asking whether he meant to spend the night on the road.

"What am I to tell him?"

"That I have nothing to say."

Madame Blanche was asking:

"Did I hurt you?"

"No."

It was no business of hers. Having pulled up his trousers he opened the door, to hear his secretary saying into the telephone:

"I assure you I did tell him. . . . No . . . I can't . . . You don't know him . . . What?"

Feeling his presence behind her, she started.

"What does he want?"

"Just a minute, please," she said again into the telephone.

Then, putting her hand over the mouthpiece, she explained:

"He insists on my asking you a question."

"What question?"

"Whether it's true that you and Chalamont are reconciled."

She spoke again into the mouthpiece:

"Just a moment. . . . No. . . . I asked you to hold on. . . ."

The Premier stood motionless, as though wondering what line to take, and all at once he grabbed the receiver and rapped out, before hanging up with a jerk:

"Go and ask him yourself. I wish you good day."

Then, turning to Milleran, he inquired, in a voice almost as disagreeable as the journalist's:

"Do you know why he rang up this morning?"

"No."

"To make sure I was still alive."

She tried to laugh, as though he were joking.

"I mean it!"

"But . . ."

"I know what I am taking about, *Mademoiselle* Milleran."

It was only on particular occasions that he addressed her in that way, with sarcastic emphasis. He went on, enunciating each syllable separately:

"For him, this morning, I ought logically to be dead. And he has expert knowledge!"

What did it matter whether she understood or not! He was not talking to her but to himself, or perhaps to History, and what he said was the literal truth.

If he were alive, really alive, it would be unthinkable for Chalamont . . .

"Turn on the radio, please. It's ten o'clock. The President will be beginning his audiences at the Elysée. You'll see!"

She didn't know what she was to see. Bewildered, she was looking anxiously at Madame Blanche, who was going off to the kitchen with her battered bowl.

"*At the fourth pip it will be* . . ."

He had picked up the little clock and was putting it exactly right.

"*And here is the latest news. We have just been informed that Monsieur Philippe Chalamont, who was called to the Elysée yesterday afternoon, has paid a second visit to the President of the Republic. He has officially undertaken to form a Cabinet on a wide coalition basis, whose main lines are already known, and it is hoped, in well-informed circles, that the list of Ministers will be announced before the end of the afternoon. . . .*"

She didn't know whether to switch off or not.

"Leave it, for heaven's sake. Don't you understand it's not finished yet?"

He was right. After a pause, a crackling of paper, the announcer began again:

"*A few names have already been mentioned* . . ."

She was watching him as, pale and tense, with angry eyes, he glared at her and at the radio set, as though ready to burst into rage at any moment.

"*. . . Monsieur Etienne Blanche, Radical Socialist, is expected to be the Keeper of the Seals . . .*"

An old hand who'd been in two of the Premier's Cabinets, once at the Board of Trade and once, already, at the Ministry of Justice.

"*. . . Monsieur Jean-Louis Lajoux, Secretary of the Socialist Party, Minister of State . . .*"

He had been starting his career when the Premier left the scene, and though he vaguely remembered him, it was only as a background figure.

"*. . . Ferdinand Jusset, another Socialist . . .*"

Another old hand, about whom there was a note, slipped into a volume of La Bruyère.

"*And then Monsieur Vabre, Monsieur Montois, and . . .*"

"That'll do!" he said curtly.

He very nearly added:

"Get me Paris on the telephone. . . ."

There were at least ten numbers on the tip of his tongue, he knew them by heart, and he need only ring one of them in order to sink the Ministry that was being formed.

He was on the point of doing it, and the effort to contain himself, remain worthy of himself, was so great that he felt an attack coming on. His fingers, his knees began to shake, and as usual at such moments his nerves refused to obey him; the mechanism suddenly began to race at increasing speed.

Without a word he went hastily into his bedroom, hoping Milleran had not noticed anything and wouldn't go and fetch Madame Blanche. With feverish haste he snatched out of a drawer two sedative pills, prescribed for him to take at such moments.

In ten minutes, at most, the drug would take effect and he would relax, gradually becoming languid and a little vague, as though after a sleepless night.

Meanwhile he stood leaning against the wall, near the square window with its small panes, watching young Marie as, in her red jersey, she stood in the fog, more translucent now, but still thick, hanging out washing on a line slung between two apple trees.

He was tempted to open the window and call to her, say no matter what, for it was too stupid to expect washing to dry in this sodden atmosphere.

But why interfere? It didn't concern him.

Was there anything left that did concern him?

All he had to do was to wait, trying to keep as calm as possible, until the drug took effect.

Even Emile wasn't back from Etretat, where Gabrielle must have given him a whole lot of errands.

"Hush! . . . One . . . two . . . three . . . four . . ."

Standing motionless, he was counting his pulse, as though his life were still of importance.

CHAPTER *6*

The instructions given by Gaffé and Dr. Lalinde, with the approval of Professor Fumet, were to take one pill, not two, at a moment of crisis, and another three hours later if need be. He had deliberately doubled the dose, partly because he was in a hurry to calm his panic-stricken nerves, but chiefly as a protest, in defiance.

The result was that before the usual ten minutes were up he began to see black spots before his eyes, flickering so that he felt dizzy, and that once seated in his armchair, in which he had hastily taken refuge, he felt torpor creeping over him.

If he had been an ordinary man he would have surrendered to it with relief, but they wouldn't let him. At the slightest change in his habits or behavior they would begin by summoning the young doctor from Le Havre, who in his turn would send for the man from Rouen, and once they were together the pair would shift the responsibility to Fumet, by telephone.

Did Fumet, in his turn, report to somebody higher up, while the three police inspectors were informing their own boss of the Premier's off moments, as though he were a kind of sacred animal?

The idea made him cross, illogically, for a few minutes earlier he had been moping about being forgotten in Paris, almost in a rage because somebody was ignoring his veto.

When Milleran came in with the letters she had sorted, he was looking surly, his small eyes were tired but aggressive, and as she was about to put down the letters on his desk he stopped her with a gesture.

"Read them to me."

He had not the energy to read them himself, for his eyelids were heavy and his brain dulled.

He began by asking:

"Where's Madame Blanche?"

"In the waiting room."

This was the name given to the library farthest from his bedroom, the one that led to the front hall and was, indeed, used as a waiting room when necessary. If Madame Blanche was settled there, with a book or some magazines, it was because she wasn't pleased with the state she had found him in and expected him to be needing her, unless it was Milleran who had said something to her.

What was the use of bothering about it, mulling over the same old suspicions and resentments? He said again, resignedly:

"Read them to me."

The public believed that he had a great deal of correspondence, as he used to when he was Premier, but in actual fact the postman usually brought a mere handful of letters every morning, except on the days following the publication of an article about him in some magazine or newspaper with a big circulation.

From time to time somebody would come bothering him for

this purpose, from one country or another, invariably asking the same questions and taking the same photos, and he knew so well where they would ask him to stand that he would get into position even before the photographer opened his mouth.

The resulting correspondence was almost identical each time. He would be asked for his autograph, often on cards specially cut to be filed in a collection, or on postcard photographs of himself such as were on sale in stationers' shops.

From Oslo a girl of sixteen, writing poor French in a careful hand, sent him a list of questions, with blank spaces for the answers, explaining that her teacher had asked her to write an essay of not less than six pages on the Premier's career.

The questions began like those on a passport application form:

"*Place of birth:*

"*Date of birth:*

"*Education:*"

She could have found those particulars in any encyclopedia, even in her own country.

"*What made you choose politics as your career?*

"*Which statesman did you admire most when you began your career?*

"*Did you hold certain theories when you were very young, and have any of them altered as time went on?*

"*If so, why?*

"*What recreations have you gone in for?*

"*Which of them do you still keep up?*

"*Are you satisfied with your life?*"

Milleran had been surprised when he had sent a serious reply to the girl, who in a few years would doubtless have settled down as a wife and mother.

An old couple—younger than he was, though!—ingenuously requested him to help them end their days in the way they had always dreamed of, by making them a present of a cottage in the country, not too far from Bergerac, where the husband had just been pensioned off from his job as a postman.

A lot of people supposed him to be rich. Humble people wouldn't have understood how a man who had led the country so often and for such long periods, living in palatial government houses and surrounded by official pomp, could be left with no private fortune at the age of eighty-two.

Yet so it was, and the Chamber had voted him a pension without his asking for it. The government also paid Madame Blanche's salary and, since he had left Paris, Emile's wages.

Were they afraid it might be said later on that France had left one of her great men to die in poverty?

So even at Les Ebergues, after retiring from public life, he was not completely independent, he remained a kind of civil servant.

"After all, there are funds for preserving historic monuments!" he sometimes said jokingly.

At other times he would point out that owners of premises classed as of historic interest were forbidden by law to make the slightest structural alteration in them. Didn't he come under the same heading? Had he any right to reveal himself in a light different from that in which the history books displayed him?

The care taken in this respect was such that three policemen took turns outside his door, and he felt convinced that his telephone was regularly tapped, his correspondence, especially letters from well-known foreigners, opened before being sent on to him. Or did Milleran take it upon herself to report to the authorities about what he wrote and whom he saw?

"*Dear Sir,*

"*I am at present writing a large-scale work on a man with whom you were well acquainted, and venture . . .*"

He was not jealous, although there were many letters of that kind. For some twenty years there had been five of them, known as the Grand Old Men, each representing his own country more or less uninterruptedly, and between them they had controlled world policy.

They used to meet periodically, on one continent or another, nearly always in some well-known spa, for conferences to which journalists and photographers would flock in hundreds.

The slightest word uttered by one of them, the faintest frown on emerging from a meeting, would be reported in press communiqués with banner headlines in all the newspapers.

Sometimes they had quarrels, followed by spectacular reconciliations, often staged merely for their own amusement; some of their talks, whose outcome the world awaited in breathless suspense, had turned only on trivial subjects.

The Englishman, who in private was the most humorous and cynical of the five, would look at his watch on arriving.

"How long are we supposed to argue before agreeing on this communiqué?"

And he would produce from his pocket a ready-drafted announcement.

"If only they were decent enough to leave us some cards, we could have a game of bridge. . . ."

They all belonged to the same generation, except the American, who had died young, at sixty-seven, before any of the others. They had summed one another up so precisely that each knew the true worth of all the others, and even their little eccentricities.

"Gentlemen, with my country about to go to the polls, it is imperative for me today to put my foot in it, as our journalist friends will report presently. So we will announce that I banged on the table and that my obstinacy has brought the conference to a deadlock."

There was nearly always a garden surrounding the luxury hotels that were taken over on these occasions, and as soon as one of the five ventured into it he would be set upon by reporters and photographers.

All five were accustomed to power and fame, and yet the varying shares of publicity they received had now and then caused sulks and subacid comments from one to another; these white-haired statesmen, depicted in profile on their countries' stamps, descended on such occasions to behaving like a bunch of actors.

In the margins of his book the Premier had noted some traits of this kind, not all of them, only the most typical, especially those with a certain human quality.

And now, when, except for Cornelio, who had lost his wits, he was the last survivor of the group, he still felt a slight twinge when somebody wrote to ask him for information about one of them, and not about himself!

In London, New York, Berlin, Stockholm, all over the world,

people were still writing books about him and about the others, and he sometimes caught himself feeling tempted to make up the whole of each of them!

"I'll answer that tomorrow. Remind me. You may go on reading."

An unknown man wanted his help in obtaining a post in the prison administration.

"I come from Evreux, like yourself, and when I was young my grandfather often talked to me about you, for you lived in the same street and he knew you well. . . ."

Milleran was watching him furtively, wondering whether he had dozed off, but his white, smooth-skinned hand, which now had the unquestionable beauty of an inanimate object, signed to her to continue.

"Dear Sir,

"I have applied everywhere, I have knocked on every door, and you are my last hope. The whole world acknowledges your benevolence and your deep understanding of human nature, and I am confident that you will understand me, you who . . ."

A professional sponger.

"Next one!"

"That's all, sir."

"Didn't I have an appointment for today?"

"Yes, the Spanish general was coming, but he sent a message to say he's ill with influenza at San Sebastian. . . ."

Speaking of generals, there was one who seemed likely to outlive them all, and of whom the Premier thought with some envy and a touch of annoyance. He was ninety-three years old, but he turned up every Thursday, alert and inclined to be waggish, at the meetings of the Académie Française, of which he was a member. A month ago there had been an article about him in a weekly paper, including a photo where he appeared in shorts, barechested, doing exercises in his garden under the indulgent eye of his wife, who sat on a bench in the background as though watching a child at play.

Was it really worth it?

At Evreux, at this very moment, someone was laying out Xavier

Malate, whose worries were at an end. He was through with everything. And he, who had been haunted by the idea of burial, would have nobody to walk behind his hearse, unless some old maid automatically turned up to follow it, as occasionally happens.

For a long time the Premier had paid no attention to the deaths of people in his circle, most of whom were his elders. He considered they had had their day, even those who died at fifty.

Then, when men hardly older than himself began to die as well, he had sometimes felt a certain selfish satisfaction, if not downright pleasure.

Someone else had been taken, and he was spared!

But the ranks of his own generation had gradually thinned, the Five Grand Old Men had begun to drop out, and on each occasion nowadays he caught himself counting, without grief but feeling vaguely apprehensive, as though it began to occur to him that his turn might really come one day.

He had never attended funerals, except on the very rare occasions when he was obliged to represent the government of the day. He had avoided death chambers, every kind of ceremonial death watch, not because they depressed him, but because he considered that kind of pomp to be in bad taste.

He would simply send in his card, or have himself represented by a member of his staff, and to his staff, too, he left the task of drawing up letters or telegrams of sympathy.

But Xavier Malate's death today had made a different impression on him, though he couldn't say exactly in what way. The drug had slowed down his mental processes, as though he were half asleep, and his thoughts were at one remove from reality.

For instance, he kept seeing the face of an old woman with thin hair and very long teeth. Heaven knew what had conjured it up, and there was no reason why she should resemble Eveline Archambault, whom he hadn't seen since she was just a little girl.

All the same he felt certain it was she, as she looked nowadays, and her face wore a curiously sweet expression, tinged with silent reproach.

She had doubtless prayed all her life that he might find religion before he died, as though words said to a priest could make any difference to anything. Like him she was seated in an armchair, an old rug over her knees, and a kind of stale smell emanated from her.

In the end he realized that the rug was the one that used to be wrapped around his mother's legs in the last weeks of her life. But what about the rest?

But for the fear of seeming ridiculous, he would have told Milleran to ring up Evreux again, the Town Hall, for instance, to inquire about Eveline, to find out whether she was still alive, if she were ill, if she had all she wanted.

He felt tired. He knew it was the natural effect of the drug he'd taken, but it gave him a depressingly helpless sensation, and if he'd had the right, he would have gone to bed.

A neighbor's cow, escaped from the barn, was running around the orchard, knocking against the boughs of the apple trees, pursued by a little boy armed with a stick.

That little boy would still be living long after he himself was dead. All those around him would outlive him, as would most of the earth's present population.

Would Emile tell the truth about Les Ebergues, later on? Perhaps so, for he liked vulgar stories and people would give him bigger tips if he made them laugh.

He had not been the first to use the cliff-top farm as a country house; before him a lawyer from Rouen—dead too now!—used to bring his family there for the holidays. The Premier had only made the additions required for his own convenience, such as the tunnel that now linked what were originally two separate buildings.

Names were of no importance to him, so he had not altered the one the property went by when he bought it.

The local people had told him that the word "*ébergues*" referred to portions of the codfish prepared for use as bait, and as Fécamp was a codfishers' port and fishing was the mainstay of the whole coast, he had been satisfied with that explanation. Probably the skipper of a fishing smack or the owner of a small fleet had lived in the house at one time?

But one day when Emile was tearing away the ivy that had

crept over the parapet of an old well, he had brought to light an inscription, roughly cut in the stone:

Les Ebernes
1701

The Premier had happened to mention this to the schoolmaster, who was also Secretary of the District Council and sometimes came to borrow books from him. The schoolmaster had had the curiosity to look up the old land-survey maps, and had found the property marked on them by the same name as that on the well.

However, nobody could tell him what "*ébernes*" were, until at last he found the explanation in the big *Littré* dictionary:

"*Eberner:* to wipe excrement off a child.

"*Eberneuses:* women who wipe excrement off children."

What kind of women had once lived in the house and been given the nickname that had stuck to the place afterwards? And what later and more prudish occupant had given that cunning twist to the spelling of the name?

He had mentioned that, too, in his secret memoirs, but would they ever be published? He was not sure whether he still wanted them to be. When the future of the country was at stake he had always been prompt to take the most fateful decisions, with no fear of committing an error, but, faced with the question of what he should reveal about his own life, he became hesitant and was tormented by scruples.

The picture the world had formed of him was cut and dried, it took no account of the changes wrought by time, it was rudimentary and often downright false, and his legend included one particular chapter he had always tried to correct, but in vain.

It had appeared in the scandalmongering rags of the day, and later in a national newspaper, under the heading: "A Gentleman and His Tailor."

For thirty years his opponents had made the most of it during every election campaign. Only the title had altered from time to time, the variants including "Tradesman's Entrance" and "The Countess's Chambermaid."

The chambermaid and the Countess, for they had been real people, were both dead now, but the "Gentleman," who was about the same age as the Premier, still survived and could be seen every afternoon at the races, upright as ever, but with creaky joints.

This was the notorious Créveaux case, which had kept the Premier out of several successive Cabinets, just as another man had been barred from office for ten years by a certain letter hidden between the pages of *Le Roi Pausole*.

The difference was that he himself had been innocent, at least of the charge brought against him. He was hardly more than forty, and had just joined a Cabinet for the first time—as Minister of Public Works, in which capacity he was about to be visited by Xavier Malate.

Wasn't it odd the way things linked up through time and space, wreathing together mockingly, as it were? Could it have been on the actual day of Xavier's visit that . . .

Anyway, that didn't matter. In those days Marthe de Créveaux, Marthe de C., as the spiteful columnists used to call her, held regular receptions in her private mansion in the Rue de la Faisanderie, where it was her ambition to bring together everybody who was anybody in Paris diplomatic and political circles, admitting no one else except a few writers, provided they were members or prospective members of the Académie Française.

At that time the new Minister had never set foot in her house, for he went about very little even in those days, and was regarded as an uncouth, solitary being, so that the caricaturists were beginning to depict him in the guise of a bear.

Was it this reputation that had impelled Marthe de Créveaux to get hold of him, or was it because shrewd observers were beginning to foretell that he would soon be someone to be reckoned with?

The only daughter of a rich Bordeaux merchant, she had acquired a title by marrying the Comte de Créveaux, and thus launched herself in society as well. After that, Créveaux had resumed his bachelor habits, and there were days when Marthe, in her ground-floor dining room, was entertaining a covey of ministers and ambassadors at luncheon, while her husband, in the second-floor suite he called his bachelor flat, was surrounded by a gay bunch of actresses and dramatists.

The Minister of Public Works had not been more than twice to the house in the Rue de la Faisanderie before it was rumored that the Countess had taken him in hand, just as she had chosen to play Egeria to two or three political men before him. There was some truth in the rumor. She was familiar with a world of which the future Premier knew very little, and she had decided to polish him up.

Was she beautiful, as the newspapers declared? After hearing her talked about, one was surprised, on seeing her for the first time, to discover that she was a small, helpless-seeming woman, looking much younger than one had expected, with nothing forceful or self-willed in her manner.

Though she spent her whole time launching and protecting men she found interesting, each of them felt he wanted to protect her from the others and from herself.

He wasn't certain he'd ever been fooled. Frankly, he had known what he wanted in those days, and he'd known she could help him to get it. Besides, he was flattered at being selected, when he was no more than a promising beginner, and even the luxurious atmosphere of her house had played its part.

Within a fortnight people were growing accustomed to speaking of them in one breath, and whenever the Comte de Créveaux met the young Minister he would hold out his hand with ironical emphasis and exclaim:

"Our very dear friend . . ."

Contrary to what had been supposed, and was still believed by some people who claimed to be in the know, physical attraction had played very little part in their relationship, and though Marthe, whose sexual needs were small, had given it to be understood that they were passionately in love, they had very seldom been in bed together.

Her great idea was to give him lessons in social behavior, and she had even set about teaching him how to dress.

It was embarrassing to remember all this, at the age of eighty-two when one was living in a little house on the Normandy coast where death would be one of the next visitors.

Because of this memory and a few others, he would have refused to have his life over again, if it had been offered to him.

For weeks and months had he not studied the attitudes and
the manner she taught him, which she declared to be those be-
fitting the perfect statesman?

And he, whose style of dress was correct and restrained, but
with no attempt at smartness, had finally yielded to Marthe's insistence and paid a visit to the most fashionable tailor of the day,
in the Faubourg Saint-Honoré.

"He's the only possible man, darling, unless you go to London for your clothes. He's my husband's tailor, by the way."

Nowadays he wondered whether he wouldn't prefer to have
some dishonorable action on his conscience, as Chalamont had,
rather than such a humiliating memory.

He could see the tailor, patronizing and ironical, his own reflection in the mirror, with one coat sleeve not yet tacked in
place. . . .

Hadn't he believed it mattered, if only for a short time, and
hadn't he gone to the point of changing the shape of his hats, the
color of his ties and gloves?

He'd taken to riding in the Bois, too, very early each morning.

The people who addressed him as "Minister" had no suspicion that he was behaving like a boy in calf love. Furthermore, in
Marthe de Créveaux's house there was a young woman who was
to get very much into the news because of him, and her name was
Juliette.

She acted as companion as well as lady's maid, for Marthe
couldn't bear to be alone and had to have someone with her even
when she went shopping or to have a dress tried on, with the car
following her from door to door. It was Juliette, too, who kept
the list of her appointments, reminded her about them, answered
the telephone, paid for small purchases in shops.

She came of a good middle-class family, dressed in trim navy
or black, and looked every inch the convent-educated girl.

Was she a nymphomaniac even in those days? Probably, and
he had probably not been the first to discover the fact.

On various occasions she had been alone on the ground floor
with the future Premier, while Marthe was getting dressed,

and she had played her game so well that one fine day, tried beyond his strength, he had taken her, on a sofa in the drawing room.

It became a habit, a necessity, and for her there could be no pleasure without danger, which she deliberately carried to the furthest limit, devising the most perilous situations.

The inevitable happened: Marthe de Créveaux caught them, and wounded pride, instead of prompting her to keep the secret, led to a scene of tragicomic fury that brought all the servants running.

Thrown out of the house together with Juliette, the Premier had had no choice but to take a room for her in a quiet hotel, for he couldn't take her to the Ministry and would not have her in his flat on the Quai Malaquais.

The next day a minor newspaper had given a fairly accurate description of the incident, in a few lines, winding up with what purported to be the Comtesse de Créveaux's comment:

"When I think that I knocked off the man's corners and even bought his clothes for him!"

Had she really said that? It was possible, the words sounded just like her. She had not foreseen that they were to dog him right through his career and add greatly to his difficulties.

For the journalists, delighted with the windfall, had made an investigation, and the result had been the famous "Gentleman and His Tailor" article.

It asserted that Marthe de C. had sent the young Minister to her husband's tailor, whose address was given, and that it was Créveaux who, in due course, had paid the bill.

As white-faced as Chalamont had been when he wrote that letter, the Minister of Public Works had seized the telephone, rung up the tailor. He could recall nothing more agonizing than his feelings as he had listened to the voice at the other end of the line.

It was true! The journalists had not made it up. The tailor, his voice polite but unruffled, offered his apologies: he had believed . . . he had thought . . .

"So you took me for a pimp?" he had shouted into the telephone.

"Oh, Minister, I assure you that . . ."

Ordinarily he waited to pay his tailor, like any other shop-keeper, till the bill was sent in. It was barely three months since he had been to the Faubourg Saint-Honoré, and he had felt no surprise at not hearing from the man. After all, didn't some firms, especially in the luxury trade, send in their accounts only once a year?

Did Marthe de Créveaux pay in this way for the clothes of every man she took under her wing? He had never known be-cause he had never seen her again, though she had written to him "to get rid of a misunderstanding and make peace" when he had become Premier.

Her end had been sad, for she, who had been so feverishly ac-tive, was bedridden with paralysis for five years, and when at last she died she was so wasted that she weighed no more than an eight-year-old girl.

Juliette had not remained on the Minister's hands for long; she was taken over by a journalist who introduced her to the newspaper world, where she soon made good on her own merits.

She had interviewed her ex-lover on several occasions, and had never failed to be astonished because he took no advantage of his renewed opportunity, as most men on whom she made a profes-sional call no doubt did.

Her death had been more sudden than that of her former mis-tress, but no less sensational, for she was among the passengers on board a plane that crashed in flames in Holland on its way to Stockholm.

As for himself, he had sent the tailor a check, of course, but hundreds of thousands of people were still convinced that . . .

And after all, didn't it come to much the same thing?

He didn't like the man he had been in those days. He didn't like himself as a little boy or as an adolescent, for that matter.

And nowadays the play-acting of the Five Grand Old Men, the airs they had put on, seemed to him to have been ridiculous.

Was all his indulgence reserved for the old man he had grown into, who was gradually drying up, like the Countess, until he'd become nothing but parchment stretched over a skeleton, with a brain spinning emptily in his bony skull?

For what did he think about all day long, while people crept like mice about the great man whose slightest sneeze was turned into a drama?

About himself! Himself! Always about himself!

He prowled round and round himself, sometimes with satisfaction, but usually discontented and bitter.

He had already told his story once, his story as the public wanted to have it, and no mere marginal notes scribbled later on would suffice to show him in his true light.

It was all false, because it was all described from a false angle.

The corrective notes were also false, being nothing but a shot at countering the legend.

As for the real man, as he had been and as he now was . . .

He stared uncomprehendingly at Gabrielle, who was standing in front of him, perhaps forgetting that she came every day at this time to tell him the same thing:

"Lunch is ready, sir."

It was Gabrielle's privilege to make this announcement, and she would not have left young Marie to do it for anything in the world. But surely, at the age of seventy, she should have got beyond such childishness?

The fog pressing against the dining-room windows was so dense that it seemed almost like a snowy landscape beneath a heavy, unbroken, motionless expanse of cloud, such as one sometimes sees in winter, when earth and sky are indivisible.

Young Marie had at last replaced her red jersey by a black dress and a white apron. She had been taught to hold the old man's chair while he bent forward, and then give it a gentle push, and this frightened her; she was always afraid of taking too long and letting him sit down on nothing.

"It seems you have another little sister?"

"Yes, sir."

"Is your mother pleased?"

"I don't know."

What was the use? Why utter meaningless words? The menu was almost as monotonous as the evening one. Half a grapefruit, for the vitamins, followed by three ounces of grilled meat, which had to be cut up for him now that his false teeth had got so loose, two potatoes and some boiled greens. Dessert would be an apple, a pear, or a few grapes, of which he wasn't allowed to eat the skins.

Would Chalamont, in Paris, follow tradition by inviting his new colleagues to a fashionable restaurant, where the main lines of his Cabinet's policy would be laid down over dessert?

In his own day the choice had almost always been a private room at Foyot's, near the Senate, or at Lapérouse's.

Men who'd often been in the same team would be there, swapping memories of previous Cabinets, old stagers would invariably be offered the same inglorious posts, and there were nearly always some newcomers, still ignorant of the rites, who would keep an uneasy eye on the old-timers.

Even the voices, the clatter of forks and the tinkle of glasses seemed to have a special resonance at those luncheons, and the headwaiters, who knew all the guests, hurried around with conspiratorial smiles, playing their part in the distribution of portfolios.

Different, but no less typical, was the noise made by the reporters and press photographers lunching in the main restaurant on the ground floor, who were just as conscious as the group upstairs of their role in the day's events.

Those two hours, in point of fact, were the most agreeable in the life of a government. Later in the afternoon, after the Ministers had been presented at the Elysée and been photographed on the steps with the President in their midst, his face wearing the inevitable smile, the time came to draft the ministerial statement, and then the difficulties began, with endless wrangling about each word, each comma.

Each of them had family matters and practical problems to consider as well. Were they to move into the various Ministries without waiting for the vote of confidence in the Chamber? Would there be room for the children? What furniture of one's own should one take along, and what dresses would one's wife need for official receptions?

He had been through this experience on twenty-two occasions, his biographers had made the tally for him, and on eight of them he had been the central figure.

Today it was Chalamont's turn, and suddenly something unex-

pected happened: remembering the bustle in Foyot's dining
rooms, the Premier tried to visualize his one-time subordinate in
that setting; but although he had spent more time with that man
than with anyone else, been in closer contact with him than with
any other, he was surprised to find himself unable to recall his
features.

Yet it was only two days since he'd seen his photograph in the
papers. Chalamont had altered in the last ten years, as was to be
expected. But his memory didn't even present him with the
Chalamont of ten years ago. It conjured up a young man of
twenty-five whose expression, though already determined, was
anxious, to whom he remembered saying at the time:

"You'll have to learn to control your feelings."

"I know, Chief. I assure you I'm trying hard."

He had always called him "Chief," adopting the term by which
a great surgeon or doctor is addressed by his juniors. He was no
sentimentalist. He was cold and cynical. All the same his cheeks
would sometimes flush, all of a sudden, with a bright color that
his usual pallor made all the more remarkable.

Did Chalamont, too, look back over his life now and then, or
was he, at sixty, still too young for that? Would he be willing to
have his time over again, and if so . . .

The Premier remembered precisely in what circumstances his
former secretary could not keep from blushing, despite his self-
control. It was whenever he felt, rightly or wrongly, that someone was trying to make him feel small.

He had formed an opinion about his own character which he
believed to be accurate, and which may indeed have been so. He
clung to this, and at the least threat to his self-confidence the
blood would instantly rush to his head.

He never argued, never protested. He made no attempt to re-
tort, but maintained a cautious silence; yet his flaming cheeks
alone betrayed his feelings.

In the Premier's office in the Hôtel Matignon the blood had
not risen to his cheeks; on the contrary, it had seemed to drain
out of his whole body.

"Are you tired?" young Marie inquired, suddenly arriving from
worlds away.

He looked at the hand he had just brushed across his face, then he gazed around him, as though awaking from sleep. His plate was hardly touched.

"Perhaps I am," he confessed in an undertone, so as not to be heard in the kitchen.

He made as if to rise, whereupon young Marie rushed to pull out his chair, and he looked so bent and feeble that she took hold of his arm.

"Thank you . . . I'm not hungry any longer. . . ."

She didn't know whether to follow him or not. She watched him as he moved away, shoulders bowed, long arms dangling, while he went with a wavering step into the passage leading to his study. She must have thought he might be going to fall, for she held herself ready to leap after him.

But he didn't even need to lean against the wall, and when at last he disappeared young Marie shrugged her shoulders, turned to clear the table.

When she went back to the kitchen with the dishes and plates, Milleran asked anxiously:

"What's happening?"

"I don't know. I think he's gone to bed. He looks tired."

But the Premier was not in bed, and when Milleran tiptoed into the study she found him asleep, with half open-mouth, in the Louis-Philippe armchair. His lower lip was slightly pendulous, as though from great weariness, or disgust.

CHAPTER 7

This time he really had gone to sleep, for he didn't hear Madame Blanche come when Milleran fetched her, nor was he aware that she was standing beside him, watch in hand, feeling his pulse with a light finger. Neither did he know that she had telephoned to the doctor, in lowered tones, or that while she was about it Milleran sat on a chair facing him, gazing steadily at him with a grave, sad face.

Then the women signed to each other and whispered together. Milleran made way for Madame Blanche and went to her office.

More than half an hour went by like this, in a silence broken only by the regular ticking of the little clock, and at last the sound of a motor was heard, and a car drew up. Emile had said something to somebody, his voice hushed, too.

There was a kind of impromptu ballet going on around him, for now Madame Blanche, in her turn, made way for Dr. Gaffé, who, after taking the patient's pulse again, sat down facing him, as erect and formal as in a waiting room.

At one moment Emile had come in and put a log back into the fire, and the Premier had had no suspicion of all these furtive comings and goings. Yet he would have sworn that he had all along been aware of sitting supine in his armchair, with his lips parted and his breath whistling through them.

Had there really been a temporary separation between his mind and his body, the latter sitting inert while the former, still agile, flew in circles like a bird, sometimes into unknown worlds, sometimes through a universe not far removed from reality?

How could he have known, for instance, that when the effort became too exhausting he knitted his bushy eyebrows, or that he occasionally groaned at his helplessness? Yet later on they confirmed his impression that he had frowned and groaned. So what about it?

His own conviction was that he had got far enough outside himself to return and take a look at the almost inert carcass which was beginning to seem alien to him, and for which he felt more revulsion than pity.

During those two hours he had seen a vast number of faces, and had gone in pursuit of some of them, wondering what they were doing at his bedside. Others were familiar, but all the same he couldn't understand how they got there, the presence of the stationmaster of a little town in southern France, for example, where he had spent a brief holiday several years in succession.

Why was he here today? The old man knew the stationmaster had died long ago. But that little girl, whose hair had been arranged in ringlets and tied with a wide tricolor ribbon so that she could present him with a bouquet? Did her being here mean that she was dead too?

That was what had been worrying him most, while Gaffé waited, watching him, not daring to light a cigarette. He was trying to disentangle those among all these people who were still alive and those who were already in the other world, and his impression was that the frontier between life and death was hard to trace, that perhaps, even, there wasn't one.

Was that the great secret? He knew that during those two hours, when he had been intensely alive despite his body's inertia, he had a dozen times been on the point of solving all problems.

What made the job so difficult and disheartening was that he could never remain for long on the same plane. Perhaps his mind was not nimble enough, or lacked balance. Or could it be a question of weight? Or of habit? He was going up and down, sometimes gradually, sometimes by leaps and bounds, coming out into different worlds, some of which were fairly close to what is called reality, fairly familiar, while others were so remote and unlike that neither people nor objects were recognizable.

He had seen Marthe de Créveaux again. But she wasn't at all as he remembered her. It was not only that, as the papers had said when she died, she weighed no more than a little girl, but she looked like one, she had a little girl's innocence, and she was stark naked.

At the same time he blamed himself for remembering her only in order to clear his conscience, not so much from the business of the tailor as from the affair of the Legion of Honor. For it wasn't true that he had never shown partiality. That was a legend he had built up, like the others, the legend of the upright, uncompromising politician, doing his duty without fear or favor.

All the same, he had given the Legion of Honor to one of Marthe's protégés, an obscure country squire whose only title to such distinction was his ownership of a pack of hounds.

And a few days later hadn't he given an official reception to an African potentate who must be propitiated for degrading practical reasons, though his proper place was in prison?

He had never asked pardon of anyone, and he was not going to begin at his time of life. Who but himself had any right to judge him?

He went on struggling. Of the faces that approached, glancing at him as thronging passers-by, in a street, cast a glance at the victim of an accident and go on their way, most were vacant-eyed, and he kept trying to stop one and ask whether this were not a procession of the dead that he was witnessing.

If so he too must be dead. And yet not quite, for they refused to treat him as one of themselves.

What was he, then, following zigzag flight like some clumsy night bird?

Very well! If it was because of Chalamont that they were cold-shouldering him, he would leave Chalamont in peace. He had understood. He'd understood long ago, even perhaps at the Hôtel Matignon, but he had refused to show pity then, because he believed he had no right to do so.

He hadn't shown himself any pity, either. Why should he have shown any to his assistant?

"Time to pay, gentlemen!"

A voice shouted the words, like the attendant in a cheap dance hall who calls out in the intervals:

"Pass along the money, please!"

Had he been indignant when Chalamont had informed him that, after careful consideration, he had decided that his career would benefit if he were to have an *established position*, in other words if he married a woman with enough money to enable him to live in some style?

He'd been so far from indignant that he had attended the wedding as one of the witnesses.

Everything derives from everything. Everything counts. Everything helps. Everything changes. There is no waste. The day the wedding took place, at Saint-Honoré-d'Eylau, the die was cast and the Premier ought to have known it.

The moment had come when Chalamont had been summoned to pay for his situation, to repay his wife and his father-in-law, failing which he would be *displaced* in their esteem. . . .

Just as Marthe de Créveaux's lover had had to bestow a decoration on a stag hunter.

All this was on the lowest level, where he kept returning and getting bogged down. But in the course of the two hours he had made other discoveries, explored regions where he felt so much a stranger that he was not even certain what he had seen there.

He had felt cold, and that, too, was an attested fact, for the doctor was to tell him, later, that he had shivered more than once. Now it was his meeting with his father and Xavier Malate that had made him feel cold. He couldn't remember where he had met them, or what had passed between them, but he had seen them, and what had particularly struck him was that they had seemed to be on such cordial terms.

He had not expected that. It bothered him. It upset all his notions of human values. And why did the two of them, who had nothing in common except the fact of being dead, look at him with one and the same expression? It wasn't pity. That word had been withdrawn from circulation. Neither was it indifference. It was—the expression was inaccurate and bombastic, but he couldn't find a better—it was a *sublime serenity*.

In his father's case that might be all right. He was willing to concede the point. But that Malate should be endowed with sublime serenity, merely because he had died under the surgeon's knife! . . .

He didn't know what would happen next, and wondered whether he was going to wake up in the Louis-Philippe armchair at Les Ebergues. He was not sure whether he wanted to, but all the same he felt a little anxious.

They had caught him unawares, giving him no time to prepare for his departure, and it seemed to him that he had a great many things to do, a lot of questions to settle.

It was a pain in his right arm that proved to him that he was still in the body, and he opened his eyes, to discover, without surprise, that facing him sat Dr. Gaffé, who felt called upon to give him an encouraging smile.

"Had a good sleep, sir?"

Night was falling, and the doctor, at last able to move, got up to turn on the light. Milleran stirred in her office next door, walked quietly out to the first room, doubtless to tell Madame Blanche that he was awake now.

"So you see," said the old man gravely, "it appears that I'm not dead."

Why did Gaffé think fit to protest at this, when he was expecting it to happen from one day to the next, and there was no reason why it shouldn't be today?

The Premier had not been joking, he had merely taken note of a fact.

"Did you suddenly feel unwell during luncheon?"

He almost began to put on his usual act, replying in ambiguous or boorish monosyllables. But why bother?

"For no sufficient reason I lost my temper, so I took two sedative pills."

"Two!" exclaimed the doctor, relieved.

"Two. Now the effect has worn off."

Except that he was left with a nasty taste in his mouth, stiff limbs.

"Let's see your blood pressure. . . . No! Don't get up . . . Madame Blanche will help me to take your coat off. . . ."

He submitted meekly and didn't ask about his blood pressure, the figure of which, for once, the doctor forgot, or preferred not, to tell him.

In addition to this, Gaffé paraded his stethoscope over his chest and back, with the dedicated air he took on at such times.

"Cough, please . . . Again . . . Good . . . A deep breath . . ."

He had never been so biddable, and neither the doctor nor Madame Blanche could guess why—neither could Milleran, pricking up her ears in the next-door room.

The truth was that in his secret heart he had decided that it was all over. He couldn't have said at what precise moment this feeling of detachment had come over him, but it must have been during the strange journey of exploration he had made while his carcass lolled motionless and he was temporarily released from it.

It hadn't been painful, much less agonizing: he felt rather like a bubble rising to the surface of the water all of a sudden, for no apparent reason, and bursting, to mingle with the atmosphere. An easy separation, bringing him a relief so great that he could have cried out in delight, like a child watching the ascent of a red balloon:

"Oh!"

He would have liked to joke with them, in gratitude for their attentiveness and all they were doing for him, but they wouldn't understand and would probably have thought he was lightheaded.

He had never been lightheaded. So he had no standard of comparison, but he felt convinced that never in his life had he been so rational as at present.

"I suppose," said Gaffé quietly, after a glance at Madame Blanche, "that if I asked you to go to bed you'd dislike the idea? Simply as a precaution, of course. You yourself admit that you've been under a strain just lately. . . ."

He had said nothing of the kind. Milleran must have told the doctor that, while he was supposed to be asleep . . .

"There's frost in the air. It's going to be a very cold night, and there's no doubt that twenty-four hours' rest in bed . . ."

He thought it over, as a straightforward suggestion, and responded with an equally straightforward one:

"Suppose we put it off till this evening?"

In point of fact he was tempted to do as Gaffé wanted, but he had something else to see to first. And both the doctor and Madame Blanche would doubtless have been astonished if they could have read his thoughts.

He was eager to get away from the lot of them, Milleran, Emile, Gabrielle, young Marie. He was tired. He'd done his share and now he was giving up. Had it been possible, he would have asked them to put him into clean pajamas and lay him down in his bed, close the shutters against the fog outside, put out the lights, except the tiny moonlike disk of the night light.

Then, with the sheets up to his chin, curled up in utter, self-contained silence, in a solitude broken only by his weakening pulse, he would ebb slowly away, a little melancholy but quite without bitterness, and very rapidly, released both from shame and pride, he would settle his last accounts.

"*I beg your pardon* . . ."

Whose? That, as he had discovered, did not matter. There was no need of any name.

"*I did my best, with all the strength of a man and all a man's weaknesses.* . . ."

Would he see around him the attentive faces of Xavier Malate, Philippe Chalamont, his father, and others as well, those of Eveline Archambault, Marthe, the stationmaster, and the little girl with the bouquet?

"*I realize it's nothing to be proud of.* . . ."

They gave him no encouragement. He didn't need encouragement. He was all alone. The others had been merely witnesses, and he had learned that witnesses have no right to set up as judges. Neither had he. No one had. . . .

"*Forgive me.* . . ."

No sound of any kind, except the blood still pumping jerkily through his veins, and a crackling of logs in the next room.

He would keep his eyes open to the very last.

CHAPTER *8*

"Madame Blanche, would you mind going to the kitchen and waiting until I call? I have things to see to with Milleran. I promise not to take long, and not to get excited."

Gaffé had granted him his respite and given him an injection to pep him up, saying he would come back about seven o'clock.

"To be quite frank, as you've always asked me to be with you," he had said, "there's a slight wheezing sound in your bronchial tubes. But I don't think it's anything to worry about, for your temperature and pulse don't suggest there's any infection so far."

They were not accustomed to finding him so meek, and it made them uneasy, but what could he do to avoid worrying them? Whatever line he took it would not stop their exchange of anxious glances. There was no understanding, any longer, between him and them. Or rather, he still understood them, but they couldn't follow him any more.

"Will you come with me, Milleran, so that we can have a big cleaning-up?"

She followed him, bewildered, into the first office, where he did not bend down right away to the bottom shelf, but took out Volume III of *Vidal-Lablache,* where there was a document of disastrous import to a man who had been in past Cabinets and would doubtless be in future ones.

Still holding this, he put back the book and went on to another and yet another, plucking out now a letter, now a scrap of paper that had been crumpled, as its creases still showed.

"Why have you turned so pale, Milleran? You look as though you were going to faint."

Yet he wasn't looking at her. He simply knew. Then, turning at last to the Pierre Louÿs volume, he went on again, in an encouraging tone with no shade of blame or anger:

"You knew all this, didn't you?"

Thereupon, as he straightened up again, adding Chalamont's confession to the other papers in his hand, she burst into tears, took a few steps toward the door as though to run away into the darkness, changed her mind, came back to fling herself at his feet, and tried to grab his hand.

"Forgive me, sir . . . I didn't want to, I swear I didn't. . . ."

This immediately restored his peremptory, authoritative manner, for he could never abide tears, bursts of emotion, any more than he could tolerate certain kinds of rudeness or silliness. He wouldn't have any woman writhing on the ground, kissing his hand and dropping tears on it.

He commanded her:

"Get up!"

Then, his tone already gentler:

"Steady, Milleran . . . There's nothing to be excited about. . . ."

"I assure you, sir, that . . ."

"You did as you were told to do, and quite right too. *By whom?*"

He was in a hurry for her to recover herself, to emerge from this melodramatic atmosphere, and in order to help her he went to the length of patting her shoulder, an unusual gesture with him.

"Who was it?"

"Superintendent Dolomieu."

"When?"

She hesitated.

"When I was still in Paris?"

"No. About two years ago. I had a day off and went to Etretat, and he was there, waiting for me. He said it was part of his official duty, he was giving me instructions on behalf of the government. . . ."

"The government was quite right, and I should probably have done the same myself. You were asked to copy the papers?"

She shook her head, and another sob jerked out. There was still a shiny, damp track down one of her cheeks.

"No. Inspector Aillevard has a photostat machine in his room. . . ."

"So you used to give him the papers and he returned them next day?"

"Sometimes only an hour later. Not one is missing. I took care he gave them all back to me."

She couldn't understand the Premier's attitude, couldn't manage to believe in it. Instead of being angry or downcast, as she would have expected, he showed a calm she had seldom known him to display, and his face was lit by a smile.

One would have thought he found it a good game, which amused him more than anyone.

"As things are now, it won't matter much if we destroy these papers, will it?"

She was trying to smile too, almost succeeding, for there was something detached and airy about him which was infectious. This was the first time he had ever seemed to regard her as an equal, so that their relationship took on a personal touch.

"Perhaps it would be better, all the same, for the originals to be got rid of. . . ."

He showed her the Chalamont letter.

"Did you find that?"

She nodded, not without a shade of pride.

"Funny thing! If Chalamont has chosen an inquisitive fellow as his Minister of the Interior, and if the chap happens to send for his chief's file . . ."

He knew Dolomieu, who had been under his orders and was Director of General Information at the Rue des Saussaies. Would he take advantage of Chalamont's access to power to get himself appointed Director of the Sûreté Nationale, or even Prefect of Police?

What did it matter, after all!

"Since you know where these papers are, come and help me. . . ."

In the first room she only missed two, whose places of concealment he pointed out to her with childish satisfaction.

"So you hadn't found those?"

In the second room, she had found all his hiding places; in his study she had missed only one.

If the policeman on duty was watching them through the window he must have been surprised to see the Premier and his secretary bending over the hearth, throwing in papers that burned with tall, roaring flames.

"We shall have to burn the books as well."

"What books?"

So she hadn't thought of the American edition of his memoirs, and she was astounded to see its pages black with notes, probably wondering when he could have written them without her knowledge.

"No point in burning the bindings, they're too thick, and we mustn't put too many pages at a time into the fire."

It was a long job tearing out the pages a few at a time and stirring them with the tongs to help them burn. While she was squatting down and attending to it, he stood behind her.

"Madame Blanche as well?" he asked, knowing she would understand.

She did understand, gave an affirmative gesture, added, after a moment's reflection:

"She couldn't have done otherwise. . . ."

He hesitated to name anyone else.

"Emile?"

"From the very beginning."

In other words, Emile had already been reporting on his behavior to the Rue des Saussaies when he was still a Cabinet Minister, then Premier.

Hadn't he always known it at the back of his mind, he who had considered it his duty to have other people spied on?

Or had he been ingenuous? Cunning? Needing to feel that he was an exception, that the rules didn't apply to him?

"And Gabrielle?"

"That's not the same thing. In Paris, when you were away from home, an inspector came now and then to ask her questions. . . ."

He had been standing for too long, and he felt the need to sit down, in his place, his armchair, in his usual position. It was as comforting as getting home and slipping on one's old clothes. The tall, dancing flames were roasting him down one side and on one cheek, but it would soon be over. As his elbow knocked against the silent radio set, where it stood on the desk, unneeded from now on, he said:

"Take this too. . . .'

She misunderstood him, or pretended to misunderstand, so as to do her bit to cheer up a situation that was depressing her:

"You want to burn the radio?"

He gave a faint chuckle.

"Give it to whoever you like."

"May I keep it myself . . . ?"

She stopped herself just in time from adding:

". . . as a souvenir."

He had understood, but he didn't scowl. He had never seemed so gentle in all his life, and he was like one of those old men who are to be seen in the country or the suburbs, sitting in sunny doorways, gazing for hours on end at a tree or some drifting clouds.

"I'm sure Gaffé will have telephoned to Dr. Lalinde."
Now he had confided in her, she was ready to reciprocate.
"Yes. He said he was going to."
"Was he very frightened when he found me asleep?"
"He didn't know you'd taken the medicine."
"What about you?"

She didn't answer, and he realized he mustn't begin to pester them with questions. They, too, had done what they could, like Xavier, like Chalamont, like that swine Dolomieu.

What did the word "swine" remind him of?

"*That swine* . . ."

He couldn't recall it, and yet when the word had been spoken it had seemed to be of considerable importance.

There was a name on the tip of his tongue, but why make the effort? Now he'd come full circle, that kind of thing had ceased to concern him.

It was a strange impression, agreeable and a little terrifying, not needing to think any longer.

A few more flames, a few pages writhing and then falling to ashes between the tongs, and all threads would be severed.

Gabrielle would come to announce that the Premier's dinner was waiting for him. The Premier would follow her obediently, would sit down on the chair offered by young Marie, with her perpetual dread of his sitting down on air. He wasn't hungry. He would eat, to please them. He would answer the questions put to him by Gaffé when he came, perhaps accompanied by Lalinde, around seven o'clock, and he'd allow his pulse to be taken yet again, let himself be put to bed as he'd promised.

He wouldn't be sarcastic with any of them, not even ironical with Lalinde, who was always a shade pompous.

He would only be unfailingly patient from now on, only taking care not to cry out, not to call for help, when the moment arrived. He meant to see to that by himself, decently, with discretion.

Whether it came tomorrow, in a week, or in a year, he would wait, and when his glance fell on Sully's memoirs, he murmured:

"You can put that book away."

What was the sense of reading other people's recollections any longer? It didn't interest him, neither did any other book, and they could have burned the whole library for all he cared.

"There we are!"

There had been nothing dramatic about it, when all was said and done, and he was almost pleased with himself. There was even a gleam of mischief in his gray eyes as he thought about his household's reactions.

Seeing him so calm and gentle, wouldn't they shake their heads sadly and whisper behind his back:

"Have you noticed how he's sinking?"

Gabrielle, no doubt, would add:

"Like a lamp dying down. . . ."

Merely because he'd ceased to concern himself with their little affairs.

"Are you asleep?" Milleran inquired anxiously, noticing all of a sudden that his eyes were closed.

He shook his head, raised his lids, smiled at her as though she were not only Milleran, but the whole of the human race.

"No, my child."

He added, after a moment's silence:

"Not yet."

Noland,
October 14, 1957

The Train
Translated from the French by Robert Baldick

CHAPTER *1*

When I woke up, a yellowish light which I knew so well was filtering into the bedroom through the holland curtains. Our windows, on the first floor, have no shutters. None of the houses in the street has any. I could hear, on the bedside table, the ticking of the alarm clock, and, beside me, my wife's regular breathing, which was almost as loud as that of patients, at the movies, during an operation. She was then seven and a half months pregnant. As when she was expecting Sophie, her huge belly forced her to sleep on her back.

Without looking at the alarm clock, I slipped one leg out of bed. Jeanne stirred and stammered in a faraway voice:

"What time is it?"

"Half past five."

I have always got up early, especially after my years in the sanatorium where, in summer, they used to bring us the thermometer at six in the morning.

My wife had already ceased to be aware of what was happening around her and one of her arms had stretched out across the place I had just left.

I dressed silently, carrying out, in order, the ritual movements of every morning, and glancing now and then at my daughter, whose bed at that time was still in our room. Yet we had furnished the prettiest room in the house for her, a front room communicating with ours.

She refused to sleep in it.

I went out of the room carrying my slippers in one hand, and put them on only at the foot of the stairs. It was then that I heard the first boats' hooters over at Uf Lock, which is about two miles away. The regulations state that the locks must be open to barge traffic at sunrise, and every morning there is the same concert.

In the kitchen I lit the gas and put the water on to boil. Once again, it looked like being a hot, sunny day. During the whole of that period, we had nothing but glorious days and even now I could still point out, hour by hour, the position of the pools of sunlight in the various rooms in the house.

I opened the back door to the glass porch which we had put on so that my wife can do the washing there in all weathers and my daughter play there. I can picture the doll's pram, and the doll a little farther off, on the yellow tiles.

I avoided going straight into my workshop because I wanted to obey the rules, as I used to say at that time when speaking of my timetable. A timetable which had established itself, little by little, made up of habits rather than obligations.

While the water was warming up, I poured some corn into an old blue enamel pan with a rusty bottom, which could no longer be used for anything else, and crossed the garden to go and feed the hens. We had six white hens and one cock.

The dew was sparkling on the vegetables and on our solitary lilac, whose flowers, which were early that year, were beginning to wither, and I could still hear, not only the hooting of the boats on the Meuse, but also the panting of the diesel engines.

I want to make it clear right away that I was not an unhappy man, nor a sad man either. At the age of thirty-two, I considered that I had gone beyond all the plans I had made, all my dreams.

I had a wife, a house, and a four-year-old daughter who was rather high-strung, but Dr. Wilhems said that that would pass.

I had a business of my own and my clientele grew from day to day, especially in the last few months of course. Because of what had been happening, everybody wanted to have a radio. I never stopped selling new radios and repairing old ones, and since we lived close to the quayside where the boats stopped for the night, I had the bargees as customers.

I remember that I heard the door open in the house on the left, where the Matrays, a quiet old couple, lived. Monsieur Matray, who worked as a cashier in the Bank of France for thirty-five or forty years, is another early riser and starts every day by going into his garden for a breather.

All the gardens in the street look the same, each as wide as the house and separated from one another by walls just so high that you can see nothing but the top of your neighbor's head.

For some time past, old Monsieur Matray had got into the habit of watching out for me, on account of my sets which could pick up short waves.

"No news this morning, Monsieur Féron?"

That day, I went back inside before he asked me the question and I poured the boiling water onto the coffee. The familiar objects were in their places, those that Jeanne and I had allotted them or which they had ended up by taking, almost of their own accord, with the passing of time.

If my wife had not been pregnant, I would have begun to hear her footsteps on the first floor, for she normally got up straight after me. All the same I insisted, out of habit, on making myself my first cup of coffee before going into my workshop. We observed a certain number of rites of that sort, and I suppose the same is true of every family.

The first pregnancy had been painful, the delivery difficult.

Jeanne attributed Sophie's nervous temperament to the forceps which had had to be used and which had bruised the child's head. Ever since her second pregnancy had started, she had been dreading a troublesome delivery and she was haunted by the idea of giving birth to an abnormal child.

Dr. Wilhems, in whom she had absolute confidence, could not manage to reassure her, except for a few hours at a time, and at night she found it impossible to fall asleep. Long after we had gone to bed, I could hear her trying to find a comfortable position and she nearly always ended up by asking in a whisper:

"Are you asleep, Marcel?"

"No."

"I wonder if I'm suffering from a deficiency of iron. I've read in an article . . ."

She tried to drop off to sleep, but often it was two o'clock in the morning before she succeeded and afterwards it was not uncommon for her to sit up with a cry.

"I've had another nightmare, Marcel."

"Tell me about it."

"No, I'd rather forget about it. It's too horrible. Forgive me for stopping you from sleeping, and when you work so hard too. . . ."

Recently she had been getting up about seven o'clock and coming downstairs after that to make breakfast.

With my cup of coffee in one hand, I went into my workshop and opened the glass door which looked out onto the yard and the garden. I was entitled, at that moment, to the first ray of sunshine of the day, a little to the left of the door, and I knew exactly when it would reach my bench.

It isn't a real bench, but a big, heavy table which came from a convent and which I bought at a sale. There are always two or three sets on it which are in the process of being repaired. My tools, arranged in a rack on the wall, are within easy reach. All round the room the deal shelves I had put up were littered with sets, each of which bore the customer's name on a label.

I ended up of course by turning the knobs. It was almost a game with me to put off that moment. I used to tell myself in defiance of all the laws of logic:

"If I wait a little longer, it may be today. . . ."

Straightaway, that particular morning, I realized that something was happening at last. I had never known the air so crowded. Whatever wave length I picked, broadcasts were overlapping, voices, whistles, phrases in German, Dutch, English, and you could feel a sort of dramatic throbbing in the air.

"During the night, the German armies launched a massive attack on . . ."

So far it was not France but Holland which had just been invaded. What I could hear was a Belgian station. I tried to get Paris but Paris remained silent.

The patch of sunshine was trembling on the gray floor, and at the bottom of the garden our six hens were fussing around the cock Sophie called Nestor. Why did I wonder all of a sudden what was going to become of our little poultry yard? I was almost moved to tears by its fate.

I turned some more knobs, searching the short waves where everybody seemed to be talking at once. In that way I picked up, for a brief moment, a military band which I promptly lost, so that I have never known to what army it belonged.

An Englishman was reading a message I could not understand, repeating each sentence as if he were dictating it to a correspondent, and after that I came across a station I had never heard before, a field transmitter.

It was obviously very close, and belonged to one of the regiments which, since October, since the beginning of the phony war, had been camping in the region.

The voices of the two men were as clear as if they had been talking to me on the telephone, and I supposed that they were in the neighborhood of Givet. Not that it matters in the slightest.

"Where is your colonel?"

That one had a strong southern accent.

"All I know is that he isn't here."

"He ought to be."

"What do you want me to do about it?"

"You've got to find him. He sleeps somewhere, doesn't he?"

"I suppose so, but not in his bed."

"In whose bed, then?"

A dirty laugh.

"Here one night, there the next. . . ."

Some atmospherics prevented me from hearing the rest, and I caught sight of Monsieur Matray's white hair and pink face over the wall, at the place where he had installed an old packing case to serve as a stepladder.

"Any news, Monsieur Féron?"

"The Germans have invaded Holland."

"Is that official?"

"The Belgians have announced it."

"And Paris?"

"Paris is playing music."

I heard him dash indoors shouting:

"Germaine! Germaine! This is it! They've attacked!"

I too was thinking that this was it, but the words had a different meaning for me than for Monsieur Matray. I am rather ashamed of saying this, but I felt relieved. I even wonder whether ever since October, indeed ever since Munich, I had not been waiting impatiently for this moment, whether I had not been disappointed every morning, when I turned the knobs of the radio, to learn that the armies were still facing each other without fighting.

It was the 10th of May. A Friday, I am almost sure of that. A month earlier, at the beginning of April, the 8th or 9th, my hopes had risen when the Germans had invaded Denmark and Norway.

I don't know how to explain myself and I wonder if there is anybody capable of understanding me. It will be pointed out that I was in no danger, as, on account of my shortsightedness, I was exempt from military service. My prescription is sixteen diopters, which means that, without my glasses, I am as helpless as somebody in total darkness, or at least in a thick fog.

I have always been terrified of finding myself without my glasses, for example of falling down in the street and breaking them, and I always have a spare pair in my pocket. That's to say nothing of my health, of the four years I spent in a sanatorium, between the ages of fourteen and eighteen, of the check-ups I had to undergo until a few years ago. None of that has anything to do with the impatience I am trying to describe.

I had little hope, at first, of leading a normal life, still less of getting a decent job and starting a family.

Yet I had become a happy man, I want to make that perfectly clear. I loved my wife. I loved my daughter. I loved my house, my habits, and even my street, which, quiet and sunny, ran down to the Meuse.

The fact remains that on the day war was declared I felt a sense of relief. I found myself saying out loud:

"It was bound to happen."

My wife looked at me in astonishment.

"Why?"

"I don't know. I felt certain about it, that's all."

It wasn't France and Germany, or Poland, England, Hitler, Nazism or Communism which, to my mind, were involved. I have never taken any interest in politics and I don't know anything about it. It would have been as much as I could do to quote the names of three or four French Ministers from having heard them on the radio.

No. This war, which had suddenly broken out after a year of spurious calm, was a personal matter between Fate and me.

I had already experienced one war, in the same town, Fumay, when I was a child, for I was six years old in 1914. I saw my father go off, in uniform, one morning when the rain was pouring down, and my mother was red-eyed all day. I heard the sound of gunfire for nearly four years, especially when we went up in the hills. I remember the Germans and their pointed helmets, the officers' capes, the posters on the walls, rationing, the poor bread, the shortage of sugar, butter, and potatoes.

One November evening I saw my mother come home naked, her hair cropped short, screaming insults and foul words at some youths who were trooping after her.

I was ten years old. We lived in the center of the town, in a first-floor flat.

She dressed without taking any notice of me, a mad look in her eyes, still muttering words I had never heard her use before, and suddenly, ready to go out, with a shawl around her head, she seemed to remember that I was there.

"Madame Jamais will look after you until your father comes home."

Madame Jamais was our landlady and lived on the ground floor. I was too terrified to cry. She didn't kiss me. At the door she hesitated, then she went out without saying anything else and the street door slammed.

I am not trying to explain. I mean that all this may have nothing to do with my feelings in 1939 or 1940. I am putting down the facts as they came back to me, without any falsification.

I contracted tuberculosis four years later. I had two or three other illnesses one after another.

Altogether, my impression, when war broke out, was that Fate was playing another trick on me and I was not surprised for I was practically certain that that was going to happen one day.

This time it wasn't a microbe, a virus, a congenital deformity of heaven knows what part of the eye—the doctors have never been able to agree about my eyes. It was a war which was hurling men against one another in tens of millions.

The idea was ridiculous, I realize that. But the fact remains that I knew, that I was ready. And that waiting, ever since October, was becoming unbearable. I didn't understand. I kept wondering why what was bound to happen didn't happen.

Were they going to tell us, one fine morning, as at Munich, that everything had been settled, that life was going back to normal, that this great panic had just been a mistake?

Wouldn't such a turn of events have meant that something had gone wrong with my personal destiny?

The sunshine was growing warmer, invading the yard, falling on the doll. Our bedroom window opened and my wife called out:

"Marcel!"

I stood up, went out of the workshop and leaned my head back. My wife looked as if she were wearing a mask, as she had during her first pregnancy. Her face, with the skin all taut, struck me as touching but almost unfamiliar.

"What's happening?"

"You heard?"

"Yes. Is it true? Are they attacking?"

"They've invaded Holland."

And my daughter, behind her, asked:

"What is it, Mummy?"

"Lie down. It isn't time to get up."

"What did Daddy say?"

"Nothing. Go to sleep."

She came down almost at once, smelling of the bed and walking with her legs slightly apart, because of her belly.

"Do you think they'll let them get through?"

"I haven't the faintest idea."

"What does the government say?"

"It hasn't said anything yet."

"What do you intend to do, Marcel?"

"I haven't thought about it. I'm going to try to get some more news."

It was still from Belgium that it was coming, given out by a dramatic staccato voice. This voice announced that at one o'clock in the morning some Messerschmitts and Stukas had flown over Belgian territory and had dropped bombs at several points.

Panzers had entered the Ardennes, and the Belgian government had addressed a solemn appeal to France to help it in its defense.

The Dutch, for their part, were opening their dykes and flooding a large part of the country, and there was talk, if the worst came to the worst, of halting the invader in front of the Albert Canal.

In the meantime my wife was making breakfast and setting the table, and I could hear the clatter of crockery.

"Any more news?"

"Tanks are crossing the Belgian frontier pretty well everywhere."

"But in that case . . ."

For certain moments of the day, my memories are so precise that I could write a detailed account of them, whereas for others I remember above all else the sunshine, the springtime smells, the blue sky like the one on the day I took my first Communion.

The whole street was waking up. Life was beginning in houses more or less similar to ours. My wife went to open the street door to take in the bread and milk and I heard her talking to our next-door neighbor on the right, Madame Piedboeuf, the schoolmaster's wife. They had an ideal little girl, curly-haired and pink-cheeked, with big blue eyes and long doll's eyelashes, who was always dressed as if for a party, and for the past year they had had a little car in which they used to go for a drive every Sunday.

I don't know what the two women said to each other. From the noises I could hear, I gathered that they weren't the only ones outside, that women were calling to one another from doorstep to doorstep. When Jeanne came back, she looked pale and even more drawn than usual.

"They're going!" she told me.

"Where?"

"South, anywhere. At the end of the street I saw more cars going past with mattresses on the roof, Belgians mostly."

We had already seen them go by before Munich, and in October a certain number of Belgians had once again traveled to the south of France, rich people, who could wait.

"Do you intend to stay here?"

"I haven't the faintest idea."

I was telling the truth. I who had seen this event coming from so far away, who had waited for it for so long, I had not made any decisions in advance. It was as if I were waiting for a sign, as if I wanted Fate to decide for me.

I wasn't responsible any more. Perhaps that's the word, perhaps that's what I was trying to explain just now. Only the day before, it had been up to me to manage my life and that of my family, to earn a living, to arrange for things to happen in the way things have to happen.

But not now. I had just lost my roots. I was no longer Marcel Féron, radio engineer in a newish district of Fumay, not far from the Meuse, but one man among millions whom superior forces were going to toss about at will.

I was no longer firmly attached to my house, to my habits. From one moment to the next, I had, so to speak, jumped into space.

From now on, decisions were no longer any concern of mine.

Instead of my own palpitations, I was beginning to feel a sort of general palpitation. I wasn't living at my tempo any more, but at the tempo of the radio, of the street, of the town which was waking up much faster than usual.

We ate in silence, in the kitchen, as usual, listening hard to the noises outside, without appearing to do so, on account of Sophie. Anyone would have thought that our daughter herself was hesitating to ask us any questions and she watched us in silence, one after the other.

"Drink your milk."

"Will we have any milk there?"

"What do you mean, there?"

"Why, where we are going. . . ."

Tears started running down my wife's cheeks. She turned her head away while I looked sadly at the familiar walls, at the furniture which we had chosen piece by piece five years earlier, before we got married.

"Go and play now, Sophie."

And my wife, once she was alone with me, said:

"Perhaps I'd better go and see my father."

"What for?"

"To find out what they are doing."

She still had her father and mother, and three sisters, all married, two of whom lived at Fumay, one of them the wife of a confectioner in the Rue du Château.

It was because of her father that I had set up in business on my own, for he was ambitious for his daughters and would not have allowed any of them to marry a workman.

It was he, too, who had made me buy the house on a twenty-year mortgage. I still had fifteen years of installments to pay, but in his eyes I was a property owner and that reassured him for the future.

"You never know what might happen to you, Marcel. You're cured, but people have been known to have relapses."

He had started in life as a miner in Delmotte's slate-pits, and had become a foreman. He had his own house too, and his own garden.

"You can arrange to buy a house in such a way that, if the husband happens to die, the wife doesn't have to pay anything more."

Wasn't it funny thinking about that on that particular morning, when nobody in the world could be sure of the future any more?

Jeanne dressed and put on her hat.

"You'll keep an eye on Sophie, won't you?"

She went off to see her father. The cars went by, more and more of them, all heading south, and two or three times I thought I heard some planes. They didn't drop any bombs. Perhaps they were French or English: it was impossible to tell, for they were flying very high and the sun was dazzling.

I opened the shop while Sophie was playing in the yard. It isn't a real shop, for the house was not built for use as business premises. My customers have to go along a corridor and an ordinary window has to serve as a shop window. The same is true of the dairy shop, a little farther on. It is often like that in the suburbs, at least in the north. It means that we are forced to leave the front door open and I have fitted the shop door with a bell.

A couple of bargees came in for their radios. They weren't ready but they insisted on taking them all the same. One of them was going downstream toward Rethel, while the other, a Fleming, wanted to get home at all costs.

I washed and shaved, watching my daughter through the window from which I could see all the gardens in the street full of flowers and grass, which was still a fresh green. People were talking to each other over the walls and I could hear a conversation between the Matrays, on the same floor as I was, for the windows were open.

"How do you expect to take all that with you?"

"We'll need it."

"We may need it, but I don't see how we're going to carry those suitcases to the station."

"We'll take a taxi."

"If we can find one! I wonder if there'll still be any trains."

I was suddenly afraid. I pictured the crowds pouring down every street toward the little station just as the cars were streaming toward the south. It struck me that we ought to be leaving, that it was no longer a matter of hours but of minutes, and I reproached myself for having allowed my wife to go and see her father.

What advice could he give her? What did he know that I didn't?

The fact of the matter was that she had never ceased to belong to her family. She had married me, lived with me, given me one child, was going to give me another. She bore my name but remained a Van Straeten for all that, and the slightest thing was enough to send her running to see her parents or her sisters.

"I must go and ask Berthe's advice. . . ."

Berthe was the confectioner's wife, the youngest of the sisters and the one who had made the best match, which was probably why Jeanne regarded her as an oracle.

If we were leaving, it was time to go, I was sure of that, just as I was suddenly sure, without asking myself why, that we had to leave Fumay. I hadn't got a car, and for deliveries I used a hand-cart.

Without waiting for my wife to return, I went up to the attic to get the suitcases and a black trunk in which we kept old clothes.

"Are we taking the train, Daddy?"

"I think so."

"You aren't certain."

I was getting nervous. I felt angry with Jeanne for going out and was afraid that at any moment something might happen: anything, perhaps not yet the arrival of the German tanks in the town, but something like an air raid which would cut us off from each other.

Every now and then I went into Sophie's bedroom, which so to speak had never been used, since my daughter refused to sleep there, to look out into the street.

Outside three houses, including the house next door, cars were being loaded. The schoolmaster's daughter, Michèle, as curly-haired and fresh in her white dress as when she went to mass on Sunday, was holding a canary's cage while she waited for her parents to finish tying a mattress onto the roof of the car.

That reminded me of our hens and of Nestor, the cock Sophie was so fond of. It was I, three years earlier, who had put up some wire netting at the bottom of the garden and made a sort of hen-house.

Jeanne wanted fresh eggs for the child. Because of her father, of course, who had always kept hens, rabbits, and pigeons. He also had some carrier pigeons, and when there was a competition on a Sunday, he would spend motionless hours at the bottom of his garden waiting for his birds to return to the pigeon-house.

Our cock, two or three times a week, flew over the walls and I had to go from house to house looking for him. Some people complained of the damage he caused in their gardens, others of being waked up by his crowing.

"Can I take my dolly with me?"

"Yes."

"And the pram?"

"Not the pram. There won't be enough room in the train."

"Where's my dolly going to sleep?"

I very nearly snapped back that, only the night before, the doll had spent the night out in the yard. At last my wife came back.

"What you are doing?"

"I've started packing."

"You've decided to leave?"

"I think it's the best thing to do. What are your parents doing?"

"They're staying. My father has sworn not to leave his house, whatever happens. I dropped in at Berthe's too. They'll be on their way in a few minutes. They'll have to hurry, because it seems there are jams everywhere, especially Mézières way. In Belgium, the Stukas are skimming the ground to machine-gun trains and cars."

She didn't protest at my decision because of her father, but didn't seem in any hurry to go. Perhaps she too would have preferred to cling to her house?

"They say there are peasants going off in their carts with everything they can take with them, and driving their animals in front of them. I saw the station from a distance. It was swarming with people."

"What are you taking with you?"

"I don't know. Sophie's things, anyway. And we ought to take something to eat, especially for her. If you could find some condensed milk . . ."

I went to the grocer's in the next street, and, contrary to my expectations, there was nobody in the shop. It is true that most of the local people had stocked up back in October. The grocer, in his white apron, was as calm as usual and I felt slightly ashamed of my feverishness.

"Have you any condensed milk left?"

He pointed to a whole shelf full of tins.

"How much do you want?"

"A dozen tins?"

I expected him to refuse to sell me as many as that. I also bought several bars of chocolate, some ham, and a whole sausage. There were no standards left, no landmarks. Nobody was capable of saying what was going to be valuable or not.

At eleven o'clock we were still not ready and Jeanne delayed us still further by being sick. I hesitated. I felt sorry for her. I asked myself whether, in view of her condition, I had any right to take her off into the unknown. She didn't complain, bustling about and bumping her huge belly against the furniture and the door jambs.

"The hens!" she exclaimed all of a sudden.

Perhaps she had a vague hope that we would stay on account of the hens, but I had thought about them before her.

"Monsieur Reversé will take them in with his."

"They're staying, are they?"

"I'll dash around and ask him."

The Reversés lived on the quayside. They had two sons at the front and a daughter who was a nun in a convent at Givet.

"We are in God's hands," the old man told me. "If He is going to protect us, He will do it just as well here as anywhere else."

His wife, in the shadows, was telling her beads. I announced my intention of giving them my hens and my cock.

"How can I go and collect them?"

"I'll leave the key with you."

"It's a big responsibility."

I nearly decided to bring the birds around right away, but then

I thought of the trains, of the crowd besieging the station, of the planes in the sky. This was no time to go running after poultry.

I had to insist.

"Even so, we shall probably never see anything we leave behind again. . . ."

The idea didn't upset me. On the contrary, it filled me with a sort of somber joy, like that of destroying something you have patiently built up with your own hands.

What counted was going, was leaving Fumay. It didn't matter if, somewhere else, other dangers were waiting for us. True, we were running away. But as far as I was concerned, it wasn't from the Germans, from the bullets and bombs, from death.

After thinking carefully about it, I swear that that was how I felt. I had the impression that for other people this departure wasn't very important. For me, as I have already said, it was the hour of my meeting with Fate, the hour of an appointment which I had had a long time, which I had always had, with Fate.

Jeanne was sniveling as we left the house. Walking between the shafts of the handcart, I didn't even turn around. As I had finally informed Monsieur Reversé, to persuade him to take charge of my hens, I had left the house unlocked so that my customers could come and collect their radios if they wanted to. Just ordinary honesty on my part. And if anybody was going to steal something, wouldn't he have broken the door down anyway?

All that was over and done with. I pushed my handcart along and Jeanne walked along the pavement with Sophie, who was clutching her doll to her chest.

I had a hard time threading my way through the traffic jams, and once I thought I had lost my wife and daughter, until I found them a little farther on.

An army ambulance drove past at full speed with its siren wailing, and a little farther on I caught sight of a Belgian car which was pitted with bullet holes.

Other people, like us, were walking toward the station, burdened with suitcases and bundles. An old woman asked me if she might put hers on my cart, and she started pushing it along with me.

"Do you think we'll still get a train? Somebody told me the line was up."

"Where?"

"Near Dinant. My stepson, who works on the railways, has seen a trainload of wounded go by."

There was a rather wild look in most people's eyes, but that was chiefly the result of impatience. Everybody wanted to be off. It was all a matter of arriving in time. Everybody was convinced that part of the huge crowd would be left behind and sacrificed.

Were those who were not leaving taking greater risks? Behind the windowpanes, faces were watching the fugitives, and it seemed to me, looking at them, that they were stamped with a sort of icy calm.

I knew the freight service buildings where I often used to go to collect parcels. I went in that direction, beckoning to my wife and daughter to follow me, and that was how we managed to get a train.

There were two in the station. One was a troop train full of disheveled soldiers grinning at the crowd.

Nobody was getting into the other train yet. Or rather, not everybody. Gendarmes were holding back the crowd. I had left my handcart. Young women wearing arm bands were bustling about, looking after the old people and the children.

One of them noticed my wife's belly, and our daughter whom she was holding by the hand.

"This way."

"But my husband . . ."

"The men will find room later on in the freight cars."

There was no arguing. You went where you were told, willy-nilly. Jeanne turned around, not knowing what was happening to her, trying to catch sight of me among all the heads. I shouted:

"Mademoiselle! Mademoiselle!"

The girl with the arm band came back toward me.

"Give her this. It's the little girl's food."

Indeed it was all the food we had brought with us.

I saw them get into a first-class carriage, and from the foot-board Sophie waved to me—or, at least, in my direction, for she could not recognize me among the hundreds of faces.

I was jostled about. I felt in my pocket to make sure that my spare pair of glasses were still there; those glasses which were my constant anxiety.

"Don't push!" cried a little man with a mustache.

And a gendarme repeated:

"Don't push. The train won't be leaving for another hour any-way!"

The ladies with the arm bands went on filling the carriages with an endless succession of old people, pregnant women, young children, and cripples, and I was not the only one to wonder whether, in the end, there would be any room on the train for the men. I looked forward with a certain irony to seeing my wife and daughter go off while I was obliged to stay behind.

It was the gendarmes who finally got tired of holding back the crowd. They suddenly broke the cordon and everybody rushed toward the five or six freight cars at the rear of the train.

At the last minute I had given Jeanne, together with the food, the suitcase containing Sophie's things and some of hers. I was left with the heavier of the two suitcases, and with my other hand I was dragging along as best I could the black trunk, which was bumping against my legs at every step. I didn't feel the pain. I wasn't thinking of anything, either.

I hoisted myself up, pushed by the people behind me, and, trying to stay as near as possible to the sliding door, I managed to put my trunk against the side of the car and sit down on it, panting for breath, with the suitcase on my lap.

To begin with, I could see only the lower half of my companions, men and women, and it was only later that I made out their faces. At first I thought that I didn't know any of them, and that surprised me, for Fumay is a little town, with a population of about five thousand. It is true that some farm workers had come in from the surrounding country. A crowded district, which I didn't know very well, had emptied.

Everybody settled down hurriedly, ready to defend his space, and a voice shouted from the back of the car:

"Full up! Don't let any more in, you!"

There was some nervous laughter, the first, and that reduced the tension slightly. The first contact had already become easier. Everybody started making himself comfortable, arranging his suitcases and bundles around him.

The sliding doors on both sides of the car had been left open, and we looked without much interest at the crowd waiting on the platform for another train, the refreshment room and the bar being pillaged, the bottles of beer and wine being passed from hand to hand.

"Hey, you over there. . . . Yes, you, Ginger. . . . You couldn't go and get me a bottle, could you?"

For a moment I thought of going to see how my wife and daughter had settled down, and at the same time reassure them with the news that I had found a place; I didn't do so for fear of not finding it on my return.

We didn't wait an hour, as the gendarme had said, but two and a half hours.

Several times the train gave a shudder and the buffers bumped against one another, and every time we held our breath, hoping that we were moving off at last. Once, it was because some cars were being added to the train.

The men who were close to the open doors reported on what was happening to those who could not see anything.

"They're adding at least eight cars. The train stretches at least halfway round the bend now."

A sort of fellowship was being established between those who had found a place on the train and were more or less sure of getting away.

One man, who had jumped down onto the platform, counted the carriages and freight cars.

"Twenty-eight!" he announced.

We didn't care a jot about the people stranded on the platforms and outside the station. The next rush was no concern of ours, and indeed we hoped that the train would go before it started.

We saw an old lady in a wheel chair being pushed along by a nurse toward the first-class carriages. She was wearing a mauve hat and a little white veil, and she had white thread gloves on her hands.

Later on, some stretchers were carried in the same direction, and I wondered whether people already in the carriages were going to be turned out, for a rumor started spreading that the hospital was being evacuated.

I was thirsty. Two of my neighbors dropped onto the line, ran over to the platform, and came back with bottles of beer. I didn't dare imitate them.

Little by little I started getting used to the faces around me, old men, for the most part, for the others had been called up, working-class women and country women, a fifteen-year-old boy with a long scraggy neck, and a girl of nine or ten whose hair was tied with a shoelace.

I finally recognized somebody after all, indeed two people. First Fernand Leroy, who had been at school with me and had become a clerk at Hachette's bookshop, next door to the confectioner's run by my sister-in-law.

From the other end of the car, where he was wedged in a corner, he gave me a little wave which I returned although I had had no occasion to speak to him for years.

As for the second person, he was a picturesque Fumay character, an old drunkard whom everybody called Jules and who distributed handbills outside the movie houses.

It took me some time to identify a third face, even though it was nearer to me, because it was hidden from me by a man with shoulders twice as broad. This third person was a buxom woman of about thirty, who was already eating a sandwich, a certain Julie who ran a little café near the port.

She was wearing a blue serge skirt, which was too tight and riding up her hips, and a white blouse marked with rings of sweat, through which you could see her brassière.

She smelled of powder and perfume, and I remember seeing her lipstick coming off onto the bread.

The troop train moved off toward the north. A few minutes later we heard a train approaching on the same line, and somebody shouted:

"Now it's coming back!"

It wasn't the same one, but a Belgian train even more crowded than ours and with only civilians on it. There were even people standing on the footboards.

Some of them jumped onto our cars. The gendarmes came running up, shouting orders. The loud-speaker joined in, announcing that nobody was allowed to leave his place.

All the same, a few managed to get in on the wrong side of the train, among them a young brunette in a black dress covered with dust, who was carrying no luggage and hadn't even a handbag.

She climbed shyly into our car, pale-faced, sad-looking, and nobody said anything to her. One or two men just exchanged winks while she huddled in a corner.

We couldn't see the cars any more and I am sure that none of us cared. Those who were near the doors looked at nothing but the piece of sky which was visible, a sky as blue as ever, wondering whether a German squadron might not appear at any moment and start bombing the station.

Since the arrival of the Belgian train, it was rumored that some stations had been bombed on the other side of the frontier, according to certain people the station at Namur.

I wish I could convey the atmosphere and above all the state of suspense in our car. We were beginning, in the stationary train, to form a little world on its own, but which remained, so to speak, in a state of tension.

Cut off from the rest, it was as if our group was only waiting for a signal, a whistle, a hiss of steam, the sound of the wheels on the rails, to fall back entirely upon itself.

And that finally happened, when we were beginning to give up hope.

What would my companions have done if they had been told that the line was blocked, that the trains had stopped running? Would they have gone home with their bundles?

Speaking for myself, I don't think that I would have given up: I think I would rather have walked along the track. It was too late to turn back. The break had occurred. The idea of going back to my street, my house, my workshop, my garden, my habits, the labeled radios waiting on the shelves to be repaired, struck me as unbearable.

The crowd on the platform started slipping slowly behind us, and for me it was as if it had never existed, as if the town itself, where, except for the four years in the sanatorium, I had spent my life, had lost its reality.

I didn't give a thought to Jeanne and my daughter sitting in their first-class carriage, farther from me than if they had been hundreds of miles away.

I didn't wonder what they were doing, how they had borne the long wait, or whether Jeanne had been sick again.

I was more concerned about my spare pair of glasses, and every time one of my companions moved I protected my pocket with my hand.

Just outside the town we passed, on the left, the state forest of Manise, where we had spent so many Sunday afternoons on the grass. To my eyes, it was not the same forest, possibly because I was seeing it from the railway. The broom was growing thickly and the train was moving so slowly that I could see the bees buzzing from flower to flower.

All of a sudden the train stopped and we all looked at one another with the same fear in our eyes. A railwayman ran along the track. Finally he shouted something I didn't understand and the train moved off again.

I wasn't hungry. I had forgotten my thirst. I looked at the grass passing by a few yards away, sometimes only a foot or two, and the wild flowers, white, blue, and yellow, whose names I didn't know and which I felt I was seeing for the first time. Whiffs of Julie's perfume reached me, especially on the bends, mingled with the strong but not unpleasant smell of her sweat.

Her café was like my shop. It wasn't a real café. There were curtains in the windows which, when they were drawn, made it impossible to make out anything inside.

The bar was tiny, without either a metal top or a sink behind. The shelf, with five or six bottles on it, was just a kitchen fitting.

I had often glanced inside when I was passing, and I remember, on the wall, next to a cuckoo clock which didn't work and the notice about the law on drunkenness in public, a publicity calendar showing a blonde holding a glass of foaming beer. A glass shaped like a champagne glass, that was what struck me.

That isn't interesting, I know. I mention it because I thought of it at that moment. There were other smells in our car, not counting that of the car itself, which had carried some cattle on one of its recent trips and smelled of the farmyard.

Some of my companions were eating sausages or pâté. One country girl had brought a huge cheese with her and kept cutting into it with a kitchen knife.

So far we had exchanged only inquisitive glances, which were still cautious, and only those who came from the same village or the same district were talking, generally to identify the places we were passing.

"Look! Dédé's farm! I wonder if he's staying. His cows are in the meadow, anyway."

We went through stops and deserted little stations where there were baskets of flowers hanging from the lamps and travel posters on the walls.

"Look, Corsica! Why don't we go to Corsica?"

After Revin we went faster, and before arriving at Monthermé we saw a lime kiln and more rows of working-class houses.

Just as we were entering the station, the engine gave a piercing whistle like a big express. Passing the station buildings and the platforms swarming with troops, it drew up in a setting of deserted tracks and signal boxes.

A pump, next to our car, was oozing huge drops of water, one by one, and I felt my thirst coming on again. A peasant, jumping down from the train, urinated on the next track, out in the sunshine, with one eye on the engine. This made everybody laugh. We felt a need to laugh, and some of the men started cracking jokes on purpose. Old Jules was asleep, with a half-empty bottle in one hand and his haversack, containing more bottles, on his belly.

"They're uncoupling the engine!" announced the man who was relieving himself.

Two or three others got out. I still didn't dare. It seemed to me that I had to hang on at all costs, that it was particularly important for me.

A quarter of an hour later, another engine was pulling us in the opposite direction, but, instead of going through Monthermé, we took a side track running alongside the Semois toward Belgium.

I had made this trip before, with Jeanne, before she became my wife. I even wonder whether it wasn't that day, a Sunday in August, which decided our fate.

Marriage at that time didn't mean the same to me as to somebody normal. Has there been anything really normal in my life since that evening when I saw my mother come home naked and with her hair cropped?

Yet it wasn't even that event which struck me. At the time I didn't understand or try to understand. For the past four years so many things had been put down to the war that one more mystery was not likely to upset me.

Madame Jamais, our landlady, was a widow and earned a good living as a dressmaker. She looked after me for about a fortnight, until my father came home. I didn't recognize him at first. He was still wearing uniform, a different uniform from the one in which he had gone away; his mustache smelled of sour wine; his eyes were shining as if he had a cold in the head.

The fact was, I scarcely knew him, and the only photograph we had of him, on the sideboard, was the one taken with my mother on their wedding day. I still wonder why both their faces

were lopsided. Perhaps Sophie finds that in our wedding photograph our features too are lopsided?

I knew that he had worked as a clerk for Monsieur Sauveur,
the dealer in seeds and fertilizers whose offices and warehouses,
occupying a long stretch of the quayside, were linked by a private track to the freight station.

My mother had pointed Monsieur Sauveur out to me in the
street, a rather short, fat man with a very pale face, who must
have been sixty at the time and walked slowly, cautiously, as if he
were afraid of the slightest shock.

"He's got a heart disease. He may drop dead in the street any
minute. The last time he had an attack, they only just managed to
save him, and afterwards they had to call in a great specialist
from Paris."

When I was a little boy I sometimes followed him with my
eyes, wondering whether the accident was going to happen in
front of me. I couldn't understand how, with a threat like that
hanging over him, Monsieur Sauveur could come and go like
everybody else without looking sad.

"Your father is his right-hand man. He started working for
him as an office boy, at the age of sixteen, and now he can sign
for the firm."

Sign what? I found out later that my father was in fact the
managing clerk and that his position was just as important as my
mother had said.

He went back to his old job, and we gradually got used to
living together in our flat, where my mother was never mentioned, although the wedding photograph remained on the sideboard.

It had taken me some time to understand why my father's
mood changed so much from one day to the next, sometimes
from one hour to the next. He could be very affectionate and
sentimental, taking me on his knees, which rather embarrassed
me, and telling me with tears in his eyes that I was all he had in
life, that that was enough for him, that nothing mattered in life
but a son. . . .

Then, a few hours later, he would seem surprised to find me at home and would order me about as if I was a maid, bullying me and shouting at me that I was no better than my mother.

Finally I heard that he drank, or to be more precise that he had started drinking, out of grief, when he hadn't found his wife waiting for him on his return and when he had heard what had happened.

I believed that for a long time. Then I thought about it. I remembered the day of his arrival, his shining eyes, his jerky gestures, his smell, the bottles which he went to the grocer's to get right away.

I caught odd phrases when he was talking about the war with his friends, and I guessed that it was at the front that he had got into the habit of drinking.

I don't hold it against him. I have never held it against him, even when, reeling about and muttering swear-words, he would bring home a woman he had picked up in the street and lock me in my room.

I didn't like Madame Jamais wheedling me and treating me like a victim. I avoided her. I had got into the habit of going shopping after school, cooking the meals, doing the washing-up.

One evening, a couple of passers-by brought in my father, whom they had found lying unconscious on the pavement. I wanted to go for a doctor but they said that that wasn't necessary, that all my father needed was to sleep it off. I helped them to undress him.

Monsieur Sauveur only kept him on out of pity, I knew that too. Several times he was insulted by his managing clerk, who, the next day, would beg his forgiveness with tears in his eyes.

That isn't really important. What I wanted to show was that I didn't lead the same kind of life as other children of my age and that when I was fourteen I had to be sent to a sanatorium above Saint-Gervais in Savoy.

When I set off, alone on my train—it was the first time I had ever taken a train—I was convinced that I wasn't going to come back alive. This idea didn't make me sad, and I began to understand Monsieur Sauveur's serenity.

In any case, I would never be like other men. Already, at

school, my poor sight had prevented me from playing any games. And now, on top of that, I was suffering from a disease which was regarded as a taint, a disease which was almost shameful. What woman would ever agree to marry me?

I spent four years up there, rather like here in the train; I mean that the past and future didn't count, nor what was happening in the valley, still less in the faraway towns.

When I was declared to be cured and sent back to Fumay, I was eighteen. I found my father more or less as I had left him, except that his features were softer, his eyes sad and frightened.

When he saw me, he studied my reaction and I realized that he was ashamed, that in his heart of hearts he wished I hadn't come back.

I had to find a sedentary occupation. I started work as an apprentice to Monsieur Ponchot, who ran the town's big piano, record, and radio shop.

In the mountains, I had got into the habit of reading up to two books a day, and I kept it up. Every month, then every three months, I went to a specialist at Mézières to be examined, never trusting his reassuring words.

I had returned to Fumay in 1926. My father died in 1934, from a clot of blood, while Monsieur Sauveur was still going strong. I had just met Jeanne, who was an assistant in Choblet's glove shop, two doors away from where I worked.

I was twenty-six; she was twenty-two. We walked along the streets in the twilight. We went together to the movies, where I held her hand, then, on Sunday afternoon, I obtained permission to take her into the country.

That struck me as incredible. For me, she was not just a woman, but the symbol of a normal regular life.

And it was, I would swear to it, in the course of that outing in the Semois valley, for which I had had to ask her father's permission, that I acquired the assurance that it was possible, that she was ready to marry me, to start a family with me.

I was speechless with gratitude. I would gladly have gone on my knees at her feet. If I talk about it at such length, it is in order to emphasize Jeanne's importance in my eyes.

Now, in my cattle car, I didn't give a thought to her, a woman seven and a half months pregnant, for whom this journey must have been particularly difficult. My thoughts were elsewhere. I wondered why we were being shunted down a side track which led nowhere, except to a place more dangerous than the one we had just left.

As we were stopping in the open country, near a grade crossing which cut across a minor road, I heard someone say:

"They're clearing the lines to let the troop trains through. They must need reinforcements out there."

The train didn't move. We couldn't hear anything except, all of a sudden, birds singing and the murmur of a spring. One man jumped onto the bank, followed by another.

"Hey there, guard, are we going to stay here long?"

"An hour or two. Unless we spend the night here."

"The train isn't likely to move off without warning, is it?"

"The engine is going back to Monthermé, and they're sending us another from there."

I made sure that the engine really was being uncoupled; then, when I saw it go off by itself in a landscape of woods and meadows, I jumped down onto the ground, and, before doing anything else, went to have a drink at the spring, in the hollow of my hand, as I used to when I was little. The water had the same taste as it had then, the taste of grass and my own hot body.

People were getting out of all the carriages. Hesitant at first, then more self-assured, I started walking alongside the train, trying to see inside.

"Daddy!"

My daughter was calling me and waving.

"Where's your mother?"

"Here."

Two elderly women were blocking the view and would not have moved for all the gold in the world, scowling disapprovingly at my daughter's excitement.

"Open the door, Daddy. I can't manage. Mummy wants to talk to you."

The carriage was an old model. I succeeded in opening the door and was confronted with eight people in two rows, as grim and motionless as in a dentist's waiting room. My wife and daughter were the only ones under sixty, and an old man in the far corner was clearly a nonagenarian.

"Are you all right, Marcel?"

"Yes. What about you?"

"I'm all right. I was wondering what you were going to eat. Luckily, we've stopped. You see, we've got all the food."

Wedged between two women with monumental hips, she could scarcely move, and she had some difficulty in handing me a thin loaf of bread together with the whole sausage.

"But what about you two?"

"You know perfectly well we can't stand garlic."

"Is there some garlic in it?"

That morning, at the grocer's, I hadn't bothered to make sure.

"How are you fixed?"

"All right."

"You couldn't get me some water, could you? They gave me a bottle before we left, but it's so hot here that we've already drunk it all."

She handed me a bottle and I ran to the spring to fill it. There, on her knees, washing her face, I found the young woman in the black dress who had got in on the wrong side of the car after the arrival of the Belgian train.

"Where did you find a bottle?" she asked me.

Her accent was neither Belgian nor German.

"Somebody gave it to my wife."

She didn't press the point, but wiped her face with her handkerchief, and I went off toward the first-class carriage.

On the way I stumbled over an empty beer bottle and turned back to pick it up as if it were a precious object. My wife jumped to the wrong conclusion.

"Are you drinking beer?"

"No. It's to put some water in."

It was curious. We were talking to each other like strangers. Not exactly: rather, like distant relatives who haven't seen each other for a long time and don't know what to say. Perhaps it was because of the presence of the old women.

"Can I get out, Daddy?"

"If you like."

My wife looked worried.

"What if the train starts moving?"

"We haven't got an engine any more."

"You mean we're going to stay here?"

At that moment we heard the first explosion, a muffled, distant sound, but one which nonetheless made us jump, and one of the old women made the sign of the cross and shut her eyes as if she had heard a clap of thunder.

"What's that?"

"I don't know."

"You can't see any planes?"

I looked at the sky, which was as blue as it had been that morning, with just two gilded clouds floating slowly along.

"Don't let her go far, Marcel."

"I won't let her out of my sight."

Holding Sophie by the hand, I walked along the tracks looking for another bottle, and I was lucky enough to find one, bigger than the first.

"What are you going to do with it?"

I told a half-lie.

"I'm collecting them."

For I was just picking up a third bottle which had contained some wine. My intention was to give at least one to the young woman in black.

I could see her from a distance, standing in front of our car, and her dusty satin dress, her figure, her tousled hair seemed foreign to everything around her. She was stretching her legs without paying any attention to what was happening and I noticed her high, pointed heels.

"Your mother hasn't been sick?"

"No. There's a woman who talks all the time and she says the train is sure to be bombed. Is that true?"

"She doesn't know anything about it."

"You don't think it'll be bombed?"

"I'm sure it won't."

"Where are we going to sleep?"

"In the train."

"There aren't any beds."

I went and washed the three bottles, rinsing them several times to remove as far as possible the taste of the beer and the wine, and filled them with fresh water.

I went back to my car, still accompanied by Sophie, and handed one of the bottles to the young woman.

She looked at me in surprise, looked at my daughter, thanked me with a nod of her head, and climbed up into the car to put it in a safe place.

There was only one house in sight, apart from the one belonging to the grade-crossing keeper: a tiny farm, a fair way away, on the hillside, and in the yard a woman with a blue apron was feeding the hens as if the war didn't exist.

"Is that where you are? On the floor?"

"I sit on the trunk."

Julie was at grips with a red-faced man with thick gray hair who was giving her meaning looks, and every now and then the two of them burst into the sort of laughter you hear in the arbors of tavern gardens. The man had a bottle of red wine in his hand and kept giving his companion a swig from it. There were purple stains on her blouse, inside which her big breasts bounced about with every burst of laughter.

"Let's go back to your mother."

"Already?"

New subdivisions were beginning to take shape. On one side there was the world of the passenger carriages and on the other there was ours, the world of the cattle cars and the freight cars. Jeanne and my daughter belonged to the first world, I to the second, and I unconsciously showed some haste in taking Sophie back.

"Aren't you going to eat?"

I ate my bread and sausage, on the track, in front of the open door. We could not say very much to one another, with those two rows of frozen faces whose eyes kept moving from my wife to me and my daughter.

"Do you think we'll set off again soon?"

"They have to let the troop trains through. Once the line is clear, it will be our turn. Look! The engine's arriving."

We could hear it, then see it, all by itself, with its white smoke, following the bends of the valley.

"Hurry back to your place. I'm so frightened that somebody might have taken it!"

Relieved to get away, I kissed Sophie but didn't dare to kiss Jeanne in front of everybody. A spiteful voice called after me:

"You might at least shut the door!"

Nearly every Sunday in summer, first with Jeanne, then with her and my daughter, I used to go into the country to have a snack and sometimes lunch on the grass.

But it wasn't the smell or the taste of that countryside which I was rediscovering today but the smell and the taste of my childhood memories.

For years I had sat down every Sunday in a clearing, I had played there with Sophie, I had picked flowers to make garlands for her, but all that was so to speak neutral.

Why was it that today the world had recovered its savor?

Even the buzzing of the wasps reminded me of the buzzing I heard when I used to hold my breath and watch a bee circling around my bread and butter.

The faces, when I got back into the car, seemed more familiar. A sort of complicity was growing up between us, making us wink, for instance, after watching the antics of Julie and her horse dealer.

I say horse dealer without knowing. People's names didn't matter, nor their occupation. He looked like a horse dealer and that was what I called him to myself.

The couple were holding each other around the waist, and the man's big hand was squeezing Julie's breast when the train started moving again after a few jolts.

The woman in black, who was still pressed against the side of the car, a few feet away from me, had nothing to sit on. It is true that, like so many others, she could have sat down on the floor. There were even four people in one corner who were playing cards as if they were sitting around a table in an inn.

We returned to Monthermé, and a little later I caught a glimpse of Leversy Lock where a dozen motor barges were vibrating on the dazzling water. The bargees had no need of a train, but the locks were there to stop them and I could imagine their impatience.

The sky was turning pink. Three planes went over, flying very low, with reassuring tricolor roundels. They were so close that we could make out the face of one of the pilots. I could have sworn that he waved to us.

When we arrived at Mézières, dusk had fallen, and our train, instead of going into the station, drew up in a wilderness of tracks. A soldier whose rank I didn't see went along the train shouting:

"Nobody must get out! It is absolutely forbidden to leave the train."

There was no platform anyway, and a little later some guns mounted on open trucks went past us at full speed. They had scarcely disappeared before the siren sounded an air-raid warning while the same voice went on shouting:

"Stay where you are. It's dangerous to get off the train. Stay where you are. . . ."

Now we could hear the drone of a certain number of planes. The town was in darkness and in the station, where all the lights were out, the passengers were probably running into the subways.

I don't think that I was frightened. I sat perfectly still, staring at the faces opposite me, and listening to the sound of the engines, which grew louder and then seemed to fade away.

There was complete silence and our train stayed there, as if abandoned in the middle of a complicated network of tracks on which a few empty carriages were standing about. Among others, I can remember a tanker which bore in big yellow letters the name of a Montpellier wine merchant.

Despite ourselves, we remained in suspense, not saying anything, waiting for the all-clear which was not sounded for almost another half-hour. During this time, the horse dealer's hand had left Julie's breast. It settled there again, more insistent than before, and the man pressed his lips on his neighbor's.

A countrywoman muttered:

"Disgusting, I call it, in front of a little girl."

And he retorted, his mouth daubed with lipstick:

"The little girl will have to learn one day! Didn't you ever learn, in your day?"

This was the sort of coarse, vulgar remark to which I wasn't accustomed. It reminded me of the torrent of abuse my mother had poured on the youths who had followed her, jeering at her. I glanced at the dark-haired girl. She was looking somewhere else as if she hadn't heard, and didn't notice my interest.

I have never been drunk for the simple reason that I drink neither wine nor beer. But I imagine that when night fell I was in roughly the condition of a man who has had a drop too much.

Possibly on account of the afternoon sun, in the valley with the spring, my eyelids were hot and prickly; I felt that my cheeks were red, my arms and legs numb, my mind empty.

I gave a start when somebody, striking a match to look at his watch, announced in an undertone:

"Half past ten. . . . !"

Time was passing at once fast and slowly. To tell the truth, there was no time any more.

Some of my companions were asleep, others were talking in low voices. I dozed off, for my part, on the black trunk, with my head against the side of the car, and later on, in a half-sleep, while the train was still motionless, surrounded by darkness and silence, I became aware of rhythmical movements close beside me. It took me some time to realize that it was Julie and her companion making love.

I wasn't shocked, even though, possibly on account of my disease, I have always been rather prudish. I followed the rhythm as if it were music and I must admit that, little by little, a detailed picture took shape in my mind, and the whole of my body was filled with a diffused warmth.

When I dropped off to sleep again, Julie was murmuring, probably to another neighbor of hers:

"No! Not now!"

A long time afterwards, toward the middle of the night, a series of jolts shook us, as if our train were shunting about. People were walking up and down the line, talking. Somebody said:

"It's the only way."

And somebody else:

"I'll only take orders from the military commandant."

They went off arguing and the train started moving, only to halt again after a few minutes.

I stopped taking any notice of these movements which I couldn't understand. We had left Fumay, and, provided we didn't go back, the rest was a matter of indifference to me.

There were some whistle blasts, more jolts, more halts followed by the hissing of steam.

I know nothing about what happened that night at Mézières or anywhere else in the world, except that there was fighting in Holland and Belgium, that tens of thousands of people were crowding the roads, that planes were streaking across the sky nearly everywhere, and that the anti-aircraft guns fired a few random shots every now and then. We heard some bursts of gunfire, in the distance, and an endless convoy of trucks, on a road which must have passed close to the railway.

In our car, where it was pitch-dark, the sound of snoring created a curious intimacy. Now and then somebody in an uncomfortable position or having a nightmare would give an unwitting groan.

When I finally opened my eyes, we were moving, and half my companions were awake. A milky dawn was breaking, lighting up a countryside which was unfamiliar to me, fairly high hills covered with woods and farmhouses standing in huge clearings.

Julie was asleep, her mouth half open, her blouse undone. The young woman in the black dress was sitting with her back against the side of the car, and a lock of hair hanging over one cheek. I wondered whether she had stayed like that all night and whether she had been able to sleep. Her eyes met mine. She smiled at me, on account of the bottle of water.

"Where are we?" asked one of my neighbors, waking up.

"I don't know," answered the man sitting in the doorway with his legs hanging out. "We've just passed a station called Lafrancheville."

We passed another decked with flowers and deserted like the rest. On the blue-and-white sign I read the name: Boulzicourt.

The train started rounding a bend, through some fairly flat

country; the man with the dangling legs took his pipe out of his mouth to exclaim in comical despair:

"Hell!"

"What is it?"

"The swine have shortened the train!"

"What's that you say?"

There was a rush toward the door, and, hanging on with both hands, the man protested:

"Stop pushing, you! You're going to shove me out on the line. You can see for yourselves there are only five carriages in front of us. Well, what have they done with the others? And how am I going to find my wife and kids? Hell! Oh, damn it to hell!"

CHAPTER *3*

"I knew perfectly well that the engine couldn't pull all those carriages. They must have realized that in the end and decided to cut the train in two."

"The first thing to do was to tell us, wasn't it? What's going to happen to the women?"

"Perhaps they're waiting for us at Rethel. Or at Rheims."

"Unless they're going to give them back to us, like soldiers' wives, when this damned war finishes—if it ever does!"

I tried automatically to distinguish between sincerity and sham in these angry complaints. Wasn't this above all a sort of game these men were playing with themselves, because there were witnesses?

Personally I wasn't upset, nor really anxious. I stayed where I was, motionless, a little startled in spite of everything. Suddenly I had the feeling that a pair of eyes were gazing insistently at mine.

I was right. The face of the woman in black was turned toward me, paler in the dawn light, and not as clear-cut as the day before. She was trying, with her gaze, to convey a message of sympathy to me, and at the same time I had the impression that she was asking a question.

I interpreted it as:

"How are you standing up to the shock? Are you terribly upset?"

This put me in a quandary. I didn't dare to show her my lack of concern, which she would have misinterpreted. I accordingly assumed a sad expression, but without overdoing it. She had seen me on the track with my daughter and must have deduced that my wife was with me too. As far as she could see, I had just lost them both, temporarily, but lost them nonetheless.

"Courage!" her brown eyes said to me over the others' heads.

I responded with the smile of a sick man whom somebody is trying to reassure but who feels no better as a result. I am almost certain that if we had been closer to one another she would have given my hand a furtive squeeze.

In behaving like that, I didn't intend to deceive her, as one might imagine, but, with all those heads between us, it wasn't the time to explain how I felt.

Later on, if we happened to be brought together and if she gave me the opportunity, I would tell her the truth, since I wasn't ashamed of it.

I was no more surprised by what was happening to us than I had been, the day before, on hearing of the invasion of Holland and the Ardennes. On the contrary, my idea that it was a matter between Fate and myself was reinforced. It was becoming more obvious. I had been separated from my family, which was a personal attack and no mistake.

The sky was rapidly brightening, as pure and clear as the day before when, in my garden, I had been feeding the hens without knowing that it was the last time.

I was touched by the memory of my hens, and the mental picture of Nestor, his comb all crimson, struggling fiercely when old Monsieur Reversé tried to grab him.

I imagined the scene between the two low, whitewashed walls, the beating of the wings, the white feathers flying, the vicious pecks, and perhaps Monsieur Matray, if he had been prevented from leaving, climbing onto his crate to look over the wall and give advice as he usually did.

That didn't prevent me from thinking at the same time about this woman who had just shown sympathy for me when I had done nothing but give her an empty bottle picked up from the track.

While she was doing her hair with her fingers moistened with saliva, I tried to decide to what category she belonged. I couldn't make up my mind. I told myself that it didn't really matter and eventually the idea occurred to me of handing her the comb I had in my pocket, while my neighbor whom I was disturbing gave me a meaning look.

He was mistaken. I wasn't doing it for that.

We were moving fairly slowly and out in the open country when we began to hear a steady buzz which we didn't manage to place immediately, and which was just a vibration of the air to begin with.

"There they are!" exclaimed the man with the pipe, his legs still dangling in the air.

For somebody who never felt giddy, he had the best place in the car.

I discovered later on that he was a constructional ironworker.

Bending down, I saw them too, for I wasn't far from the door. The man was counting:

"Nine . . . ten . . . eleven . . . twelve. . . .   There are twelve of them. . . . Probably what they call a squadron. . . . If it was the right time of the year and they weren't making any noise, I'd swear they were storks. . . ."

I counted eleven of them, high up in the sky. Because of a trick of the light, they appeared white and luminous, and they were flying in a V-shaped formation.

"What's that fellow up to?"

Pressed against one another, we were looking up at the sky when I felt the woman's hand on my shoulder where she might easily have put it inadvertently.

The last plane in one leg of the V had just broken away from the others and seemed to be diving toward the ground, so that our first impression was that it was falling. It grew larger at incredible speed, spiraling down, while the others, instead of continuing on their way toward the horizon, started forming a huge circle.

The rest happened so quickly that we didn't have time to be really frightened. The plane which was doing the nose dive had disappeared from our sight, but we could hear its menacing roar.

It flew over the train, along its whole length, from back to front, so low that we instinctively ducked.

Then it disappeared only to repeat its maneuver, with the difference that this time we heard the rattle of the machine gun above us, and other sounds, like that of wood splintering.

There were shouts, inside our car and elsewhere. The train went a little farther, then, like a wounded animal, stopped after a few jolts.

For a while there was complete silence, the silence of fear, which I was facing for the first time, and I was probably not breathing any more than my companions.

All the same, I went on looking at the scene in the sky, the plane soaring upwards again, its two swastikas clearly visible, the head of the pilot giving us a final glance, and the others, up there, circling around until he took up his position again.

"Swine!"

I don't know from whose breast the word exploded. It relieved us all and roused us from our immobility.

A little girl was crying. A woman pushed forward, repeating as if she didn't know what she was saying:

"Let me pass. . . . Let me pass. . . ."

"Are you hurt?'

"My husband . . ."

"Where is he?"

Everybody looked instinctively for a body stretched out on the floor.

"In the next car. . . . The one that's been hit. . . . I heard it. . . ."

Her face drawn, she dropped to the stones beside the lines and started running along, shouting:

"François! . . . François!"

None of us made a pretty picture and we felt no desire to look at one another. It seemed to me that everything was happening in slow motion, but perhaps that was just an illusion. I also remember something like zones of silence around isolated noises which sounded even louder as a result.

One man, then another, then a third jumped down, and their first instinct was to pass water without taking the trouble to move away, or even, in one case, to face the other way.

Farther off a continuous lament could be heard, a sort of animal howl.

As for Julie, she stood up, her blouse coming out of her crumpled skirt, and said in a drunken voice:

"Well, chum!"

She repeated this two or three times; perhaps she was still repeating it when I got out in my turn and helped the woman in black to jump down onto the ground.

Why was it that particular moment that I asked her:

"What's your name?"

She didn't consider the question stupid or out of place, for she answered:

"Anna."

She didn't ask me what I was called. I told her all the same:

"My name is Marcel. Marcel Féron."

I would have liked to pass water like the others. I didn't dare, because of her, and it hurt me to restrain myself.

There was a meadow below the track, with tall grass, barbed wire, and, a hundred yards away, a white farmhouse where there was nobody to be seen. Some hens, around a pile of manure, had all started cackling together, as excited as if they had been frightened too.

The people in the other car had got out, as flustered and awkward as we were.

In front of one of the carriages there was a more compact, solemn crowd. Some faces were turned away.

"A woman has been wounded over there," somebody came and told us. "I don't suppose there's a doctor among you?"

Why did the question strike me as grotesque? Do doctors travel in cattle cars? Could any of us be taken for a doctor?

At the front of the train, the fireman, his face and hands black, was waving his arms about, and a little later we learned that the engineer had been killed by a bullet in the face.

"They're coming back! They're coming back!"

The shout ended in a strangled cry. Everybody copied the first ones who had had the idea of throwing themselves flat on their faces in the meadow, at the foot of the embankment.

I did like the others; so did Anna, who was now following me about like a dog without a master.

The planes up in the sky were forming another circle, a little farther west, and this time we missed nothing of the maneuver. We saw one plane come spiraling down, flatten out just when it seemed bound to crash, skim the ground, soar upwards again, and sweep around to cover the same ground once more, this time firing its machine gun.

It was two or three miles away. We couldn't see the target—a village, perhaps, or a road—which was hidden by a wood of fir trees. And already it was climbing into the sky to join the flock waiting for it up there and follow them northwards.

I went, like the others, to look at the dead engineer, part of his body on the footplate, near the open firebox, his head and shoulders hanging over the side. There was no face left, just a black and red mass from which the blood was oozing in big drops onto the gray stones by the track.

He was my first dead man of the war. He was almost my first dead man, apart from my father, who had been laid out by the time I came home.

I felt sick and tried not to show it, because Anna was beside me, and because at that moment she took my arm as naturally as a girl walking along the street with her sweetheart.

I think she was less upset than I was. And yet I myself was less upset than I would have expected. At the sanatorium, where there were a lot of dead people, we were not allowed to see them. The nurses acted in good time, coming to collect a patient from his bed, sometimes in the middle of the night. We knew what that meant.

There was a special room for dying, and another, in the basement, where the body was kept until the relatives claimed it or it was buried in the little local cemetery.

Those deaths were different. There wasn't the sunshine, the grass, the flowers, the cackling hens, the flies buzzing around our heads.

"We can't leave him there."

The men looked at one another. Two of them, both elderly, volunteered to lend the fireman a hand.

I don't know where they put the engineer. Walking back along the train, I noticed holes in the sides of the cars, long scores which showed the wood as bare as when you fell a tree.

A woman had been wounded, one shoulder, we were told, practically torn off.

It was she whom we could hear groaning as if she were in labor. There were just a few other women around her, old women for the most part, for the men, embarrassed, had moved away in silence.

"It isn't a pretty sight."

"What are we going to do? Stay here until they come back to snipe at us?"

I saw an old man sitting on the ground, holding a bloodstained handkerchief to his face. A bottle, hit by a bullet, had shattered in his hand and splinters of glass had scored his cheeks. He didn't complain. I could see only his eyes, which were expressing nothing but a sort of amazement.

"They've found somebody to attend to her."

"Who?"

"A midwife on the train."

I caught sight of her, a sour-faced little old woman with a sturdy figure and her hair arranged in a bun on top of her head. She didn't belong to our car.

Without realizing, we gathered together in groups correspond-

ing to the carriages, and in front of ours the man with the pipe
went on protesting halfheartedly. He was one of the few who
had not been to see the dead engineer.

"What the hell are we waiting for? Isn't there a single bastard
here who can make that damned engine work?"

I remember somebody climbing up onto the track carrying a
dead chicken by the feet, and sitting down to pluck it. I didn't
try to understand. Seeing that nothing was happening as it
did in ordinary life, everything was natural.

"The fireman wants a hefty fellow to feed the boiler while he
tries to take the engineer's place. He thinks he can manage. It
isn't as if the traffic was normal."

Contrary to all expectations, the horse dealer volunteered,
without making a song and dance about it. It seemed to amuse
him, like those members of an audience who go up onto the stage
in response to an appeal by a conjuror.

He took off his jacket, his tie, and his wrist watch, which he
handed over to Julie before making for the engine.

The half-plucked chicken was hanging from a bar in the ceiling. Three of our companions, sweating and out of breath, came
back with some bales of straw.

"Make room, you fellows!"

The young fellow of fifteen, for his part, had brought an alu-
minum saucepan and a frying pan from the abandoned farm.

Were others doing the same in my house?

I can remember some amusing exchanges which made us laugh
in spite of ourselves.

"Let's hope he doesn't run the train down the embankment."

"What do you think the rails are for, you idiot?"

"Trains can run off the rails, even in peacetime, can't they? So
which of us two is the idiot?"

A group of people went on fussing around the engine for some
time, and it came as a surprise to hear it whistle in the end like an
ordinary train. We moved off slowly, almost at a walking pace,
without any jolting, before gradually picking up speed.

Ten minutes later we passed a road which crossed the line and
which was crowded with carts and cattle, with cars here and
there trying to get through. Two or three peasants waved to us,

more solemn and serious than we were, and it seemed to me that they looked at us enviously.

Later on, we saw a road which ran parallel with the line for some time, with army trucks driving in both directions and spluttering motorcycles weaving in and out.

I imagine, although I didn't make sure afterwards, that it was the road from Aumagne to Rethel. In any case, we were getting near to Rethel, judging by the increasing number of signals and houses, the sort of houses you find around towns.

"Do you come from Belgium?"

I couldn't think of anything else to say to Anna, who was sitting beside me on the trunk.

"From Namur. They suddenly decided, in the middle of the night, to set us free. We'd have had to wait until the morning to get our things, because nobody had the key to the place where they're locked up. I preferred to run to the station and jump on the first train."

I didn't bat an eyelid. Perhaps, in spite of myself, I looked surprised, since she added:

"I was in the women's prison."

I didn't ask what for. It struck me almost as natural. In any case, it was no more extraordinary than for me to be there in a cattle car and my wife and daughter on another train, or to have the driver killed on the footplate and, somewhere else, an old man wounded by a bottle which a machine-gun bullet had shattered in his hand. Everything was natural now.

"Are you from Fumay?"

"Yes."

"That was your daughter, was it?"

"Yes. My wife is seven and a half months pregnant."

"You'll find her at Rethel."

"Perhaps."

The others, who had been in the army and were more practical than I was, spread the straw on the floor in readiness for the coming night. It formed a sort of huge communal bed. Some were already lying down on it. The card players kept passing around a bottle of brandy which never left their corner.

We drew into Rethel and there, all of a sudden, for the first time, we became aware that we weren't ordinary people like the rest, but refugees. I say we, although none of my companions confided in me. All the same I think that in that short space of time we had come to react more or less in the same way.

It was the same sort of weariness, for instance, which could be seen on every face, a weariness very different from that which you feel after a sleepless night or a night's work.

Perhaps we hadn't quite reached a state of indifference, but each of us had given up thinking for himself.

Thinking about what, anyway? We knew absolutely nothing. What was happening was beyond us and it was no use thinking or arguing.

For heaven knows how many miles, for instance, I puzzled over the question of the stations. The little stations, the stops, as I have already said, were empty, without even a railwayman to rush out with his whistle and his red flag when the train appeared. On the other hand the bigger stations were packed with people, and police cordons had to be established on the platforms.

I finally hit on an explanation which seems to me to be the right one: namely, that the slow trains had been withdrawn.

The same was true of the roads, the empty ones probably having been closed to traffic for military reasons.

Somebody from Fumay, whom I didn't know, told me, that very morning, when I was sitting beside Anna, that there was a plan for the evacuation of the town and that he had seen a poster about it at the town hall.

"Special trains have been arranged to take refugees to reception centers in the country where everything is ready to accommodate them."

That may be true. I didn't see the poster. I rarely set foot in the town hall, and when we got to the station my wife, Sophie, and I jumped on the first train we saw.

What made me think that my neighbor was right was that at Rethel nurses, boy scouts, and a whole reception service were waiting for us. There were some stretchers ready, as if somebody already knew what had happened to us, but I learned a little later that our train wasn't the first to have been machine-gunned on the way.

"And our wives? Our kids?" the man with the pipe started shouting, even before the train had come to a stop.

"Where do you come from?" asked an elderly lady in white, who obviously belonged to the upper class.

"Fumay."

I counted at least four trains in the station. There were crowds of people in the waiting rooms and behind the barriers, for barriers had been put up as for an official procession. The place was swarming with soldiers and officers.

"Where are the wounded?"

"But what about my wife, dammit?"

"She may have been in the train which has been sent to Rheims."

"When?"

The more gently the lady in white spoke to him, the more fierce and aggressive he was—on purpose, for he was beginning to feel that he had certain rights.

"About an hour ago."

"They could have waited for us, couldn't they?"

Tears came into his eyes, for he was worried in spite of everything and perhaps he wanted to feel unhappy. That didn't prevent him, a few moments later, from falling on the sandwiches some girls were passing in big baskets from car to car.

"How many can we take?"

"As many as you like. It's useless hoarding them. You'll find fresh sandwiches at the next station."

We were given bowls of hot coffee. A nurse went by asking: "Nobody sick or wounded?"

Feeding bottles were ready and an ambulance was waiting at the end of the platform. On the next line a train full of Flemings seemed to be on the point of pulling out. They had had their sandwiches and watched us inquisitively as we ate ours.

The Van Straetens are Flemish in origin; they settled at Fumay three generations ago and no longer speak their original language. In the slate-pits, though, they still call my father-in-law the Fleming.

"Take your seats! Watch out for the doors!"

So far they had kept us for hours in stations or sidings. Now they were dealing with us as quickly as possible, as if they were in a hurry to get rid of us.

Because there were too many people on the platform, I couldn't make out the headlines of the newspapers on the bookstall. I only know that there was one in bold lettering with the word "troops."

We were moving and a girl wearing an arm band was running alongside the train to distribute her last bars of chocolate. She threw a handful in our direction. I managed to catch one for Anna.

We were going to find similar reception centers at Rheims and elsewhere. The horse dealer had returned to his place in our car after being allowed to wash in the station lavatories, and he was treated as a hero. I heard Julie call him Jeff. He was holding a bottle of Cointreau which he had bought in the refreshment room along with two oranges whose scent spread throughout the car.

It was between Rethel and Rheims, toward the end of the afternoon, for we were not moving fast, that a countrywoman stood up grumbling:

"I can't help it. I'm not going to make myself ill."

Going over to the open door, she put a cardboard box on the floor, squatted down and relieved herself, still muttering between her teeth.

That too was significant. The conventions were giving way—in any case those which had been in force the day before. Today nobody protested at the sight of the horse dealer dozing with his head on Julie's plump belly.

"You haven't got a cigarette, have you?" Anna asked me.

"I don't smoke."

It had been forbidden in the sanatorium and afterwards I hadn't been tempted to take it up. My neighbor passed her one. I hadn't any matches on me either, and because of the straw it worried me to see her smoke, although other people had been smoking since the previous day. Perhaps it was a sort of jealousy on my part, a feeling of displeasure which I can't explain.

We spent a long time in a suburb of Rheims, looking at the backs of the houses, and in the station we were told that our train would be leaving in half an hour.

There was a rush toward the refreshment room, the lavatories, and the inquiry office, where nobody had heard of women, children, and invalids from a train coming from Fumay.

Trains were going through all the time, troop trains, munition trains, refugee trains, and I still wonder how it was that there weren't more accidents.

"Perhaps your wife has left a message for you?" Anna suggested.

"Where?"

"Why don't you ask those ladies?"

She pointed to the nurses, the young women of the reception service.

"What name did you say?"

The oldest of the women took a note-pad out of her pocket on which I could see names written by different hands, often in a clumsy script.

"Féron? No. Is she a Belgian?"

"She comes from Fumay, and she's traveling with a little girl of four who's holding a doll dressed in blue in her arms."

I was sure that Sophie hadn't let go of her doll.

"She is seven and a half months pregnant," I went on insistently.

"Then go to the sickroom, in case she felt ill."

It was an office which had been converted and which smelled of disinfectant. No. They had treated several pregnant women. One of them had had to be taken straight to the nearest maternity home to have her baby, but she wasn't called Féron and her mother was with her.

"Are you worried?"

"Not really."

I was sure that Jeanne would not leave any message for me. It wasn't in her nature. The idea of bothering one of these distinguished ladies, of writing her name in a notebook, of drawing attention to herself, would never have occurred to her.

"Why do you keep touching your left-hand pocket?"

"Because of my spare pair of glasses. I'm afraid of losing them or breaking them."

We were given some more sandwiches, one orange each, and coffee with as much sugar as we liked. Some people put a few lumps in their pockets.

Noticing a pile of pillows in a corner, I asked if it was possible to hire a couple. The person I asked didn't know, and said that the woman in charge wasn't there, that she wouldn't be back for an hour.

Then, feeling a little awkward, I took two pillows, and when I got back into the car my companions rushed to get the others.

Now that I think of it, I am surprised that during that long day Anna and I should have said scarcely anything to each other. As if by common consent, we stayed together. Even when we separated, at Rheims, to go to the respective lavatories, I found her waiting for me outside the men's.

"I've bought a bar of soap," she announced with childish joy.

She smelled of soap, and her hair, which she had moistened before arranging, was still wet.

I could count the number of times I had taken a train before that journey. The first time, at the age of fourteen, when I had to go to Saint-Gervais, I had been given a card with my name, my destination, and a note saying:

"In case of accident or difficulties, please inform Madame Jacques Delmotte, Fumay, Ardennes."

Four years later, when I returned home, aged eighteen, I no longer needed a note of that sort.

After that I never went anywhere except to Mézières, periodically, to see the specialist and have an X-ray examination.

Madame Delmotte was my benefactress, as people called her, and I had ended up by adopting that word too. I can't remember the circumstances in which she came to take an interest in me. It was soon after the First World War and I was not yet eleven.

She must have heard about my mother's disappearance, my father's behavior, my situation as a virtually abandoned child.

At that time I used to go to the church club, and one Sunday our curate, the Abbé Dubois, told me that a lady had invited me to her house for chocolate the following Thursday.

Like all Fumay, I knew the name of Delmotte, since the family owns the main slate-pits and consequently everybody in the town is more or less dependent on them. Those Delmottes, in my mind, were the employer Delmottes.

Madame Jacques Delmotte, who was then about fifty, was the charity Delmotte.

They were all brothers, sisters, brothers-in-law, or cousins; their fortune had a common origin but they nonetheless formed two distinct clans.

Was Madame Delmotte, as some people claimed, ashamed of her family's hardness? Widowed at an early age, she had made a doctor of her son, and he had been killed at the front.

Since then she had lived with two maidservants in a big stone house where she spent her afternoons on the veranda. From the street you could see her knitting for the old people in the alms-house, in a black dress with a narrow white lace collar. Dainty and pink, she gave off a sugary smell.

It was on the veranda that she gave me chocolate to drink and biscuits to eat while asking me questions about school, my friends, what I wanted to do later on, etc. Making no mention of my mother and father, she asked me if I would like to serve at mass, with the result that I was a choirboy for two years.

She invited me to her house nearly every Thursday and some-times another little boy or girl shared our snack. We were invari-ably given home-made biscuits of two sorts, bright yellow ones with lemon flavoring and brown ones with spices and almonds.

I can still remember the smell of the veranda and the warmth in winter, which wasn't the same as anywhere else and struck me as subtler and more pervasive.

Madame Delmotte came to see me when I had what was diag-nosed at first as dry pleurisy, and it was she, in her car driven by Désiré, who took me to see a specialist at Mézières.

Three weeks later, thanks to her, I was admitted to a sanato-rium where I wouldn't have obtained a bed without her interven-tion.

It was she too who, when I got married, gave us the silver bowl which stands on the kitchen sideboard. It would look better in a dining room, but we haven't got one.

I think that Madame Delmotte, indirectly, played an important part in my life and, more directly, in my departure from Fumay.

As for her, she had no need to leave, for, having become an old lady, she was already in her flat at Nice, as she was every year at the same season.

Why did I begin thinking about her? For I did think about her, sitting in my cattle car, where it was dark again, feeling Anna's shoulder against mine and wondering whether I dared to take her hand.

Madame Delmotte had made a choirboy of me and Anna had just left prison. I wasn't interested in finding out why she had been sent to prison and for how long.

I suddenly remembered that she had no luggage, no handbag, that when the gates had been opened the authorities hadn't been able to give back their things to the prisoners. So in all probability she hadn't any money on her. And yet, a little earlier, she had told me that she had just bought a bar of soap.

Jeff and Julie, lying side by side, were kissing each other full on the lips and I could make out the scent of their saliva.

"Don't you feel sleepy?"

"What about you?"

"Perhaps we could lie down?"

"Perhaps."

Both of us were forced to bump against our neighbors, and I would have sworn that there were legs and feet all over the place.

"Are you all right?"

"Yes."

"You aren't cold?"

"No."

Behind me, the man I had taken for a horse dealer hoisted himself imperceptibly onto his neighbor, who, as she spread her legs, brushed against my back. We were so close to one another and my senses were so alert that I knew the exact moment of penetration.

Anna too, I would swear to that. Her face touched my cheek, her hair, her parted lips, but she didn't kiss me and I didn't try to kiss her.

Others besides ourselves were still awake and must have known. The movement of the train was shaking us all; after a while the noise of the wheels on the rails became a sort of music.

I am possibly going to express myself crudely, out of clumsiness, precisely because I have always been a prudish man, even in my thoughts.

I wasn't discontented with my way of life. I had chosen it. I had patiently realized an ideal which, until the previous day—I repeat this in all sincerity—had satisfied me completely.

Now I was there, in the dark, with the song of the train, red and green lights passing by, telegraph wires, other bodies stretched out in the straw, and close beside me, within reach of my hand, what the Abbé Dubois called the carnal act was taking place.

Against my own body, a woman's body pressed itself, tense, vibrant, and a hand moved to pull up the black dress, to push the panties down to the feet which kicked them off with an odd jerking movement.

We still hadn't kissed each other. It was Anna who drew me toward her, on top of her, both of us as silent as snakes.

Julie's breathing grew quicker and louder just as Anna was helping me to enter her, and I suddenly found myself there.

I didn't cry out. But I came close to doing so. I came close to talking incoherently, saying thank you, telling of my happiness, or else complaining, for that happiness hurt me. Hurt me with the attempt to reach the unattainable.

I should have liked to express all at once my affection for this woman whom I hadn't known the day before, but who was a human being, who in my eyes was becoming *the* human being.

I bruised her unconsciously, my hands trying to grasp the whole of her.

"Anna . . ."

"Hush!"

"I love you."

"Hush!"

For the first time in my life I had said "I love you" like that, from the depths of my heart. Perhaps it wasn't she that I loved, but life? I don't know how to put it: I was inside her life, and I should have liked to stay there for hours, never to think of anything else, to become like a plant in the sun.

Our lips met, each mouth as moist as the other. I didn't think of asking her, as I used to during my experiences as a young man:

"Can I?"

I could, seeing that she wasn't worried, seeing that she didn't push me away but on the contrary held me inside her.

Finally our lips parted at the same time as our arms and legs relaxed.

"Don't move," she whispered.

And, with both of us invisible to each other, she stroked my forehead gently, following the lines of my face with her hand, like a sculptor.

Still in a whisper, she asked me:

"Did you enjoy that?"

Hadn't I been right in thinking that I had an appointment with Fate?

As usual, I woke up at dawn, about half past five in the morning. Several of my companions, mostly peasants, were already sitting, wide awake, on the floor of the car. So as not to wake the others, they just said good morning to me with their eyes.

Although one of the sliding doors had been shut for the night, you could feel the biting cold which always precedes sunrise, and, afraid that Anna might catch cold, I spread my jacket over her shoulders and her chest.

So far I hadn't really looked at her. I took advantage of her being asleep to examine her solemnly, somewhat disturbed by what I saw. I was rather inexperienced. Until then I had scarcely seen anybody except my wife and daughter, and I knew how both of them looked in the early morning.

When she wasn't pregnant and oppressed by the weight of her body, Jeanne seemed younger at dawn than she did during the day. With her features erased as it were, she took on the pouting expression of a little girl, roughly the same as Sophie, innocent and satisfied.

Anna was younger than my wife, I put her down as twenty-two, twenty-three at the most, but her face was that of someone much older, as I noticed that morning. I also realized, looking at her more closely, that she was a foreigner.

Not only because she came from another country, I didn't know which, but because she had a different life, different thoughts, different feelings from the people at Fumay and all the others I knew.

Instead of letting herself go, to get rid of her weariness, she had curled up, on the defensive, with a crease in the middle of her forehead, and now and then the corners of her mouth twitched as if she had felt a pain or experienced a disagreeable mental picture.

Her flesh didn't look like Jeanne's flesh either. It was firmer, more solid, with muscles capable of suddenly becoming taut, like those of a cat.

I didn't know where we were. There were poplars lining meadows and cornfields which were still green. Billboards kept slipping by as usual, and once we passed close to an almost deserted road where there was nothing to remind us of the war.

I had some water in my bottles, a towel, a shaving brush, and everything I needed in my suitcase; I took the opportunity to have a shave, for I had been ashamed, ever since the day before, of the reddish hairs, a quarter of an inch long, which covered my cheeks and my chin.

When I finished, Anna was looking at me, motionless, and I didn't know how long she had been awake.

She must have taken the opportunity, as I had a little earlier, to look at me inquisitively. I smiled at her while I was wiping my face and she returned my smile, in what struck me as an embarrassed way, or as if her thoughts were somewhere else.

I could still see the crease in her forehead. Propping herself up on her elbow, she found my jacket covering her.

"Why did you do that?"

If she hadn't spoken first, I wouldn't have known whether to use the *tu* or the *vous* form of address. Thanks to her, everything became easy.

"Before sunrise it was rather chilly."

She didn't react like Jeanne either. Jeanne would have been profuse in her thanks, would have felt obliged to protest, to show that she was touched.

Anna simply asked me:

"Did you get any sleep?"

"Yes."

She spoke in a low voice, on account of the people who were still asleep, but didn't think it necessary, as I had done, to give a friendly glance to those of our companions who were already awake and who were looking at us.

I wonder whether it wasn't that which, the day before, as soon as she had slipped into our car, had struck me about her. She didn't live with other people. She didn't mix. She remained alone among others.

It may seem ridiculous to say that, after what had happened the previous evening. All the same, I know what I mean. She had followed me along the track when I hadn't called her. I had given her an empty bottle, without asking her for anything in exchange. I hadn't spoken to her. I hadn't asked her any questions.

She had accepted a place on my trunk without feeling the need to say thank you, just as with the jacket now. And, when our bodies had drawn together, she had bared her belly and guided my movements.

"You aren't thirsty?"

There was some water left in the second bottle, and I gave her some in a camping cup which my wife had put in the suitcase.

"What time is it?"

"Ten past six."

"Where are we?"

"I don't know."

She ran her fingers through her hair, still looking at me thoughtfully.

"You're a cool one," she finally concluded, talking to herself.

"You always stay cool. Life doesn't frighten you. You haven't any problems, have you?"

"Can't you shut up, the two of you?" grumbled fat Julie.

We smiled and sat down on the trunk to watch the countryside go by. I took her hand. She let me, a little surprised I think, especially when I raised it to my lips to kiss her fingertips.

A long time afterwards, the sight of the congregation coming out of a village church reminded me that it was Sunday, and I was amazed at the thought that, two days before at the same time, I had been at home, wondering whether we ought to leave.

I saw myself again throwing corn to the hens while the water was boiling for my coffee; then I recalled Monsieur Matray's head appearing over the wall, my wife at the window, her face at once drawn and puffy, and later my daughter's anxious voice.

It was as if I could still hear the comical dialogue, on the radio, about the colonel who couldn't be found, and I understood it better now that I was plunged in the muddle myself.

We were moving slowly again. A bend in the line took us nearly all the way around the village, which was perched on a hillock.

The church and the houses weren't the same shape or the same color as in our part of the world, but the congregation outside the church was behaving in accordance with an identical ritual.

The men in their black clothes, all old because the others were at the front, were standing about in groups, and you could tell that it wouldn't be long before they went into the inn.

The old women were going off one by one, hurrying along and keeping close to the walls, while the girls in bright dresses and the youths stood waiting for one another, holding their missals in their hands, and the children started running immediately.

Anna was still looking at me, and I wondered if she knew what mass on Sunday was like. Before Sophie was born, Jeanne and I used to go to high mass at ten o'clock. Afterwards we went for a stroll around the town, greeting our acquaintances, before stopping at her sister's to collect our cake.

I paid for it. I had insisted on paying for it, accepting nothing but a discount of twenty per cent. Often the cake was still warm, and on the way home I could smell the sugar on it.

After Sophie, Jeanne got into the habit of going to the seven-o'clock mass while I looked after the child, and later, when the little girl could walk, I took her with me to the ten-o'clock mass while my wife cooked lunch.

Was there a high mass that morning at Fumay? Were there still enough members of the congregation? Had the Germans bombed or invaded the town?

"What are you thinking about? Your wife?"

"No."

That was true. Jeanne figured only incidentally in these thoughts. I was thinking just as much about old Monsieur Matray and the schoolmaster's curly-haired little girl. Had their car managed to make its way through the chaos on the roads? Had Monsieur Reversé been to get our hens and our poor Nestor?

I wasn't upset. I asked myself these questions objectively, almost playfully, because everything had become possible, even, for example, the razing of Fumay to the ground and the shooting of its population.

That was just as plausible as our driver's death in the cab of his engine, or, in my case, making love in the middle of forty people with a young woman whom I hadn't known two days before and who had just come out of prison.

More and more of the others had sat down like us, looking around with vacant eyes, and a few were taking food out of their luggage. We were getting near a town. On the billboards I had read some names which were familiar to me, and when I saw that we were at Auxerre I had to make an effort to remember the map of France.

I don't know why I had got it into my head that we were going to go through Paris. We had avoided the capital, probably going by way of Troyes during the night.

Now we found ourselves under the big glass roof of a station whose atmosphere was different from the one where we had stopped before.

Here it was a real Sunday morning, a prewar Sunday, with no reception service, no nurses, no girls wearing arm bands.

A score of people in all were waiting on the green benches on the platforms, and the sunshine, filtering through the dirty panes and reduced to light-dust, gave an unreal quality to the silence and solitude.

"Hey there, guard, are we going to stay here long?"

The guard looked at the front of the train, then at the clock. I don't know why, for he replied:

"I haven't the faintest idea."

"Have we got time to go to the refreshment room?"

"You've got an hour at least, I should say."

"Where are they taking us?"

He went off shrugging his shoulders, indicating that this question didn't come within his province.

I wonder whether we weren't rather annoyed—I say we on purpose—at not being welcomed, at finding ourselves suddenly left to our own resources. Expressing in his fashion the general feeling, somebody called out:

"So nobody's feeding us any more?"

As if it had become a right.

Right away, seeing that we were now in a civilized part of the world, I said to Anna:

"Are you coming?"

"Where?"

"To have something to eat."

Our first instinctive action, for all of us, once we were on the platform, where we suddenly had too much room, was to look at our train from one end to the other, and it was a disappointment to find that it was no longer the same train.

Not only had the engine been changed, but, behind the tender, I counted fourteen Belgian carriages, as clean-looking as on ordinary trains.

As for our cattle cars and freight cars, there were only three of them left.

"The swine have cut us in two again!"

The doors opened in front, and the first person to get out was a huge, athletic priest, who went over to the stationmaster with an air of authority about him.

They talked together. The stationmaster seemed to be agreeing to something, and afterwards the priest spoke to the people who had stayed in the carriage, and helped a nun in a white coif to get down onto the platform.

There were four nuns in all, two of them very young, with baby faces, to help out and line up like schoolchildren about forty old men dressed in identical gray woolen suits.

It was an old people's home which had been evacuated, and we learned later that the train to which we had been joined while we were asleep came from Louvain.

The men were all very old, and more or less infirm. Beards had grown, thick and white, on faces as clear-cut as in old pictures.

The extraordinary thing was their meekness, the indifference which you could read in their eyes. They allowed themselves to be taken to the second-class refreshment room, where they were installed as in a refectory while the priest spoke to the manager.

Once again Anna looked at me. Was it because of the priest and the nuns, because she thought that I was familiar with that world? Or was it because the old men in a line reminded her of prison and a discipline which I didn't know but of which she had experience?

I don't know. We kept darting these brief, probing glances at each other like this, only to resume an impassive expression immediately afterwards.

THE LIÈGE FORTS IN GERMAN HANDS.

I read this headline on a newspaper on the stall, and, in smaller letters:

PARACHUTISTS ATTACK ALBERT CANAL.

"What do you want to eat? Do you like croissants?"

She nodded.

"Light coffee?'

"Black. If we've got time, I'd like to tidy up first. Would you mind lending me your comb?"

As we had sat down at a table and all the others had been taken, I didn't dare to get up to follow her. Just as she was going through the glass door, I felt my heart sink, for the idea occurred to me that I might never see her again.

Through the window I could see a quiet square, some taxis on a rank, a hotel, and a little blue-painted bar where the waiter was wiping the tables on the terrace.

There was nothing to stop Anna from going.

"Had any news of your wife and daughter?"

Fernand Leroy was standing in front of me, a bottle of beer in his hand, an ironical look in his eye. I said no, trying not to blush, for I realized that he knew what had happened between Anna and myself.

I have never liked Leroy. The son of a sergeant-major in the cavalry, he used to explain to us at school:

"In the cavalry, a sergeant-major is much more important than a lieutenant or even a captain in any other branch of the army."

He always managed to get other boys punished instead of him and the masters were taken in by his innocent expression, something which didn't prevent him from making faces behind their backs.

I learned, later on, that he had failed his *baccalauréat* twice. His father was dead. His mother worked as a cashier in a movie house. He got a job at Hachette's bookshop and, two or three years later, married the daughter of a rich contractor.

Did he marry her for her money? That's none of my business. It was without any malicious intent that I in turn asked:

"Isn't your wife with you?"

"I thought you knew. We're getting a divorce."

If it hadn't been for him, I should have gone to look for Anna. Time seemed to drag. My hands were getting moist. I was filled with an impatience I had never known before, which, though much stronger, was comparable only to the feeling which had gripped me the previous Friday, in the station at Fumay, when I was wondering whether we would manage to get away.

A waitress came over and I ordered coffee and croissants for two while Leroy put on his horrible smile again. People like him, I thought to myself, are capable of dirtying everything with a glance, and all the time I was waiting I really hated him.

It was only when he saw Anna pushing open the door that he moved away in the direction of the bar, saying:

"I'll leave the two of you."

Yes, the two of us. We were the two of us again. My face must have shown the joy I felt, for Anna had scarcely sat down opposite me before she murmured:

"Were you afraid I wouldn't come back?"

"Yes."

"Why?"

"I don't know. I suddenly felt lost and I nearly ran after you on the platform."

"I haven't any money."

"And if you'd had some?"

"I wouldn't have gone even then."

She didn't say whether this was because of me, but just asked me for some small change which she took to the woman in charge of the ladies' washrooms.

The old men were eating in silence, as they must have done in the institution. The tables had been put together. The priest was at one end, the oldest of the nuns at the other. It was half past ten in the morning. Presumably to provide two meals in one, or because nobody knew what lay ahead of us, each of them had been given some cheese and a hard-boiled egg.

Some of them, who had no teeth left, were munching with their gums. One of them was dribbling so badly that a nun had tied a paper napkin around his neck and was keeping a close watch on his movements. A good many were red-eyed and had thick blue veins standing out on their hands.

"Don't you want to go and wash up too?"

I not only went to have a wash, but I took a clean shirt out of my suitcase in order to change. My traveling companions were in the washrooms, stripped to the waist, washing, shaving, and combing their wet hair. The roller towel was black and had a doggy smell.

"You know how many fellows had her last night?"

I caught my breath and felt a bar across my chest, something which taught me that I was jealous.

"Three, as well as the fat fellow! I counted them, seeing that I hardly slept a wink because of them. But they had to cough up their twenty francs, just like they did in her pub. Have you ever been in her pub?"

"Once, with my brother-in-law."

"Who's your brother-in-law?"

"You saw him when you got married and when you registered your kids. He's the clerk in the register office."

"Is he here?"

"They aren't allowed to leave. That's what they say, anyway. All the same, I saw with my own eyes a police officer scramming on his motor-bike with his wife up behind him."

Why had I felt frightened? It was all the more ridiculous in that I am a light sleeper and Anna had so to speak slept in my arms.

I also discovered, there in the washrooms, that there had been other couplings during the night, in the corner opposite ours, including some with a huge countrywoman who was over fifty. They even said that old Jules, after a few others had had her, had tried his luck and that she had been hard put to it to push him away.

Wasn't it odd that nobody had made the slightest approach to Anna? They had seen her get on the train by herself, so they knew that she wasn't with me, that we had met by chance. There was no reason, in the minds of those men, why I should enjoy an exclusive privilege.

Yet they just looked at her from a distance. It was true—and that struck me now—that nobody had spoken to her. Had they recognized that she belonged to another race? Did they distrust her?

I rejoined her. The stationmaster came along twice to have a chat with the priest. In that way, as long as the old men stayed at table, we were in no danger of seeing the train leave without us.

"Do you know where we're going?"

It was the man with the pipe who had suddenly reappeared, clean-shaven, his pockets stuffed with packets of tobacco, of which he had bought a whole stock.

"For the moment my instructions are to send you on to Bourges, via Clamecy, but all that may change from one minute to the next."

"And after that?'

"They'll decide at Bourges."

"Are we allowed to get off when we like?"

"You want to leave the train?"

"I don't. But there are some people who might like the idea."

"I don't see how they could be prevented, nor why anybody should prevent them."

"Back there they stopped us from leaving the train."

The stationmaster scratched his head and gave serious thought to the question.

"It depends whether you're regarded as evacuees or refugees."

"What's the difference?"

"Were you forced to leave, in a group?"

"No."

"In that case, you're refugees. Did you pay for your ticket?"

"There was nobody in the ticket office."

"Theoretically . . ."

It was getting too complicated for him, and with an evasive gesture he rushed off in the direction of Platform 3, where a train was due, a real train, with ordinary passengers who knew where they were going and had paid for their tickets.

"You heard what he said?"

I nodded.

"If only I knew where I could find my wife and kids! Back there, they treat you like soldiers or prisoners of war: do this, do that, don't get out on the platform. They give you an orange juice and sandwiches, the women up in front, the men at the back, shoved together like cattle. They cut the train in two without telling you, they machine-gun you, they separate you—in fact, you aren't human beings any more.

"And then here, all of a sudden, you've got complete freedom. Do what you like! Go and jump in the river if you feel like it. . . ."

Perhaps the next day, or that evening, the station at Auxerre would be different. My favorite memory, seeing that we had enough time, is of walking about outside with Anna. It seemed so wonderful to be in a real square, walking on real pavingstones, among people who weren't worried yet about planes.

We saw groups of people slowly making their way home from

church, and we went into the little blue-painted bar where I drank a lemonade while Anna, after a furtive glance, ordered an Italian apéritif.

It was the first station since we had left which we had seen from the outside, with its big clock and its frosted-glass porch, the shadowy entrance hall contrasting with the sunny square and the multicolored magazines all around the kiosk.

"Where do you come from, you two?"

"Fumay."

"I thought that was a Belgian train."

"There are Belgian carriages and French carriages."

"Last night we had some Dutch people. It seems they're being taken to Toulouse. What about you?"

"We don't know."

The waiter raised his head and looked at me incredulously. It was only later that I understood his reaction.

"What, you don't know? You mean you just let them trundle you around wherever they like?"

Some towns had entered the war, while others hadn't as yet. Because that was so, we had seen from the train quiet villages where everyone was going about his business and little towns invaded by convoys.

It didn't depend entirely on how close the front was. Indeed, was there such a thing as a front?

At Bourges, for instance, in the middle of the afternoon, we found a reception service as in the north, a platform swarming with families waiting among suitcases and bundles.

They were Belgians again. I wondered how they could have arrived before us. They must have traveled along another line, not as busy as ours, but they had had a similar experience, only more serious, near the frontier.

Several planes had machine-gunned them. Everybody had got out—men, women, and children—to lie down in the ditch. The Germans had returned to the attack twice, putting the engine out of action and killing or wounding a dozen people.

We were forbidden to leave the train so that we shouldn't get mixed up, but conversations started with the people on the platform while we were being given something to eat and drink.

At Auxerre I had bought a couple of packed meals. We took the sandwiches all the same and put them aside, for we were becoming cautious.

The Belgians on the platform were dazed and gloomy. They had walked for two hours on the pebbles and sleepers along the track before reaching a station, carrying what they could, but leaving most of their things behind.

As usual, the man with the pipe was the best-informed of us all, first because of his strategic position near the door, and then because he was not afraid of asking questions.

"You see that blonde over there in a dress with blue dots? She carried her dead child all the way to the station. It seems it was a very small place. Everybody came to see them and she gave the baby to the mayor, who's a farmer by trade, to be buried."

She was eating absent-mindedly, with a vacant look in her eyes, sitting on a brown suitcase tied up with ropes.

"A train went to pick them up and left the dead and wounded at a bigger station, they don't know which. Here, they made them get off their train because they needed the carriages, and they've been waiting since eight o'clock this morning."

They, too, looked at us enviously, without understanding what was happening to them. A pretty, fresh-faced nurse, without a single mark on her starched uniform, was feeding a baby from a bottle while the mother was hunting through her luggage for some clean diapers.

We didn't see their train come in, so I don't know when they managed to leave, or where they were taken in the end. It's true that I didn't know where my wife and daughter were either.

I tried to find out, and asked the woman who seemed to be in charge of the reception service. She answered calmly:

"Don't worry. Everything has been provided for. There will be lists printed."

"Where shall I be able to see these lists?"

"At the reception center you're going to. You're Belgian, aren't you?"

"No. I'm from Fumay."

"Then what are you doing on a Belgian train?"

I heard that question ten, twenty times. People came close to resenting our presence on the train. Our three wretched cars, as the result of heaven knows what mistake, weren't where they ought to have been, and we narrowly missed getting the blame.

"Where are they sending the Belgians?"

"As a general rule, to Gironde and the Charente departments."

"Is this train going there?"

Like the stationmaster at Auxerre, she preferred to answer with a vague gesture.

Contrary to what you might imagine, I thought of Jeanne and my daughter without overmuch anxiety, indeed with a certain serenity.

Once, my heart had missed a beat, when I had heard about the train which had been machine-gunned and the dead child which its mother had been obliged to leave at a little station.

Then I had told myself that that had happened in the north, that Jeanne's train had been ahead of ours and had therefore crossed the danger zone before us.

I loved my wife. She was just as I had wanted her and had brought me exactly what I expected from my partner in life. I had no complaints to make of her. I wasn't looking for any either, and that was why I resented Leroy's ambiguous smile so keenly.

Jeanne had nothing to do with what was happening now, any more than the ten-o'clock mass, for instance, my sister-in-law's confectionery business, or the labeled radios on the shelves in my workshop.

I sometimes say "we" when talking of the people in our train because, on certain points, I know that our reactions were the same. But on this point I speak for myself, although I am convinced that I wasn't the only one in my position.

A break had occurred. That didn't mean that the past had ceased to exist, still less that I repudiated my family and had stopped loving them.

It was just that, for an indeterminate period, I was living on another level, where the values had nothing in common with those of my previous existence.

I might say that I was living on two levels at once, but that for the moment the one which counted was the new one, represented by our car with its smell of the stables, by faces I hadn't known a few days before, by the baskets of sandwiches carried by the young ladies with the arm bands, and by Anna.

I am convinced that she understood me. She no longer tried to cheer me up by telling me, for instance, that my wife and daughter were in no danger and that I would soon find them again.

Something she had said that morning came back to me.

"You're a cool one."

She took me for a strong-minded character, and I suspect that that is why she attached herself to me. At that time I knew nothing of her life, apart from the reference she had made to the Namur prison, and I know little more now. It is obvious that she had no ties, nothing solid to lean on.

But, in fact, wasn't she the stronger of the two of us?

At the Blois station, unless I am mistaken, where another reception service was waiting for us, she was the first to ask:

"There hasn't been a train here from Fumay, has there?"

"Where's Fumay?"

"In the Ardennes, near the Belgian frontier."

"Oh, we've had so many Belgians going through!"

On the roads, too, we could now see Belgian cars following one another bumper to bumper, in two lines, so that jams occurred everywhere. There were also some French cars, but far fewer, mainly from the northern departments.

I didn't know the Loire, which was sparkling in the sunshine, and we caught sight of two or three historic châteaux which were familiar to me from picture postcards.

"Have you been here before?" I asked Anna.

She hesitated before answering "yes" and squeezing the tips of my fingers. Did she guess that she was hurting me a little, that I would have preferred her not to have a past?

It was absurd. But hadn't everything become absurd and wasn't this what I had been looking for?

The horse dealer was asleep. Fat Julie had drunk too much and was holding her bosom in both hands, looking at the door with the expression of somebody who expects to be sick any minute.

There were bottles and scraps of food all over the straw, and the fifteen-year-old boy had found a couple of army blankets somewhere.

Everybody had his special place, his corner which he was sure of finding again after getting down onto the platform when we were allowed to leave the train.

It seemed to me that there were fewer of us than at the beginning of our journey, that four or five people were missing, but, not having counted them, I couldn't be sure, except about the little girl whom the nuns, seeing her with us, had taken off to their carriage as if we were devils.

At Tours, that evening, we were given big bowls of soup, with pieces of boiled beef and some bread. Night was beginning to fall. I was impatient to rediscover our intimacy of the previous night. I must have shown it, for Anna looked at me with a certain tenderness.

The latest news was that we were being taken to Nantes, where our final destination would be decided on.

Wrapping himself up in a blanket, somebody called out:

"Good night, everybody!"

A few cigarettes were still glowing, and I waited, motionless, my eyes fixed on the signals which I kept confusing with the stars.

Jeff was still asleep. All the same there were some furtive movements near Julie until her voice suddenly broke the silence:

"No, boys! Tonight I want a bit of shut-eye. You'd better get that into your heads."

Anna laughed in my ear and we waited another half-hour.

CHAPTER *5*

One of the old men from the infirmary died during the night. I don't know which, for he was taken off at Nantes in the morning, his face covered with a towel. The Belgian consul was waiting on the platform and the priest went into the stationmaster's office with him for the formalities.

The reception service here was bigger than before, not only in the number of ladies with arm bands, but because there seemed to be some people concerned with organizing the movements of refugees.

I hoped that I was at last going to see the sea, for the first time in my life. I gathered that it was a long way off, that we were in an estuary, but I caught sight of some ships' masts and funnels, I heard some hooters, and near to us a whole trainful of bluejackets alighted: they lined up on the platform and marched out of the station.

The weather was as unbelievably glorious as it had been on the previous days, and we were able to wash and have breakfast before leaving.

I had a moment's anxiety when an assistant stationmaster started talking to somebody who looked like an official, pointing to our three shabby cars, as if there were some question of uncoupling them.

It was becoming increasingly obvious that, incorporated in the Belgian train through no fault of ours, we presented a problem, but finally we were allowed to go.

Our biggest surprise was fat Julie. A few moments before the whistle blew, she appeared on the platform, radiant, fresh-complexioned, wearing a floral cotton dress without a single crease in it.

"What do you think Julie's been doing, boys, while you've been wallowing in the straw? She's been and had a bath, a real hot bath, in the hotel opposite. And on top of that she's managed to buy herself a dress on the way!"

We were traveling down toward the Vendée, where, an hour later, I caught a glimpse of the sea in the distance. Deeply stirred, I reached for Anna's hand. I had seen the sea at the movies and in colored photos, but I hadn't imagined that it was so bright or so huge and insubstantial.

The water was the same color as the sky, and, since it was reflecting the light, since the sun was both up above and down below, there was no longer any limit to anything and the word "infinite" sprang to my mind.

Anna understood that it was a new experience for me. She smiled. We were both of us lighthearted. The whole car was gay all day.

We now knew more or less what was waiting for us, for the consul had visited the first carriages to cheer up his fellow countrymen, and the man with the pipe, always on the watch, had brought us the news.

"It seems that the Belgians' destination is La Rochelle. That's their marshaling yard, so to speak. They've set up a sort of camp there with huts, beds, and everything."

"And what about us? Seeing that we aren't Belgians?"

"Oh, we'll manage."

We were moving slowly and I kept reading place names which reminded me of books I had read: Pornic, Saint-Jean-de-Monts, Croix-de-Vie . . .

We caught sight of the Île d'Yeu, which, in the dazzling sunlight, you might have taken for a cloud stretched out on a level with the water.

For hours our train seemed to be taking the longest route, as if we were on an excursion, going off on side tracks to stop in the open country and then coming back again.

We were no longer afraid of getting off and jumping on again, for we knew that the engineer would wait for us.

I realized why we were following such a circuitous route, and also perhaps why we had taken such a long time coming from the Ardennes.

The regular trains, with normal passengers who paid for their tickets, were still running, and on the main lines there was also a continual traffic of troop trains and munition trains which had priority over the rest.

In nearly every station, as well as the ordinary staff, we started seeing an officer giving orders.

As we belonged to none of these categories, we kept being shunted into a siding to make room.

Once I overheard a telephone conversation in a pretty station red with geraniums, where a dog was stretched out across the doorway of the stationmaster's office. The stationmaster, who was feeling hot, had pushed his cap back and was toying with his flag, which was lying on the desk.

"Is that you, Dambois?"

Another stationmaster explained to me that this wasn't an ordinary telephone. If I remember rightly, it is called the block telephone and you can only speak to and hear the nearest station on it. That is how notice of a train's approach is given.

"How are things with you?"

There were some hens behind some chicken wire, just like at home, and a well-kept garden. The stationmaster's wife was doing the rooms upstairs and came to the window now and then to shake her duster.

"I've got the 237 here. . . . I can't keep them much longer, because I'm expecting the 161. . . . Is your siding free? . . . Is Hortense's café open? . . . Tell her she's going to have a crowd of customers. . . . Right! . . . Thanks. . . . I'll send it on to you. . . ."

The result was that we spent three hours in a tiny station next to an inn painted pink. The tables were taken by storm. Everybody drank. Everybody ate. Anna and I stayed outside, under a pine tree, and at times we felt embarrassed at having nothing to say to each other.

If I had to describe the place, I could only talk of the patches of sunshine and shadow, of the pink daylight, of the green vines and currant bushes, of my feeling of torpor and animal well-being, and I wonder whether, that particular day, I didn't get as close as possible to perfect happiness.

Smells existed as they had in my childhood, the quivering of the air, the imperceptible noises of life. I think I have said this before, but as I am not writing all at one go but scribbling a few lines here, a page or two there, in secret, on the sly, I am bound to repeat myself.

When I began my story, I was tempted to start with a foreword, for sentimental rather than practical reasons. You see, at the sanatorium the library consisted mainly of books dating back before 1900, and it was the fashion for authors in the last century to write a foreword, an introduction, or a preface.

The paper in those books, yellow and speckled with brown spots, was thicker and shinier than in present-day books, and they had a pleasant smell which, for me, has clung to the characters in the novels. The black cloth of the bindings was as shiny as the elbows of an old jacket, and I found the same cloth again in the public library at Fumay.

I dropped the idea of a foreword for fear of seeming conceited. It is true that I may repeat myself, get mixed up, even contradict myself, for I am writing this mainly in the hope of discovering a certain truth.

As for the events which don't concern me personally, I record them, when I witnessed them, to the best of my recollection. To find certain dates I would have had to look up the back numbers of the newspapers, and I don't know where to find them.

I am sure about the date of Friday the 10th, which must be in the history books now. I am sure too, more or less, about the itinerary we followed, although, even on the train, some of my companions started mentioning names of stations which we hadn't seen.

A road which was deserted in the morning, in those days, could be swarming with life an hour later. Everything went terribly fast and terribly slowly. People were still talking about fighting in Holland when the Panzers had already reached Sedan.

Again, my memory may occasionally play tricks on me. As I said about the last morning at Fumay, I could reconstruct certain hours minute by minute, whereas with others I can only remember the general atmosphere.

It was like that on the train, especially with the fatigue, the dull, dazed feeling which resulted from our way of life.

We no longer had any responsibilities, any decisions to make. Nothing depended on us, not even our own fate.

One detail, for instance, has worried me a lot, because I am rather pernickety and tend to think over an idea for hours until I have got it right. When I wrote about the plane machine-gunning our train, about the fireman gesticulating beside his engine, and about the dead driver, I didn't mention the guard. Yet there ought to have been a guard, whose job it was to make the necessary decisions.

I didn't see him. Did he exist or didn't he? Once again, things didn't necessarily happen in a logical way.

As for the Vendée, I know that my skin, my eyes, the whole of my body have never drunk in the sunshine as greedily as they did that day, and I can say for sure that I appreciated every nuance of the light, every shade of green of the meadows, the fields, and the trees.

A cow, stretched out in the shade of an oak, all white and brown, its wet muzzle twitching endlessly, ceased to be a familiar animal, a commonplace sight, to become . . .

To become what? I can't find the words I want. I am no good

at expressing myself. The fact remains that tears came into my eyes looking at a cow. And, that day on the terrace of a pink-painted inn, my eyes remained for a long time fixed in wonderment on a fly circling around a drop of lemonade.

Anna noticed. I became aware that she was smiling. I asked her why.

"I've just seen you as you must have been when you were five."

Even the smells of the human body, particularly that of sweat, were pleasant to rediscover. Finally, I had found a part of the world where the land was on a level with the sea and where you could see as many as five church steeples at once.

The country people went about their work as usual, and when our train stopped they just looked at it from a distance, without feeling the need to come and inspect us or ask us questions.

I noticed that there were far more geese and ducks than there were at home, and that the houses were so low that you could touch the roofs, as if the inhabitants were afraid of the wind carrying them away.

I saw Luçon, which made me think of Cardinal Richelieu, then Fontenay-le-Comte. We could have arrived at La Rochelle in the evening, but the stationmaster at Fontenay came and explained to us that it would be difficult to disembark us in the dark and install us in the reception center.

You have to remember that, on account of the air raids, the gas lamps and all the other street lights were painted blue and people had to hang black curtains in their windows, so that at night, in the towns, the passers-by carried flashlights and the cars drove at a walking pace, with just their side lights on.

"They're going to find you a quiet spot to spend the night in. And somebody'll bring you food and drink."

It was true. We approached the sea only to leave it behind again, and our train, which had no timetable to observe and seemed to be looking for a resting place, ended up by stopping in a meadow, near to a way station.

It was six o'clock in the evening. You couldn't feel the chill of twilight yet. Nearly everybody got out to stretch their legs, except for the old men in the care of the priest and the nuns, and I saw middle-aged women with grim faces bending down to pick daisies and buttercups.

Somebody said the old men in the coarse gray uniforms were mental patients. That may have been the case. At La Rochelle they were met by nurses and more nuns who piled them into a couple of coaches.

I had already had an idea, and I went over to Dédé, the fifteen-year-old boy, to buy one of his blankets from him. It was more difficult than I had expected. He haggled more stubbornly than a peasant at a fair, but I got my way in the end.

Anna watched us with a smile, unable, I imagine, to guess the object of our bargaining.

I was enjoying myself. I felt young. Or rather I didn't feel any age in particular.

"What were you talking about so earnestly?"

"An idea of mine."

"I know what it is."

"I doubt it."

"Bet you I do."

As if I were a boy and she were a little girl.

"Tell me what you're thinking, to see if you've guessed."

"You don't want to sleep on the train."

It was true, and I was surprised that she had thought of it. To my mind, it was a rather crazy idea, which couldn't occur to anybody but myself. I had never had an opportunity to sleep in the open air, as a child because my mother wouldn't have allowed it and besides it would have been difficult in a town, and later on account of my illness.

As soon as the stationmaster had spoken of finding us a quiet spot in the country, the idea had occurred to me, and now I had got hold of a blanket which would protect us from the dew and safeguard our intimacy.

A yellow car arrived with a jovial nurse and four boy scouts of sixteen or seventeen. They brought us sandwiches, bars of chocolate, and a couple of cans of hot coffee. They also had some blankets, which were reserved for the children and the old men.

The doors banged. For a good hour, in the slowly fading light, there was a confused hubbub in which cries in Flemish could be heard the loudest.

If it hadn't been for that night's halt, I would never have known that there were some babies in the Belgian carriages. But the nurse knew, thanks to the block telephone, and she had brought along some feeding bottles and a big bundle of diapers.

That was of no interest to our car. Not because they were Belgians but because the children didn't belong to our group. Besides, the French people in the other two freight cars, although they had got on the train at the same time as us at Fumay, were just as foreign to us.

Cells had been formed, airtight, self-contained. And in each cell smaller cells could be observed, such as the card players or the couple consisting of Anna and myself.

Frogs started croaking, and new sounds could be heard in the meadows and the trees.

We went for a stroll without holding hands, without touching each other, and Anna smoked one of the cigarettes I had bought her at Nantes.

The idea of talking about love never occurred to us, and I wonder today if it was really love that we felt for each other. I mean love in the sense which is usually given to the word, for to my mind it was much more.

She didn't know what I did for a living and showed no desire to find out. She knew that I had had tuberculosis, for I had happened to remark, on the subject of sleep:

"At the sanatorium they used to turn the lights out at eight o'clock."

She looked at me immediately and that movement was characteristic of her, as was her glance which I would find difficult to describe. It was as if an idea had struck her all of a sudden, not an idea born of reflection, but something palpable if fleeting which she had caught instinctively in flight.

"Now I understand," she murmured.

"You understand what?"

"You."

"What have you found out?"

"That you've spent several years shut up."

I didn't press the point but I think that I understood in my turn. She had been shut up, too. The name of the place where you are condemned to live between four walls is of small importance.

Didn't she mean that it leaves a mark, and that she had recognized that mark in me without knowing how to explain it?

We walked slowly back to the darkened train where nothing could be seen but the firefly glimmer of cigarettes and we could hear a few voices whispering.

I collected the blanket. We looked for a place, our place, some soft earth, some tall grass, a gentle slope.

A clump of three trees hid us from sight and there was also a big, smelly patch of cow dung in which somebody had walked. The moon wouldn't rise before three o'clock in the morning.

We stood for a while rather awkwardly facing one another, and to keep my composure I started arranging the blanket.

I remember Anna throwing away her cigarette, which went on glowing in the grass, taking off her dress with a movement I hadn't seen before, and then removing her underclothes.

She came up to me then, naked, surprised by the cold which made her shiver once or twice, and gently pulled me down on the ground.

I realized right away that she wanted it to be my night. She had guessed that I was looking forward to it, just as she had guessed so many of my thoughts.

It was she who took the initiative all the time; she too who pushed away the blanket so that our bodies should be in contact with the ground, with the smell of the earth and the grass.

When the moon rose, I was still awake. Anna had put her dress on again and we were rolled up in the blanket, pressed against each other, on account of the cool of the night.

I could see her dark hair with its glints of red, her exotic profile, and her pale skin whose texture was unlike anything I had ever known before.

We had blended so closely into each other that we had only a single smell.

I don't know what I thought about while I was looking at her.

I was in a serious mood, neither gay nor sad. The future didn't worry me. I refused to let it intervene in the present.

I suddenly noticed that, for the past twenty-four hours, I hadn't worried once about my spare pair of glasses, which were probably lying somewhere in the meadow or in the straw in our car.

Every now and then her body was shaken by a shudder and the crease in her forehead deepened, as if at a bad dream or in a spasm of pain.

I finally dropped off to sleep. Instead of waking up of my own accord, as I usually did, I was roused from sleep by the sound of footsteps. Somebody was walking close to us, the man with the pipe, whom I called the concierge. A whiff of his tobacco, unexpected in that country dawn, came to my nostrils.

He was an early riser like me, and doubtless something of a hermit, in spite of his wife and children for whom he kept clamoring with exaggerated ill-humor. He was walking with the same steps that I used to walk with in my garden in the morning, and our eyes met.

I thought he had a kindly look about him. With his sloping shoulders and his lopsided nose, he looked like a friendly gnome in a picture book.

Anna woke up with a start.

"Is it time to go?"

"I don't think so. The sun hasn't risen yet."

A slight mist was rising from the ground and some cows were lowing in a distant barn from which a gleam of light was filtering. Somebody was presumably milking them.

The day before, we had noticed a tap behind the brick shelter at the way station. We went there to clean ourselves up. There was nobody around.

"Hold the blanket."

Anna undressed in a flash and dashed some icy water over her body.

"Go and get my soap, will you? It's in the straw, behind your trunk."

Once she had dried herself and got dressed again, she said:

"Your turn!"

I hesitated.

"They're beginning to get up," I objected.

"What about it? Even if they see you stark naked?"

I followed her example, my lips blue with cold, and she rubbed my back and chest with the towel.

The yellow car returned, bringing back the same nurse and the same scouts, who looked like overgrown children or unfinished men.

They brought us more coffee, some bread and butter, and feeding bottles for the babies.

I know nothing of what happened on the train that night, nor whether it is true, as rumor had it, that a woman gave birth to a child. I find that hard to believe, for I didn't hear anything.

They treated us like schoolchildren on holiday, and the nurse, although she was under forty, ordered us about like an infants' class.

"Heavens above, what a smell of dirty feet! When you get to the camp, you'll have to have a good wash, all of you. And you, Grandpa, did you empty all those bottles by yourself?"

She spotted Julie.

"Hey, Fatty, what are you waiting for? Are you having a lie-in this morning? Get a move on! An hour from now, you'll be at La Rochelle."

There, at last, the sea was close to us, the port adjoining the station, with steamers on one side, and on the other side fishing boats whose sails and nets were drying in the sun.

I took possession of the scene immediately and let it get right under my skin. If there were several trains on the tracks I didn't pay any attention to them, and I didn't see anything at all. I didn't pay any attention either to the more or less important individuals who came and went, giving orders, girls in white, soldiers, boy scouts.

The old men were helped out of the train and the priest counted them as if he were afraid of losing or forgetting some.

"Everybody over to the reception center, opposite the station."

I picked up my trunk and the suitcase which Anna had tried to take out of my hands, leaving her nothing to carry but the blanket and our empty bottles, which might come in useful again.

Some armed soldiers watched us pass and turned around to look at Anna, who was following close behind me, as if she suddenly felt lost and frightened.

I didn't understand why until a little later. Outside, the scouts pointed to the deal huts which had been put up in a public park, only a few feet from the dock. There was a smaller hut, hardly any bigger than a newspaper kiosk, which was being used as an office, and we found ourselves queuing with the others outside the open door.

Our group had broken up. We were mixed up with the Belgians, who were the bigger party, and we had no idea what was going to happen to us.

From a distance we witnessed the loading of the old men into the coaches. A couple of ambulances drove away too. The towers of the town could be seen some way off, and some refugees who were already installed in the camp came and looked at us inquisitively. A lot of them were Flemings and were delighted to find some fellow countrymen.

One of them, who spoke French, asked me with a pronounced accent:

"Where do you come from?"

"Fumay."

"Then you shouldn't be here, should you? This is a camp for Belgians."

We exchanged anxious glances, Anna and I, while we waited our turn in the sun.

"Have your identity cards ready."

I hadn't got one, because at that time they were not compulsory in France. I hadn't a passport either, never having been abroad.

I saw some of the people coming out of the office go over to the huts, while others were sent to wait on the pavement, probably for transport to take them somewhere else.

Getting closer to the door, I overheard some snatches of conversation.

"What's your trade, Peeters?"

"I'm a fitter, but since the war . . ."

"Do you want a job?"

"I'm not a slacker, you know."

"Have you got a wife, children?"

"My wife's over there, the one in the green dress, with the three kids."

"You can start work tomorrow at the factory at Aytré, and you'll get the same wage as the French. Go and wait on the pavement. You'll be taken to Aytré, where they'll find you lodgings."

"You mean that?"

"Next."

Next came old Jules, who, one of the last to arrive, had slipped into the queue.

"Your identity card."

"I haven't got one."

"You've lost it?"

"I've never had one."

"You're Belgian, aren't you?"

"French."

"Then what are you doing here?"

"I'm waiting for you to tell me."

The man spoke in a low voice to somebody I couldn't see.

"Have you any money?"

"Not enough to buy myself a drink."

"You haven't any relatives at La Rochelle?"

"I haven't any relatives anywhere. I'm an orphan from birth."

"We'll see about you later. Go and have a rest."

I could feel Anna getting more and more nervous. I was the second Frenchman to come forward.

"Identity card."

"I'm French."

The man looked at me, irritated.

"Are many of you on the train French?"

"Three cars full."

"Who's been looking after you?"

"Nobody."

"What are you thinking of doing?"

"I don't know."

He nodded toward Anna.

"Is she your wife?"

I hesitated only a second before saying "yes."

"Settle down in the camp for the moment. I don't know what to do about you. This wasn't expected."

Three of the huts were new and roomy, with two rows of mattresses on bails. A few people were still lying down, possibly because they were ill or because they had arrived during the night.

Farther on, an old circus tent made of coarse green canvas had been put up, and they had simply strewn some straw on the ground.

It was there that we put our things down in a corner, Anna and I. People were just beginning to move into the camp. There were a lot of empty spaces. I could see that that wasn't going to last and thought that we would be more likely to be left in peace in the tent than in the huts.

In a smaller, rather shabby tent, some women were busy peeling potatoes and cleaning whole bucketfuls of vegetables.

"Thank you," murmured Anna.

"Why?"

"For what you said."

"I was afraid they might not let you in."

"What would you have done?"

"I'd have gone with you."

"Where?"

"That doesn't matter."

I hadn't much money with me, most of our savings being in Jeanne's handbag. I could have got a job. I wasn't unwilling to work.

For the moment, though, I wanted to keep my status as a refugee. Above all, I wanted to stay in this camp, near the port, near the boats, and to roam among the huts where women were washing their linen and hanging it out to dry, where children were crawling about on the ground, their bottoms bare.

I hadn't left Fumay to have to think and take on responsibilities.

"If I had told them I was a Czech . . ."

"You are a Czech?"

"From Prague, with Jewish blood from my mother. My mother is Jewish."

She didn't speak in the past tense, which suggested that her mother was still alive.

"I haven't got my passport. I left it behind at Namur. With my accent they might have taken me for a German woman."

I must admit that a disagreeable thought occurred to me and my face clouded over. Wasn't it she who had as it were chosen me, almost immediately after our departure from Fumay?

In our car, I was the only man under fifty, apart from the boy with the blankets. I had nearly forgotten my former schoolmate Leroy, and now I wonder all of a sudden why he wasn't in the army.

In any case I hadn't made any advances. It was she who had come to me. I recalled her precise gestures, the first night, next to Julie and her horse dealer.

She hadn't any luggage, any money; she had ended up by begging a cigarette.

"What are you thinking about?"

"You."

"I know. But what are you thinking?"

I was thinking that she had foreseen, as far back as Fumay, that sooner or later she would be asked for her papers, and that she had provided herself in advance with a guarantor. Me!

We were standing between two huts. There was still a little trampled grass left on the path; some washing was drying on clotheslines. I saw her pupils narrow, her eyes mist over. I wouldn't have thought her capable of crying, and yet they were real tears which were trickling down her cheeks.

At the same time her fists clenched and her face grew so dark that I thought that she was going to hurl a torrent of reproaches and abuse at me through her tears.

I tried to take her hand, which she snatched away.

"Forgive me, Anna."

She shook her head, scattering her hair over her cheeks.

"I didn't really think that. It was just a vague idea, the sort we all have at certain moments."

"I know."

"You understand me?"

She wiped her eyes with the back of her hand, sniveling unaffectedly.

"It's finished," she announced.

"Did I hurt you badly?"

"I'll get over it."

"I hurt myself too. Stupidly. I realized right away that it wasn't true."

"You're sure of that?"

"Yes."

"Come along."

She took me off toward the quayside and we both looked across the masts rocked by the tide at the two bulky towers, like fortress keeps, which flanked the entrance of the port.

"Anna!"

I spoke in an undertone, without turning to look at her, my eyes dazzled by the sunlight and colors.

"Yes?"

"I love you."

"Hush!"

Her throat swelled as if she were swallowing her saliva. Then she spoke of something else, in a voice which had become natural again.

"You aren't afraid of somebody pinching your things?"

I started laughing, laughing as if I would never stop, and I kissed her while seagulls, in their flight, passed a few feet above us.

CHAPTER *6*

There are the official landmarks, the dates, which must be available in books. I suppose that everybody, depending on the place where he was at that time, his family responsibilities, his personal anxieties, has his own landmarks. Mine are all connected with the reception center, the center as we used to call it, and distinguished by the arrival of a certain train, by the fitting out of a new hut, by an apparently commonplace incident.

Without knowing it, we had been among the first to arrive, a couple of days after the trains had unloaded some Belgian refugees, so that the center hadn't been broken in yet.

Had the huts, which had been put up a few weeks before and were still new, been intended for this purpose? The question never occurred to me. Probably the answer is yes, seeing that, long before the German attack, the authorities had evacuated part of Alsace.

Nobody, in any case, expected things to happen so quickly, and it was obvious that the people in charge of the camp were improvising from day to day.

On the morning we arrived, the newspapers were already talking of fighting at Monthermé and on the Semois; the next day the Germans were building bridges for their tanks at Dinant; and on May 15th, unless I am mistaken, at the same time as the withdrawal of the French government was announced, the daily papers quoted in large type the names of places in our part of the world, Montmédy, Raucourt, Rethel, which we had had so much trouble reaching.

All this admittedly existed for me as it did for the others, but it was happening in a far-off, theoretical world from which I was as it were detached.

I should like to try to define my state of mind, not only in the early days, but during the whole time I spent at the center.

The war existed, more tangible with every day that passed, and very real, as we had discovered for ourselves when our train had been machine-gunned. Dazed and bewildered, we had crossed a chaotic zone where there had been no fighting as yet but where battles would follow one after another.

Now that had happened. The names of towns and villages, which we had read in passing, in the sunshine, could now be read in big letters on the front page of the newspapers.

That zone, beyond which we had been surprised to find people coming out of church and towns in their Sunday best, was extending every day, and other trains were following the same route as ours, other cars were shuddering along the roads, bumper to bumper, with mattresses and prams on top, old men and dolls inside.

This long caterpillar had already reached La Rochelle, crawling past us in the direction of Bordeaux.

Men, women, and children were dying as our engineer had died, their eyes staring up into the blue sky. Others were bleeding like the old man who had held his reddened handkerchief to his face, or groaning like the woman with her shoulder shot away.

I ought to be ashamed of admitting it: I didn't participate in this drama. It was outside us. It no longer affected us personally.

It was as if I had known, when I had left Fumay, what I was going to find: a little circle made to measure for me, which would become my shelter and in which it was essential for me to establish myself.

Since the reception center was intended for Belgian refugees, we had no right to be there, Anna and I. That is why we made ourselves as inconspicuous as possible, forgoing the first distributions of soup for fear of being noticed.

A low kitchen range had been installed in the open air, then two, then three, then four, with huge copper pans, real vats, like those used on farms for cooking pig-food.

Later a new prefabricated hut was put up to serve as a kitchen, with fixed tables at which we could sit down to eat.

Followed by Anna, who never left me, I watched the comings and goings. I had soon understood the organization of the camp, which was in fact a continuous improvisation.

One man was in charge of the whole camp, a Belgian, the man who had questioned me on my arrival and whom I avoided as much as possible. He was helped by a number of girls and scouts, including some older scouts from Ostend who had come off one of the first trains.

The refugees were sorted out as well as possible into the useful and useless, that is to say those who were capable of working and those—old men, women, and children—who could only be given shelter.

Theoretically the camp was a stop where people shouldn't have spent more than a few hours or a night.

The factories engaged on defense work, at Aytré, La Pallice, and elsewhere, were clamoring for labor, and woodcutters were needed in a nearby forest to keep the bakeries supplied with firewood.

Coaches took the skilled workers and their families to these places, where local committees tried to find accommodations for them.

As for the unaccompanied women, the fatherless families, the unemployable persons, they were sent to towns which hadn't any industry, such as Saintes or Royan.

The aim we set ourselves, Anna and I, right away, was to stay at the camp and get ourselves accepted there.

The nurse who had come in a car to bring us food on the last evening of our journey was called Madame Bauche and struck me as the most important person, so that, like a schoolboy who wants to get into his teacher's good books, I gave her all my attention.

She was not very tall, plump, almost fat, aged, as I have said already, between thirty and forty, and I have never seen anybody display so much energy with such unruffled good humor.

I don't know whether she was a registered nurse. She belonged to the upper crust of La Rochelle society, and was married to a doctor or an architect, I can't remember which, for there were four or five other women with her, from the same place, and I used to get their husbands' jobs mixed up.

As soon as a train was announced, she was the first at the station, not, like a lot of others, wearing arm bands, to distribute kind words and chocolate, but to find out those in the crowd who were most in need of help.

As the invasion gathered speed, they became more and more numerous, and she could be seen taking the cripples, the babies, the more helpless of the old people into one of the huts, where, on her knees, in a white smock, she washed sore feet, dressed wounds, and led behind a blanket, which did duty as a curtain, those women who needed special attention.

More often than not she was still there at midnight, making a silent tour of inspection with the aid of a pocket flashlight, comforting women in tears, scolding men who were making too much noise.

The electric system, which had been installed in a hurry, was unsatisfactory, and when I offered to repair it Madame Bauche asked me:

"Do you know about that sort of thing?"

"It's my trade in a manner of speaking. All I need is a ladder."

"Go and find one."

I had noticed a building under construction in a group of new blocks of flats. I went to the site, and as there was nobody there to ask, I walked off with a ladder with Anna helping me. That ladder stayed at the camp as long as I did, without anybody coming to claim it.

I also replaced some broken windows, mended some taps and water pipes. Madame Bauche didn't know my surname, or where I came from. She called me Marcel and got into the habit of sending for me whenever anything went wrong.

After two or three days I had become the general handyman. Leroy had disappeared with the first batch, sent off in the direction of Bordeaux or Toulouse. Of all the people in our car, old Jules was the only one who remained at the camp, where he was tolerated because he played the fool.

In town I met the man with the pipe, the one I used to call the concierge. Looking very harassed, he told me in passing that he was on his way to the Prefecture to demand news of his wife, and I never saw him again.

That happened on the second or third day. The day before, Anna had washed her panties and her brassière, which she had hung out to dry in the sun, and as we wandered about the camp we exchanged conspiratorial glances at the thought that she was naked under her black dress.

There was a big tower at the end of the quay, the Clock Tower, which was a more massive construction than those flanking the entrance to the port, and which you went under to get to the main street.

This archway was to become a familiar sight for us, as were the arcaded streets which were unbelievably busy, for, over and above the population and the refugees, the town had troops and sailors stationed in it.

When I suggested buying Anna a change of underwear, she made no objection. It was essential. I had wondered whether I might not take the opportunity to buy her a light-colored dress of the sort you could see in all the shop windows. She must have thought about it too, for she guessed everything that entered my head.

"You know," I said to her, "I'd offer to give you a dress . . ."

She didn't feel obliged to protest politely, as so many others would have done, if only as a matter of form, and she looked at me with a smile.

"Well? What were you going to add?"

"That I hesitate to do so, out of selfishness. For me, your black dress is almost part of you. You understand? I wonder whether I wouldn't be disappointed to see you wearing something else."

"I'm happy as I am," she murmured, squeezing my fingertips.

I could feel that that was true. I was happy too. As we were passing a cosmetics shop I stopped.

"You don't use powder or lipstick?"

"I used to, before."

She didn't mean before me, but before Namur.

"Would you like to have some again?"

"That depends on you. Only if you prefer me with make-up."

"No."

"Then I'd rather not."

She didn't want to have her hair cut either; it was neither long nor short.

There was something I never thought about, not only because I refused to think about it, but because it never entered my head: the fact that our life together didn't have any future.

I didn't know what was going to happen. Nobody could know. We were living through an interval, outside space, and I savored those days and nights greedily.

I was greedy for everything, for the changing spectacle of the port and the sea, the fishing boats of different colors which went off in Indian file at high tide, the fish which was unloaded in baskets or flat boxes, the crowds in the streets, glimpses of the camp and the station.

I was even hungrier for Anna, and for the first time in my life I wasn't ashamed of my sexual desires.

On the contrary. With her, it had become a game which struck me as very pure. We talked about it gaily, frankly, inventing a whole code, adopting a certain number of signs which allowed us to exchange certain secret thoughts in public.

The center of this new world was the greenish tent which could be seen from a long way off dominating the huts, and, inside this tent, our own corner in the straw, what we called our stable.

We had arranged our belongings there, the things I had taken out of my luggage and other things which I had bought, such as mess tins for the soup and a compact spirit stove with everything we needed to brew our morning coffee, outside, between a couple of huts, facing the boats.

The others, especially those who were only staying there for a night, looked at our corner in surprise and, I feel sure, with envy, just as I in the past had sometimes looked at a real stable, with horses living snugly on their litter.

I used to talk about our litter too, and I didn't like changing our straw too often, so that it remained impregnated with us.

It wasn't only there that we made love, but all over the place, often in the most unexpected spots. That had begun with the boat, one evening when we were looking at the fishing smacks rocking beside the quay while the creaking of the pulleys imitated the cry of the seagulls.

Knowing that in all probability I would never go to sea, I looked longingly at the open hatchway of one of the boats, whose deck was piled with lobster pots. Next my eyes turned to Anna, then back to the boat, and she started laughing with a laugh which formed part of our secret language.

"You want to?"

"What about you?"

"You aren't afraid we might be taken for thieves and arrested?"

It was after midnight. The quay was deserted, all the lights camouflaged. Any footsteps could be heard a long way off. The hardest thing about it was going down the iron ladder embedded in the stone. The last few rungs were slimy.

We managed all the same and slipped through the hatchway into the darkness below, where we bumped into more baskets, cans, and objects we couldn't identify.

There was a smell of fish, seaweed, and paraffin. Finally Anna said:

"This way. . . ."

I found her hand, which guided me along, and the two of us collapsed onto a hard, narrow bunk, pushing aside some oilskins which were in our way.

The tide rocked us gently to and fro. Through the hatchway we could see a patch of sky and a few stars; a train whistled over by the station. It wasn't a new arrival. Some carriages were moving backwards and forwards, shunting around as if they were trying to tidy up the tracks.

There were no fences yet around the camp. We could come in and go out as we liked. There was nobody mounting guard. We just had to move softly so as not to wake our neighbors.

Later on, fences were put up, not to shut us in, but to prevent prowlers from mixing with the refugees and stealing things, as had happened once or twice.

Often, too, in the evening, we used to roam around the station, and one night when there was no traffic we lay down on the bench farthest away from the station buildings.

That amused us. It was a sort of challenge, and once we made love behind some bales of straw, close to Madame Bauche, who was bandaging sore feet and talking to us at the same time.

Every day I devoted a certain amount of time to looking for my wife and daughter to the best of my ability.

They hadn't been deceiving us, I can't remember where, at Auxerre or Saumur, or perhaps it was at Tours, when they had told us of lists which would be posted up. Some were beginning to appear on the door of the office, where groups collected every morning to consult them.

Only they were lists of Belgian refugees. A lot of them were at Bordeaux, at Saintes, at Cognac, at Angoulême. Some had gone as far as Toulouse, and a good many were living in villages I had never heard of before.

I looked through the lists just in case. Every day, too, I went to see an official at the station who had promised to find out what had become of our train. He had made it a point of honor and it annoyed him intensely to be unable to find any trace of it.

"A train can't disappear like that," he muttered, "even in wartime. Sooner or later, I'm bound to find out where it's gone."

Thanks to the block telephone system linking one station to another, he had put his colleagues on the trail, and they were beginning to talk about the ghost train.

We went to the town hall, Anna and I. Crowds used to gather outside all the offices, for at that time everybody needed a piece of information, a permit, a paper bearing an official stamp.

Here too lists were posted up, of French people this time, but my wife's name still wasn't on them.

"If you're looking for somebody, you'd do better to try the Prefecture."

We went there. The courtyard was bright, the corridors and the offices bathed in sunshine, with clerks in shirt sleeves and a lot of girls in summer dresses. I had left Anna in the street, seeing that I couldn't pass her off as my wife when it was my wife I was trying to trace.

I saw her from the window, standing on the curb, raising her head, then walking up and down, grave, thoughtful. Already I felt impatient to rejoin her, and I reproached myself for leaving her, even for such a short time.

They were issuing petrol coupons to motorists. The Place d'Armes, the quays, the streets were crowded with hundreds of cars from all points of the compass. Their owners were here, at the Prefecture, waiting in the longest of the queues for the precious coupon which would enable them to continue their exodus.

The day before, in the line of cars making their way toward Rochefort, I had caught sight of a hearse from Charleroi in which a whole family was installed, and I suppose that their luggage was occupying the place of the coffin.

"Are you looking for something?"

"I'd like to know where my wife . . . ."

It seems that there were already thousands of us, and there would soon be tens of thousands, in the same plight. Not only were people still fleeing from Belgium and the north, but panic had taken hold of the Parisians since the government had left the city, and it was said that, apart from the cars, a long procession of men and women on foot was now winding along the roads.

In the villages close to the main roads, the bakers' shops were being taken by storm, and there wasn't a single bed available in the hospitals.

"Fill out this form. Leave me your name and address."

Out of prudence, I didn't mention the reception center and I put down *poste restante*. Already, however, old Jules and I were no longer the only French people in the camp.

I can still picture to myself the ugliest train, in the heat of a fine afternoon, when the girls of a local school had just gone by, in a line, along the pavement, on their way to a fête.

What we, like Madame Bauche, called ugly trains were those which had suffered the most en route, trains in which people had died, in which women had given birth without proper attention.

There had been a lunatics' train, for instance, ten carriages full of lunatics evacuated from an asylum. In spite of all the precautions taken, two of them escaped and got as far as the big clock before they were caught.

I can't remember whether the train I am talking about had come from Douai or from Laon, for I tend to get the two towns mixed up. It was carrying only a few wounded people, who had had medical attention on the way, but the eyes of all the passengers, men, women, and children, were still glazed with terror.

One woman was trembling violently and she went on trembling all night, her teeth chattering and her hands pushing away her blanket.

Others talked incoherently or kept on repeating the same story in a monotonous voice.

They were being entrained, at Douai or at Laon, two hundred yards from the station which was packed with people. Some of them were waiting for late-comers or for relatives who had gone to the refreshment room to buy something when, without any warning having been sounded, some planes had suddenly appeared in the sky.

"The bombs fell like that, Monsieur. . . . Sideways. . . . You could see them falling on the station and the houses opposite, and everything started trembling and blowing up, roofs, stones, people, the carriages standing a little way off. . . . I saw a leg hurled into the air, and I myself, although we were a fair distance away, I was thrown to the ground on top of my son. . . ."

The sirens had finally started wailing, those of the fire engines too, and from the heaps of stones, bricks, and twisted metal corpses could be seen poking out, pieces of broken furniture, occasionally a familiar object which had miraculously remained intact.

The newspapers announced the formation of a new government, the retreat toward Dunkirk, the blocking of railway lines all over the place, while Anna and I continued our quiet existence as if it were going to last forever.

Anna knew as well as I did that this wasn't so, but she never made any mention of it. Before me, she had shared other existences, other more or less prolonged moments of different lives, and I preferred not to think about what was going to happen after me.

It had wrung my heart seeing her from the window in the Prefecture, alone on the pavement, as if we were already parted. I had been filled with panic. When I had rejoined her, I had seized hold of her arm as if I had been separated from her for several days.

I would be ready to swear that it didn't rain once during the whole of that period apart from a solitary storm, I remember that now, which left pockets of water in the roof of our tent. The weather seemed unreal, it was so wonderful, and I can't imagine La Rochelle otherwise than in the heat of the sun.

The fishermen used to bring us fish. The scouts, every morning, went around the market where their baskets were filled with vegetables and fruit. They had a handcart like the one which I had abandoned at Fumay in the station yard. I accompanied them several times, putting myself between the shafts for the fun of it, while Anna followed on the pavement.

We nearly had some ugly incidents, in the camp and at the station, when the radio announced the capitulation of Belgium. At that time there were almost as many French refugees as Belgians, and whole factories were being evacuated. I saw some Flemings and Walloons who were crying like children, and others who came to blows and had to be separated.

Every day that passed nibbled away some of my meager capital of happiness. That isn't the right word, but as I can't find another, and as people are always talking about happiness, I am obliged to make do with the word myself.

Sooner or later, at the town hall, at the Prefecture, at the post office, I would find news of Jeanne and my daughter. The baby was nearly due, and I hoped that the journey and all the excitement hadn't brought on a premature delivery.

The Paris newspapers were publishing lists of readers who gave news to their families in that way, and for a moment I thought of using the same method. But at Fumay we never read any of the Paris papers. Which was I to choose? We would have had to agree on one beforehand, something which we hadn't done. There was no likelihood of Jeanne buying all the daily papers every day.

The Germans were advancing so fast that there was a lot of talk of treason and fifth-column activities. It appeared that in one of our huts they had arrested a man who said he was Dutch, and who had a portable radio transmitter in his luggage.

I don't know whether that was true. Madame Bauche, whom I asked about it, couldn't confirm the story, but she had seen some plain-clothes detectives prowling around the camp.

This frightened Anna, whose surname, Kupfer, sounded very Teutonic. We thought about that every time we crossed the square between the camp and the station and looked at the geraniums in all their splendor.

The municipal gardener had set them out, already in flower, shortly after our arrival. I remember seeing him, early in the morning, in the as yet pale sunshine, doing his reassuring work, when the refugee trains were arriving all the time at the station and the newspapers on the stall were full of disasters.

It seems that two hours later, while the gardener was still there, a German radio station, which broadcast propaganda in French, said something to this effect:

"It is kind of you, Monsieur Vieiljeux, to plant flowers outside your station in our honor. We shall be there a few days from now."

Monsieur Vieiljeux, whom I never saw, was the Mayor of La Rochelle, and the German radio went on sending him ironic messages, thus showing that they knew everything that was happening in the town.

The word "spy" could be heard more and more often, and people's eyes became suspicious.

"You'd better speak as little as possible when other people are around."

"I've thought of that."

She wasn't talkative. Nor was I. Even if both of us had been, there were so many forbidden subjects between us that we wouldn't have found much to say to each other.

No past or future. Nothing but a fragile present, which we sipped and savored together.

We feasted ourselves on little pleasures, on patterns of light and shade which we knew we should remember all our lives. As for our flesh, we tortured it with our desperate efforts to blend it into a single whole.

I am not ashamed to say that I was happy, with a happiness which bore the same relation to everyday happiness as the sound produced by passing a violin bow across the wrong side of the bridge bears to the normal sound of a violin. It was sharp and exquisite, and deliciously painful.

As for our sexual hunger, I am almost certain that we weren't alone in feeling it. Although we were not as crowded in the circus tent as in our cattle car, there were still about a hundred of us, men and women, sleeping under the same shelter. Not a night went by without my hearing bodies moving cautiously, panting breath and amorous complaints.

I wasn't alone in feeling outside ordinary life and its conventions. At any moment planes might appear in the sky and drop their rosary of bombs. In a fortnight or three weeks the German troops would be at La Rochelle, and nobody had any idea what would happen then.

The first time the air-raid warning sounded, we were told to lie down beside the dock, for the underground shelter which had been built near the freight station was too far away.

The anti-aircraft guns opened up. Bursts of fire came from the station. Later we were told that it was a mistake, that the planes had been French machines which hadn't given the regulation signals.

Some other planes dived over the town to lay mines around a ship, the *Champlain*, in the La Pallice roadstead. In the morning the boat blew up. We heard the explosions without knowing what was happening.

Later on, some petrol tanks started blazing two or three miles from the town, and black smoke hung in the sky for several days.

I have said this before, but I say it again: the days went by both fast and slowly. The notion of time had altered. The Germans were entering Paris, whereas Anna and I had changed nothing in our little habits. Only the atmosphere in the station was altering from day to day, becoming more confused and chaotic.

As at Fumay, I got up first and went outside to make the coffee, at the same time shaving in front of a mirror hooked onto the canvas of the tent. Part of one hut had finally been set aside as a washroom for the women, and Anna went there early, before the rush.

Then we used to stroll over to the station, where they were used to us and gave us a cheery greeting.

"Many trains today?"

"We're expecting some personnel from Renault's."

We knew the subway, the tracks, the benches. It was with a certain tenderness that we looked at the cattle cars in which there was still some straw lying about. Where was ours now, in which a little of our own smell must be lingering?

After that, Madame Bauche nearly always needed me for some job, mending a door or a window, or fitting up new shelves for food or medical supplies.

We went for our ration of soup. Now and then we gave ourselves an extra treat. Crossing the avenue, we would go into a cozy bar where I knew Anna liked to drink an apéritif while I, to keep her company, ordered a lemonade.

In the afternoon we went into town, and I would go and read the lists before dropping in at the post office.

Unless it was a little premature, our child might be born any day now, and I kept wondering who would look after Sophie while my wife was in the maternity home.

Oddly enough, I couldn't manage to picture either of them in my mind. Their features remained vague and blurred.

I wasn't too worried about Sophie, for we had had a couple of children in the camp for a week who had lost their mother on the way and didn't suffer as a result. They played with the others, as carefree as they were, and when their mother finally came to fetch them they stood motionless in front of her for quite a while, embarrassed, as if they had been playing truant.

The 16th of June is one of the dates I remember. Pétain, at Orléans, was asking for an armistice and some soldiers left the station suddenly, without their weapons, in spite of attempts by the officers to stop them.

Three days later the Germans were at Nantes. We calculated that, being motorized, they were moving fast, and we expected to see them the following day.

But it wasn't until the 22nd, a Saturday, that some motorists called out to us in passing:

"They're at La Roche-sur-Yon!"

"Have you seen them?"

They nodded as they drove on.

The following night was hot. Anna lay down first, and, standing there, I felt tears coming to my eyes at the sight of her making her hole in the straw. I said:

"No. Come along."

She never asked me where or why. You would have sworn that she had spent her life following a man, that she had been born to do just that.

We walked along listening to the sound of the sea and the creaking of the rigging. Perhaps she thought that I was looking for the shelter of a boat?

I led her like that as far as the end of the port, where the building yards begin, and then I turned into the path which ends up at the beach.

There wasn't a sound to be heard. You couldn't see any lights in the town, nothing but a dark green lantern at the end of the jetty.

We lay down on the sand, near the little waves, and we stayed for a long time without saying anything, without doing anything, listening to our heartbeats.

"Anna! I'd like you to remember always . . ."

"Hush!"

She didn't need words. She didn't like them. I think they frightened her.

I started to take her, awkwardly, gradually bringing to my love-making an impatience which resembled malice. This time she didn't help me, but lay motionless, her eyes fixed on my face, and I could read no expression in them.

For a moment it seemed to me that she had already gone and I imagined her alone again, like a lost animal.

"Anna!" I cried, in the same voice in which I would have called for help. "Try to understand!"

She took my head between her hands to murmur, choking back her sobs:

"It was good!"

She wasn't speaking of our embrace but of us, of all that had been us for such a short time. We wept, one on top of the other, while we made love. Meanwhile the sea had come up to our feet.

I needed to do something, I didn't know what. I tore her dress off her, stripped off my clothes. I said once again:

"Come along!"

The sky was bright enough for her body to stand out in the dark, but I couldn't see her face. Was she really frightened? Did she think that I meant to drown her, perhaps drown myself with her? Her body drew back, seized by an animal panic.

"Come along, silly!"

I ran into the water, where she soon joined me. She could swim. I couldn't. She went farther into the sea, then came and made rings around me.

I wonder today whether she was so very far wrong to feel frightened. Everything was possible just then. We tried to make a game of that bath, to amuse ourselves like schoolchildren on holiday, but we didn't succeed.

"Are you cold?"

"No."

"Let's run to get warm."

We ran along the sand, which stuck to our feet and the calves of our legs.

It hadn't been a good idea. On our way back to the camp, a patrol obliged us to stay hidden in a corner for nearly a quarter of an hour.

Our tent seemed to stifle us with human warmth, and after we finally curled up in our corner I didn't sleep all night.

The next day was a Sunday. Some of the refugees dressed up to go to mass. In town we saw girls in light-colored dresses, children in their Sunday best walking in front of their parents. The confectioners' shops were open and I bought a cake which was still warm, as at Fumay.

After lunch we went to eat it beside the dock, sitting on the stone with our legs dangling above the water.

At five o'clock some German motorcyclists stopped outside the town hall and an officer asked to see Monsieur Vieiljeux.

CHAPTER 7

On Monday morning I felt empty and depressed. Anna had had a restless night, shaken several times by those abrupt movements which I found it hard to get used to, and several times she had spoken volubly in her native language.

I got up at the same time as on the other days to make the coffee and to shave, but, instead of finding myself alone outside, I saw some groups of half-awake refugees who were watching German motorcyclists going past.

I had the impression of finding in their eyes the mournful resignation which they must have been able to read in mine, and that was a general reaction: it lasted several days, for some people several weeks.

A page had been turned. An epoch had ended, everybody felt sure of that, although nobody could foresee what was going to take its place.

It was no longer just our fate which was at stake but that of the world to which we belonged.

We had formed a more or less terrifying idea of the war, of the invasion, and now, just as war and invasion reached us in our turn, we saw that they were different from everything we had imagined. It is true that this was just the beginning.

For example, while my water was boiling on the little spirit stove on the ground and the Germans were still going by without bothering about us, very young, pink, and fresh as if they were going on parade, I could see two French soldiers, with their rifles slung over their shoulders, mounting guard at the door of the station.

No trains had arrived for two days. The platforms were deserted, as were the waiting rooms, the refreshment room, and the military commandant's office. The two soldiers, not having received any orders, didn't know what to do, and it wasn't until about nine o'clock that they propped their rifles against the wall and went off.

While I was lathering my cheeks with my shaving brush I heard the familiar sound of diesel engines and some boats went out fishing. There were only three or four of them. The fact remains that, while the enemy was invading the town, some fishermen went out to sea as usual to cast their nets. Nobody stopped them.

When we went toward the town, Anna and I, the cafés, the bars, the shops were open, and shopkeepers were tidying up their window displays. I remember in particular a florist arranging carnations in some buckets in front of her shop. Did that mean there were people buying flowers on a day like that?

On the pavements people were walking along, rather worried, above all perplexed, as I was, and there were some men in uniform, Frenchmen, among the crowd.

One of them, in the middle of the Rue du Palais, was asking a policeman what he ought to do, and, judging by his gestures, I gathered that the policeman was replying that he didn't know any more than the soldier did.

I didn't see any Germans in the vicinity of the town hall. To tell the truth, I don't remember seeing any walking among the townspeople. I went to consult the lists, as on other days, then on to the post office, where I waited my turn at the *poste restante* counter while Anna stood pensively by the window.

We had said scarcely anything to each other since the morning. We were both of us equally depressed, and when I was handed a message in my name I wasn't surprised, I thought that it was inevitable, that it was bound to happen that particular day.

But I went weak at the knees and had some difficulty in walking away from the counter.

I knew already. The form was printed on poor paper, with blanks which had been completed in purple pencil.

NAME OF MISSING PERSON: Jeanne Marie Clémentine Féron, *née* Van Straeten.

PLACE OF ORIGIN: Fumay (Ardennes).

PROFESSION: None.

MISSING SINCE: . . .

METHOD OF TRANSPORT: Rail.

ACCOMPANIED BY: Her daughter, aged four.

PRESENT WHEREABOUTS: . . .

My heart started beating wildly and I looked around for Anna. I saw her against the light, still by the window, gazing at me without moving.

PRESENT WHEREABOUTS: Maternity home at Bressuire.

I went over to her and held out the paper without a word. Then, without really knowing what I was doing, I made for the telephone counter.

"Is it possible to telephone to Bressuire?"

I expected to be told that it wasn't. Contrary to all logic, it seemed to me, the telephone was working normally.

"What number do you want?"

"The maternity home."

"Don't you know the number? Or the name of the street?"

"I imagine there's only one maternity home in the town."

In my memories of geography lessons at school, Bressuire was somewhere in a region you rarely heard about, between Niort and Poitiers, farther west, toward the Vendée.

"There's a delay of ten minutes."

Anna had given me back the message, which I stuffed into my pocket. I said, unnecessarily, since she knew it already:

"I'm waiting for them to put the call through."

She lit a cigarette. I had bought her a cheap handbag as well as a little suitcase in imitation leather in which to keep her underwear and her toilet things. The floor of the post office was still marked by the drops of water which had been sprinkled on it before it was swept.

Opposite, on the other side of a little square, some men who looked like local notabilities were sitting on a café terrace, arguing and drinking white wine, and the proprietor of the café, in shirt sleeves and a blue apron, was standing near them, holding a napkin.

"Bressuire is on the line in Box 2."

At the other end of the line a voice was getting impatient.

"Hello! La Rochelle . . . Speak up."

"Is that Bressuire?"

"Yes, of course it is. I'm putting you through."

"Hello. Is that the maternity home?"

"Who's speaking?"

"Marcel Féron. I'd like to know if my wife is still there."

"What name did you say?"

"Féron."

I had to spell it out: F for Fernand, and so on.

"Has she had a baby here?"

"I suppose so. She was pregnant when . . ."

"Is she in a private room or a public ward?"

"I don't know. We are refugees from Fumay and I lost her on the way as well as my daughter."

"Hold the line. I'll go and see."

Through the glass pane of the phone booth I saw Anna, who was leaning on the window sill, and it had a curious effect on me, looking at her black dress, her shoulders, her lips which were becoming unfamiliar to me again.

"Yes, she's here. She gave birth the day before yesterday."

"Can I speak to her?"

"There's no telephone in the wards, but I can give her a message."

"Tell her . . ."

I started searching for something to say and suddenly I heard a crackling sound on the line.

"Hello! . . . Hello! . . . Don't cut me off, Mademoiselle. . . ."

"Speak up, then. . . . Hurry up. . . ."

"Tell her that her husband is at La Rochelle, that all's well, that he'll come to Bressuire as quickly as he can. . . . I don't know yet if I can find any transport but . . ."

There was nobody on the line any more and I didn't know if she had heard the end of my sentence. It hadn't occurred to me to ask whether it was a boy or a girl, or whether everything had gone well.

I went to pay at the counter. Then I said automatically, as I had said so often in the course of the last few weeks:

"Come along."

It was unnecessary, seeing that Anna always followed me.

In the street she asked:

"How are you going to get there?"

"I don't know."

"They probably won't get the trains running again for several days."

I didn't ask myself any questions. I would go to Bressuire on foot if necessary. Seeing that I knew where Jeanne was, I had to join her. It wasn't a matter of duty. It was so natural that I didn't hesitate for a moment.

I must have appeared very calm and sure of myself, for Anna was looking at me with a certain astonishment. On the quay I stopped at the shop where I had bought the spirit stove. It had some coarse canvas kit bags for sale and I wanted one to replace the trunk which, even empty, was too heavy to be carted along the roads.

The German soldiers were still not mixing with the passers-by. A group which had camped on the outskirts of the town, on the old ramparts, around a field kitchen, had gone off again at dawn.

I went for the last time into the camp, into the green circus tent, where I stuffed the contents of the trunk into the kit bag. Noticing the spirit stove, I handed it to Anna.

"You can have this. I won't need it any more, and in any case I haven't got room for it."

She took it without protest and put it in her suitcase. I was preoccupied, wondering where and how we were going to say good-by.

Some women were still asleep, and others, who were busy with their children, looked at us inquisitively.

"I'll help you."

Anna hoisted the kit bag onto my shoulder and I bent down to pick up the suitcase. She followed me, holding her case. Outside, between a couple of huts, I started clumsily:

"All my life . . ."

She gave me a smile which baffled me.

"I'm coming with you."

"To Bressuire?"

I was worried.

"I want to stay with you as long as possible. Don't worry. When we get there I'll disappear."

I was relieved to see our leave-taking postponed. We didn't meet Madame Bauche and we left, like so many others, without saying good-by to her and thanking her. Yet we were the oldest inhabitants of the center, for old Jules had been taken to hospital with an attack of delirium tremens.

We made our way toward the Place d'Armes through increasingly chaotic streets. The terrace of the Café de la Paix was crowded. Civilian cars were driving about, and at the far end of the square, near the park, you could make out the mottled camouflage of the German cars.

I didn't expect to find a bus. Yet there were several outside the bus station, since nobody had given orders to suspend the service. I asked if there was a bus for Bressuire or for Niort. They told me no, that the road to Niort was jammed with cars and with refugees on foot, and that the Germans were finding it difficult to get through.

"There's a bus for Fontenay-le-Comte."

"Is that on the road to Bressuire?"

"It gets you a bit nearer."

"When does it leave?"

"The driver's filling up with petrol."

We installed ourselves in the bus, in the blazing sunshine, and to begin with we were alone among the empty seats. Then a French soldier got in, a man of about forty, from the country, with his jacket over his arm, and later half a dozen people sat down around us.

Sitting side by side, and shaken by the jolting of the bus, Anna and I kept our eyes fixed on the scenery.

"Are you hungry?"

"No. What about you?"

"I'm not hungry either."

A peasant woman sitting facing us, her eyes red with crying, was eating a slice of pâté which smelled good.

We were following a road which went from village to village, not far from the sea at first, through Nieul, Marsilly, Esnandres, and Charron, and we didn't see many Germans, just a small group in the square of each little town, in front of the church or the town hall, with the local inhabitants watching them from a distance.

We were off the route taken by the refugees and most of the troops. Somewhere, I thought I recognized the meadow and the stop where we had slept on the last night of our journey. I am not sure, because no landscape looks the same from the railway as it does from the road.

We passed a big dairy where dozens of pails of milk were shining in the sun; then we crossed a bridge over a canal, near an inn with an arbor beside it. There were blue checked tablecloths, flowers on the tables, and a fretwork chef at the roadside, holding out a stenciled menu.

At Fontenay-le-Comte there were more Germans, and more vehicles too, including trucks, but only in the main street leading to the station. At the bus station, in a square, we were told that there was no coach for Bressuire.

The idea of hiring a taxi didn't occur to me, first because that was something I had never done, and then because I wouldn't have believed that it was still possible.

We went into a café in the market place to have a snack.

"Are you refugees?"

"Yes. From the Ardennes."

"There are some people from the Ardennes working as wood-cutters in the Mervent forest. They look a bit wild, but they're good sorts, with plenty of guts. Are you going far?"

"To Bressuire."

"Have you got a car?"

We were the only customers in the place, and an old man in felt slippers came to look at us through the kitchen door.

"No. We'll walk there if need be."

"You think you can walk all the way to Bressuire? With this little lady? Wait a minute while I ask if Martin's truck has gone."

We were lucky. Martin's business, on the other side of the trees, was a wholesale ironmonger's. It had some deliveries to make at Pouzauges and Cholet. We waited, drinking coffee, and looking out at the empty square.

There was room for both of us, squeezed together in the cab, beside the driver, and after a fairly steep hill we drove through an endless forest.

"The Ardennes people are over there," said our driver, pointing to a clearing and a few huts around which some half-naked children were playing.

"Are there many Germans around here?"

"There was a lot of traffic yesterday evening and last night. It will probably start again. What we've seen has been mainly motor-bikes and field kitchens. I suppose the tanks are following."

He stopped to leave a parcel at a smithy where a plow-horse turned toward us, neighing. The day seemed terribly long to me, and in spite of our stroke of luck the journey went on and on.

I felt rather annoyed with Anna now for having come with me. It would have been better for both of us to have done with it at La Rochelle, with my kit bag on my shoulder and my suitcase in my hand.

Knowing that I was annoyed, she made herself as inconspicuous as she could between the driver and me. It suddenly occurred to me that her warm hip was touching the driver's, and I felt a surge of jealousy.

We took nearly two hours to get to Pouzauges, meeting nobody but a motorized column half a mile long. The soldiers looked at us as they went by, looked at Anna above all, and a few of them waved to her.

"You're only about fifteen miles from Bressuire. You'd better come into this café with me. I might be able to get you a lift."

Some surly-looking men were playing cards. Two others, at the back of the room, were arguing over some papers spread out between the glasses.

"Look, is anybody going Bressuire way? This lady and gentleman are refugees who have to get there before tonight."

One of the men who was arguing and who looked like an estate agent inspected Anna from head to foot before saying:

"I can take them as far as Cerizay."

I didn't know where Cerizay was. They explained that it was halfway to Bressuire. I had expected to have to overcome difficulties and show a certain heroism in order to rejoin my wife, to tramp the roads for several days and to be harassed by the Germans.

I was almost disappointed that everything was going so easily.

We waited for an hour until the discussion ended. Several times the men stood up and made as if to shake hands, only to sit down again and order another round of drinks.

Our new driver had an apoplectic complexion. With a self-important manner he made Anna sit beside him while I installed myself on the back seat. I suddenly felt the fatigue of my sleepless night; my eyelids were heavy and my lips burning hot, as if I had a fever. Perhaps I had got sunstroke?

After some time I ceased to be able to make out the conversation going on in front. I was vaguely aware of meadows, woods, and one or two sleepy-looking villages. We crossed a bridge over a river which was practically dry, before finally stopping in a square.

I thanked the driver. So did Anna. We walked two or three hundred yards before noticing, outside a baker's shop, a flour truck on which the name of a miller at Bressuire was painted.

So I didn't have to do any walking. Nor did Anna. We weren't alone together once all day.

Night had fallen. We were standing on a pavement, near the terrace of a café, with my kit bag and my suitcase at my feet. I turned aside to take a few bank notes out of my wallet. Anna understood and didn't protest when I slipped them into her hand-bag.

The square was empty all around us. I have never had such an impression of emptiness. I stopped a boy who was passing.

"Can you tell me where the maternity home is?"

"Second street on the left, right at the end. You can't miss it."

Guessing that I was going to say good-by there and then, Anna murmured:

"Let me go as far as the door with you."

She was so humble that I hadn't the heart to refuse. In one square there were some Germans fussing around a dozen big tanks and some officers shouting orders.

The street with the maternity home was on a slope, lined with middle-class houses. At the far end there was a big brick building.

Once again I put down my kit bag and my suitcase. I didn't dare to look at Anna. A woman was leaning out of a window, a child sitting on the doorstep, and only the rooftops were still lit by the setting sun.

"Well . . . ," I began.

The sound stopped in my throat and I took hold of her hands.

Despite myself I had to look at her one last time and I saw a face which seemed already blurred and indistinct.

"Good-by!"

"I hope you'll be happy, Marcel."

I pressed her hands. I let go of them. I picked up my kit bag and my suitcase again, almost staggering, and when I had nearly got to the door of the maternity home she ran up behind me to whisper in my ear:

"I've been happy with you."

Through the glass door I caught sight of some nurses in an entrance hall, a trolley, the receptionist talking on the telephone. I went in. I turned around. She was standing there on the pavement.

"Madame Féron, please."

CHAPTER *8*

It wasn't simply to straighten out my ideas, nor in the hope of understanding certain things which have always worried me, that I started writing these recollections, unknown to my wife and everybody else, in a notebook which I lock up every time anybody comes into my office.

For now I have an office, a shop with two display windows in the Rue du Château, and I employ more people than the son of my former employer, Monsieur Ponchot, who hasn't kept up with the times and whose shop is still as dark and solemn as when I used to work there.

I have three growing children, two girls and a boy. It is the boy, Jean-François, who was born at Bressuire while Sophie was being looked after by some farmers in a nearby village who had taken my wife in when the train had abandoned them.

Sophie seemed pleased to see me, but not surprised, and when, a month later, we took the train to Fumay with her mother and her little brother, she was very upset.

The birth had been easy. Jean-François is the sturdiest of the three. It is his younger sister who has given us a lot of trouble. It is true that I found Jeanne edgier than ever, getting frightened about nothing at all, and convinced that misfortune was lying in wait for her.

Isabelle, our third child, was born at the most dramatic moment in the war, when we were waiting for the Allied landing. Some people said that the landing would produce the same chaos and disorder as the German invasion. The authorities expected that all the able-bodied men would be sent to Germany, and routes were marked with arrows so that we shouldn't congest the roads needed by the army.

It was also the time of shortages. Food stocks were at their lowest point and I couldn't afford to buy much on the black market.

The fact remains that Jeanne was delivered prematurely, the baby was put in an incubator, and my wife has never really recovered. I mean morally even more than physically. She is still timid and pessimistic, and when, later on, we moved to the Rue du Château, she was convinced for a long time that we were heading for disaster and that we would end up poorer than ever.

I picked up my life where I had left it, as it was my duty and destiny to do, because that was the only possible solution and I had never imagined that it might be otherwise.

I worked hard. When the time came, I sent my children to the best schools.

I don't know what they are going to do in later life. For the moment they are like all the other children of our sort of world and accept the ideas they are taught.

All the same, especially watching my son growing up, listening to the questions he asks, and seeing the glances he darts at me, all the same I wonder.

Perhaps Jean-François will go on behaving as his mother and

his schoolmasters teach him to and as I do more or less sincerely myself.

It is also possible that one day he may rebel against our ideas, our way of life, and try to be himself.

That is true of the girls as well, of course, but it was when I tried to imagine Jean-François as a young man that I started feeling worried.

My hair has receded. I need glasses with increasingly thick lenses. I am a fairly prosperous, quiet, rather dull man. From a certain point of view, the pair we form, Jeanne and I, is really a caricature of the married couple.

And then the idea came to me of leaving my son another picture of myself. I wondered whether it wouldn't do him good, one day, to know that his father hadn't always been the shop-keeper and the timid husband he had known, with no ambition beyond that of bringing up his children to the best of his ability and helping them to climb a small rung of the social ladder.

Like that, my son, and perhaps my daughters too, would learn that there had been a different man in me, and that for a few weeks I had been capable of a real passion.

I don't know yet. I haven't made up my mind what to do with this notebook, and I hope that I have some time left in which to think it over.

In any case, I owed it to myself to reveal that idea of mine here, just as I owe it to myself, in order to be honest with myself and other people, to go on to the end of the story.

As early as the winter of 1940, life had almost gone back to normal, except for the presence of the Germans and the food situation, which was already getting difficult. I had gone back to work. Radio sets were not prohibited, and more of them were being bought than ever before. Nestor, the cock, and our hens, minus one, had returned to the bottom of the garden, and, con-trary to my expectations, nothing had been stolen from the house, not a single radio, not a single tool; my workshop was just as I had left it, except for the dust.

The spring and the autumn of 1941 must have been uneventful, for I can remember very little about them except that Dr. Wil-hems was a frequent caller. Jeanne's health was worrying him, and he later admitted to me that he was afraid of her having a nervous breakdown.

Although there has never been any mention of Anna between my wife and myself, I would swear that she knows. Did some rumor reach her ears, spread by refugees who had returned home like us? I can't remember meeting any at the time, but it isn't impossible.

In any case, that had nothing to do with her health or her worries. She has never been a passionate or a jealous woman, and, like her sister Berthe, whose husband, the confectioner, is said to be a ladykiller, she wouldn't mind me having affairs, provided they were kept discreet and didn't endanger our home.

I am not trying to get rid of my responsibilities. I am saying what I think, quite objectively. If she realized, at Bressuire, that for a while I had stopped being the same man, my behavior, from then on, reassured her.

Did she guess that she had nearly lost me? But that isn't really true. Our marriage hadn't been in any serious danger: I say that at the risk of diminishing myself in my own eyes.

It was mainly the Germans that frightened her, filling her with an instinctive, physical fear: their footsteps in the street, their music, the posters which they put up on the walls and which always announced bad news.

On account of my trade, they had ransacked my workshop and the house twice, and had even dug holes in the garden in search of secret radio transmitters.

We were still living in the same street at that time, near the quay, between the old Matrays' house and that of the schoolmaster with the curly-haired daughter. The schoolmaster and his family hadn't returned and we didn't see them again until after the Liberation, for they spent the whole of the war near Carcassonne where he was in the Resistance.

As far as I can remember, the winter of 1941-42 was a very cold one. Shortly before Christmas, when there had already been some snow, Dr. Wilhems called one morning to see Jeanne, who was just recovering from an attack of influenza. We had all had it, but she was taking some time to get over hers and was more worried than ever.

As he was taking leave of me, in the corridor, he said:

"Would you mind coming around and having a look at my radio? I've an idea that one of the tubes has burned out."

It was dark by four o'clock in the afternoon and the street lamps were still painted blue, the shop windows unlighted. I had just finished a job when I remembered Dr. Wilhems, and I told myself that I had time to go over to his house before dinner.

I told my wife and put on my windbreaker. With my toolbox in one hand, I left the warmth of the house for the cold and the darkness of the street.

I had scarcely covered a few yards before a silhouette detached itself from the wall and came toward me while a voice called me by my name.

"Marcel."

I recognized her immediately. She was wearing a beret and a dark coat. Her face struck me as paler than ever. She fell in step beside me just as when I used to say to her:

"Come along."

She looked perished with cold, and nervous, while I remained calm and clearheaded.

"I've got to speak to you, Marcel. It's my last chance. I'm at Fumay with an English airman I'm taking to the unoccupied zone."

I turned around and thought I could see the figure of a man hiding in the Matrays' doorway.

"Somebody has given us away and the Gestapo's after us. We need to hide for a few days in a safe place until they've forgotten us."

She was getting out of breath as she walked along, something which didn't use to happen to her. There were rings under her eyes and her face was tired.

I was still striding along, and just as we were turning the corner on to the quay, I began:

"Listen . . ."

"I understand."

She always understood before I had opened my mouth. All the same, I wanted to say what I had to say:

"The Germans are watching me. Twice, they . . ."

"I understand, Marcel," she said again. "I don't hold it against you. Excuse me."

I didn't have time to stop her. She had turned back, running toward the man who was waiting in the dark.

I never mentioned it to anybody. When I had repaired the doctor's radio, I went back home where Jeanne was setting the table in the kitchen while Jean-François was already eating in his high-chair.

"You haven't caught cold, have you?" she asked, looking at me.

Everything was in its usual place, the furniture, the various objects, just as we had left it all when we had left Fumay, and there was an extra child in the house.

A month later, I noticed a freshly printed poster on the wall of the town hall. There were five names on it, including an English name and that of Anna Kupfer. All five had been shot as spies, two days before, in the courtyard of Mézières prison.

I have never been back to La Rochelle. I shall never go back.

I have a wife, three children, a shop in the Rue du Château.

Noland, March 25, 1961